CONTENTS

PART 01

PART TWO

PART THREE

DEDICATION

Although this story is fictional, some things stand out as noteworthy and authentic. First; this book is dedicated to the men and women who chose to serve in our armed forces and have done so with honor and distinction. Their sacrifice, along with the sacrifices of their families, is a reality no fiction can ever describe, and they can never be acknowledged enough to repay them for their devotion.

Second; this book could not have been written accurately without the story of US Army Lieutenant Colonel Robert George ("Tony") Melzer. Tony was a signals intelligence officer attached to MACV-SOG in Vietnam, serving two terms there. Tony enjoyed telling me about the story of him configuring all the gear required for a listening post, normally arrayed in two tents with a generator for power, into one M-37 Jeep ambulance. This rugged, dependable collection of solid-state circuitry and long-range sensors took Tony up and down the far side of the border with Vietnam. His ingenuity and perseverance were priceless additions to the mission of providing advanced intelligence to the war fighters and trying to prevent the Communists from being able to wage war against our country. God bless you Tony, and thank you for your service.

My sincerest thanks to those who bumped me back and forth, and made this story into an incredible and compelling book.

FOREWORD

Many of the characters in this story were introduced in my first book, but I've laid out the story to make sure the character traits and background are understood here.

I've broken the story into three sections: setting up the story, fleshing out the characters and the threat, and then laying out the response from Randall Betts. Each section is unique and has depth, but the third section is the darkest: How far can we be pushed by evil forces that operate with impunity before we attack?

Each chapter begins with a quote from a foreign land. It gives a brief insight into what happens in the chapter, but it serves to prove that wisdom is something to be considered, and we can find it anywhere.

Once again, this is a story of personal struggle, of sacrifice and dedication, and of redemption. For Randall Betts, the redemption is on a much more personal level. I hope you enjoy this story; it has excised a lot of demons for me.

PART ONE

CHAPTER ONE: MONDAY, OCTOBER 23, 2002

Every hundred feet the world changes.

—Roberto Bolaño

It seemed like a typical fall day, but it wasn't. Randall Betts's shoes clicked as he walked briskly through the polished-stone hallways of the CIA head-quarters building. Betts was five feet, nine inches tall, and at 190 pounds carved from good workouts, he blended in with other employees roaming the hallways. But today Betts felt a bit different; he supervised an office that was critical to the mission, and today his connection to that office was in question. He ducked into the large space assigned to CTC and checked in with his small staff. This open-office area had been converted into a massive cube farm, and his section occupied one small corner of it. His deputy chief, Everett Wilson, was as chipper as ever and reported that nothing new was going on. Randall's administrative assistant and chief of reports, Evelyn Steiner, was drafting responses to requests from overseas and was totally focused on wordsmithing her cable text in a way that didn't seem haughty or parochial. It seemed that everything was humming along well. Yet for him it wasn't.

Betts was a certified clandestine operations officer for the CIA. He had joined the "Agency" after first serving a few years in the Marine Corps, followed by earning a bachelor's degree from the University of Richmond.

His degree changed from earth science (a field recommended by his girl-friend) to international studies when he decided to rush his graduation so he could join the CIA. Training for his new career was chaotic but not insurmountable. Once he was certified, he undertook some very interesting tours overseas, including one that foiled a major terrorist plot against the US Embassy in Ethiopia. Randall had gone on to serve in South America, and East Asia, and had returned to headquarters to manage a small office that was working with several different liaison accounts throughout the world.

Then 9/11 happened, and everything changed for Randall, for the CIA, and for the world.

Randall was now in charge of a small office in the Counterterrorist Center at CIA headquarters. This recently created office, the Operational Support Section (OSS), was an homage to the original clandestine operations office. Randall had been an integral part of the effort to create this support element after 9/11; he and his department chief had urged the CIA to create it to provide oversight for a multitude of projects to counter terrorist threats overseas. Randall's mission was to help arrange for the assets and resources to undertake those projects. It was a small staff, initially put under Randall's control to acquire the office space, select the talented officers needed, and begin the process of getting the attention of CIA offices worldwide. The "mission creep" to support a broad range of efforts and operational ideas subsequently blossomed into a much bigger chore.

Now it was October 2002, almost a full year after the terrorist attack on the World Trade Center and the Pentagon. It could have been much worse were it not for a brave band of souls on United Airlines Flight 93. The US government had taken the gloves off. Parts of the world previously considered unimportant were now flooded with brand new CTC officers seeking cooperation and collegial arrangements. Longtime alliances with large, lazy foreign counterparts were threatened with joining the effort to eradicate al-Qaeda or face marginalization. Every part of the globe was experiencing a reset of its relationship with the United States, and the new message was clear: get with the program, or get run over.

Randall found that getting other governments in line with the CTC's gigantic effort wasn't an issue; the cable traffic flowing into CIA HQ indicated that seemingly everyone wanted to help. Foreign powers that had previously exuded arrogance and indifference to US government officials were now racing to offer more than condolences; they were offering real assistance. Access to previously unattainable intelligence agencies was being cheerfully granted, and CTC was the main clearinghouse for all this fantastic help to bring bin Laden to justice and keep his criminal enterprise al-Qaeda from striking again. So the effort to reset relationships with US partners was not the big hurdle; it was training all the CIA employees being pushed into counterterrorism roles. Case officers, analysts, and reports managers who were traditional "South American" and "European" experts on Wednesday, September 12, were counterterrorism "experts" on Thursday the thirteenth. Training these experienced officers in the rapidly expanding world of chasing extremists and understanding the difference between Sufi Muslims and Salafists was a daunting task. When it came right down to it, understanding Islam wasn't the secret to stopping terrorists. As they learned fighting the narco-terrorists in Colombia, you cut off the base and starve the leadership, and then you'll see them fail.

And as though that wasn't enough, the rest of the federal government wanted in on this explosion. Suddenly, budget allocations were being reconfigured based on who had the most investment in counterterrorism, so the CIA found itself stretched thin to get the FBI and DOD spun up on how to locate, track, and void the warranty on those who plotted against the United States. This meant creating new and interesting courses of training that went beyond just cars and guns. This was a curriculum that would instruct well-trained and knowledgeable case officers from all over the world (and some of their foreign counterparts) on the techniques and tactics for going after radicalized extremists bent on further attacks against the United States. Randall used existing talent and commercial-service experts to fill these training requirements. It wasn't easy, and it had several setbacks, but Randall's little shop of misfit toys and gifted insiders was eventually awarded a Meritorious Unit Citation (MUC) for their work.

But this morning had little to do with supporting overseas CT projects. This morning Randall asked for a sit-down with his immediate supervisor, Joe Canelli. Joe was an experienced and thorough manager who always looked ahead when challenged with a difficult decision. He was not prone to a lot of interaction or "face time" with those in his department. He fully trusted his employees to do their jobs and did not hover over them or micromanage. While this management style may have seemed "hands-off" to some of the headquarters' staff, Randall tried to see it as a slightly more adult approach. Joe and Randall weren't sure they were going to get along at first, but once Joe found that Randall simply needed a clearly defined mission with little input or positive encouragement, he became a fan of the former Marine's leadership style.

After Randall walked the miles of corridors in the headquarters building, he arrived at CTC's main office and checked in with Yolanda, the office manager. He had discovered a whole new world of respect for these "moat dragons" in the CIA; the office managers could make or break your day if you displayed disrespect for their position. He crossed the large, open space filled with undersized cubicles and knocked on the frame of the open door at Joe's office.

"Good morning, boss. You got a minute?" said Randall. Even though he had checked with Yolanda and made an appointment to see Joe, he wasn't going to walk in without an invitation. To Randall, the rank structure described as an "informal office climate" at the CIA was false advertising. Although rank was not strictly adhered to (junior employees could easily talk to senior managers, and vice versa), there was a strict, unspoken code of command-chain communications and need-to-know limitations within the Agency. Unless your immediate supervisor committed a felony offense, you risked much by going outside of that chain or that office, and Randall respected that.

When Randall came to the door and asked for some time, Joe said what he always said.

"Sure, come in, close the door, have a seat. What's up?" With this set of instructions, Joe spun his chair to face Randall, leaned back a bit, and placed his thin, worn face into his right hand. Joe was all ears.

"I got a letter in the mail, and it looks legit, but I'd like to get someone to check it out. What it says is pretty crazy," Randall said as he handed over a single sheet of paper he had received Friday afternoon.

Joe looked it over for a minute, handed it back, and said flatly, "Yeah, it's legitimate."

Randall was a bit confused. The letter was thick-stock paper with the US Marine Corps logo at the top and a series of Pentagon offices listed with blue-ink initials at each office listing. It had three serious, distinct paragraphs with no sign-off at the end. It informed Randall that he was being reactivated for service in the USMC and was expected to appear at Marine Corps Base Quantico in two weeks for processing and reevaluation.

"How do you know? Have you seen letters like this before?" said Randall.

"It's the first time I've seen that letter, or one like it, for that matter," said Joe. "But the message about it came to the chief of CTC last week."

Now Randall was dumbfounded. Why in the world would they want him back?

Randall waited for the rest. Joe never changed the dark, unforgiving look on his face as he said, "The deputy undersecretary for the Navy, a guy that the chief of CTC beats every other week in handball, called him this morning and recommended that he never bring it up again. You're going back in, and that's all there is to it."

Randall sat back in his chair as Joe sat back in his. Randall's first question was "Why didn't somebody tell me about this?"

Joe's logic was, once again, sound: "You called in first thing and told Yolanda you wanted to talk. I knew this is what you wanted to talk about, so I waited for you to bring it to me rather than seeking you out in your office or scouring the line at the dining area coffee shop."

Randall's next question came out softer than he wanted, but the seriousness of the tone gave it the gravity it deserved. "So what do I do now? Who will take my place? How much longer can I work here?"

Joe was all business. His tone seemed to indicate indifference or lack of concern: "You are officially on 'Military Service Leave'. You have paperwork in the human resources shop to complete, and any property you've checked out in your name has to be returned. The chief of CTC has worked up a boilerplate vacancy notice for your slot and will speak informally with your deputy chief first thing tomorrow. The passport office will need your black passport back—the Marines will issue you something to replace it—and CIA Director Johnson wants to speak with you Thursday morning at eight sharp."

Randall was soaking in the details and the objectives. They all seemed to be fairly easy. Then one detail about Joe's list seemed out of place. "Thursday? What do I do until I meet with Director Johnson?"

Now Joe Canelli leaned forward, back into Randall's face, across his desk, and for the first time he could remember, his supervisor spoke in a congenial, forthright tone: "Randy, we need you here at the CIA, but the friggin' Marine Corps wants you back. So they get you, and you have enough to worry about without putting up with any more nonsense here. So sign your papers, turn in your CTC cell phone, and mail the goddamned passport to the State Department. We'll send a car to your house Thursday morning for you to meet Director Johnson. Don't worry about it. Just go play in their sandbox and come back safe, please."

"Do you know why they want me? Man, I'm thirty-six years old!" noted Randall.

"Partner, they are recalling guys from all over the globe with a USMC tattoo and the ability to draw a breath," said Joe with a conspiratorial look around the office outside of his door. "You've seen the news; you know where they're going next."

Randall cocked his head. "You can't mean going back into Baghdad?"

Joe changed his response from the posture of leaning toward Randall to easing back into his chair with a resigned, worried look on his face. "Can you believe this shit? They're taking the word of some blacklisted asset with an axe to grind with Saddam and using his outdated information to invade Iraq."

Randall had been watching the news, but the cable traffic from overseas did not portend any upcoming war with a sovereign nation. Counter-terrorism always went after nonstate actors and conducted clandestine operations against countries known for supporting acts of terror, but never at the level of invading a country. Iraq was indeed linked to acts of terror and supporting terrorist groups, but the typical response from the United States was more prone to guerrilla-type warfare and quiet operations to discourage such support. Iraq hadn't attacked New York City or the Pentagon, and just because they hadn't condemned al-Qaeda for 9/11, that didn't mean anything. The writing on the wall had been well known, with the US Secretary of State openly denouncing Iraq's aggressive actions against its neighbors and its pursuit of nuclear and biological weapons. But this was a whole new ball game, and the downsizing of the military had come to an end. The DOD was ramping up for a colossal fight with one of the largest standing armies in the world, and nothing was going to stop it. Not the Russians, not the Israelis, not the Saudis—nobody could talk the United States out of this fight.

Randall stared for a long while, then said, "Okay, boss, I'll see you sometime later."

Joe stood and shook Randall's hand hard, then said, "Come back to us, Randy; you're one of the good ones."

So, indicative of how the government works, the Thursday meeting with the Director of CIA never happened. Instead, he received a call from a Marine Corps lieutenant at Camp Lejeune Wednesday evening, informing him that he had been moved ahead for his pretraining brief to the following day. His journey back into uniformed duty had begun, whether Betts was ready or not.

CHAPTER TWO: FIVE MONTHS LATER, APRIL 1, 2003

Only a fool tests the depth of the water with both feet.

—African proverb

The monotonous whine and heavy road noise made the quiet moments something to be avoided. When Randall became aware that his unit was rolling along with nothing going on, he had to call out a drill to make sure everyone was paying attention.

"Location check! Where are we right now?" called out Marine Corps Staff Sergeant Randall Betts to everyone in his Humvee.

They were traveling "balls-to-the-wall" at just over fifty miles per hour on the dusty two-lane road called Route One, heading northwest as they returned from a major offensive against the Iraqi Army outside the southern city of al-Nasiriyah. The offensive, an attack utilizing combined arms from the Second and Third Marine Expeditionary Units, along with US Army Rangers and Delta Force commandos, had been a huge diversion to draw Iraqi Army units away from the city center so that a small special-forces team could invade a local teaching hospital and rescue US Army troops who were injured and being held as prisoners of war. The military feint had worked so that Private First Class Jessica Lynch and several colleagues, alive and dead, were recovered without a shot being fired.

Once the "attack" was completed and the rescued prisoners were flown out from the Saddam Hospital, a sizable move of military assets from the front lines of the diversionary attack to aircraft waiting on the flight line in Hillah, just south of Baghdad, resulted in a mad dash of various units through the open desert areas east of Lake Tharthar.

Randall was in the control vehicle, number two in a four-Humvee motorcade, sitting in the passenger-side front seat. Randall's vehicle crew consisted of a newly promoted corporal manning the machine-gun turret and a communications expert in the driver's-side rear seat, behind a corporal driving the vehicle like he was scared to death. The extra person in the back, just behind Randall, was a USMC major who had hitched a ride at the last minute because he wanted to arrive in Hillah ahead of the one-star general who had directed much of the action from a mobile command post. The general had elected to travel back to Hillah in the tractor-trailer-sized command vehicle, and his travel back would be much slower than the other convoys. The major surmised that being at the flight line first to ensure that everything was smooth for the general was a valuable goal, so he jumped into Randall's group at the last minute. As Randall drove on and monitored the command channel, it became clear to him that the general was giving orders and instructions pertaining to his arrival in Hillah, so this major was wasting his time. But Randall kept his mouth shut. He simply endured the extra crowding for the three-hour drive.

The four-vehicle motorcade consisted of a total of sixteen Marines plus the hitchhiking major. As part of the Weapons Support Battalion, their job was to coordinate the heavy weapons needed for the MEUs and ensure that the proper firepower got to the right place. As the supply of Mark 19 grenade launchers dwindled (they were new and shiny; all the commanders wanted them), Randall and his crew were relegated to mounting the older M2 Browning heavy-barrel machine-gun into each turret of the Humvees under his control. Randall didn't mind, as he preferred what the .50-caliber machine-gun could do in a firefight. The Mark 19 40mm grenade launcher put a lot of explosive violence into an enemy, but the M2 needed to be aimed properly, and that made it a formidable weapon in the hands of a Marine rifleman.

Randall's sudden shout of "Location check!" made everyone pay attention to where they were and thereby avoid any lack of attention on the part of his team. It wasn't a typical USMC drill. Randall had learned to do this while working with CIA case officers in dangerous neighborhoods. It was called "situational driving" and taught case officers more than just being alert; it gave them an outlet to voice their concerns and diminished their anxiety. Calling out what was going on close to the motorcade and where they were located in case they had to report it later created a great deal of situational awareness and kept everyone awake.

The driver spoke up first: "One hour and forty-six minutes into the movement from an-Nasiriyah, Staff Sergeant!"

The gunner leaned in from the turret and shouted, "Level desert with some dunes to the west, slight drop-off to the east of the roadway, Staff Sergeant!"

The commo expert waited his turn and proclaimed, "Just passed an unfinished cloverleaf, Staff Sergeant! About two klicks to our south, there was a gas station and a restaurant! I think the name of the restaurant was something like Wawa-"

"Shut up with your guesses! If you don't know the name, keep it to yourself!" barked the major. This was the first thing spoken by the officer in over an hour, and it rattled everyone in the truck.

"The name of the restaurant was Mawa," said Randall calmly. He didn't want to qualify what the major had said, as these Marines were Randall's crew, and this guy was a ride-along, regardless of his rank.

"Gimme the details of the gas station!" Randall quickly added to the communications officer.

The private replied sheepishly at first but finished his report with more confidence: "Two-story white-stone structure on the west side of Route One, Staff Sergeant! Now three kilometers to our south. Four gas pumps, large red letters in lights, and just south of the unfinished cloverleaf!"

"Not bad, Private. You see the value of providing those details if you had to vector in a medevac helicopter."

"Yes, Staff Sergeant!" The reply was one of pride. Everyone was a bit more alert now, even if it was due to the rude comments from the officer.

"Yo, garbage pile coming up on our left," said the driver.

"Pile of destroyed vehicles on our left, one klick ahead!" called the turret gunner.

This was good; the crew was starting to learn to call out potential threats as they approached.

As Randall looked through the windscreen, he could see blackened hunks piled on the driver's side of the roadway. These were not uncommon, as the plow crews that cleared these roads had pushed various mounds of debris into piles as they built small berms from the sand that blew constantly across the road.

As they were approaching, the radio crackled with a report from the lead vehicle. "Looks like a Tennessee new-car dealership coming up on our left."

Randall instantly smiled at the joke. The control unit in the lead vehicle knew that Randall was from Tennessee. They were coming up on the junked vehicles now; they were piled in neat lines horizontal to the roadway. The rear line of junked and burned cars was taller than the line closer to the road. Kind of unusual when the bulldozers didn't normally take the time to do that.

Then Randall felt the pull on his shoulder epaulet as the major behind him leaned into his ear and spoke clearly. "Tell your lead vehicle to avoid unnecessary radio traff—"

The lead vehicle exploded in front of them, sending a wall of sand and smoke and debris into the windscreen. The next sounds Randall remembered hearing were the screams of his turret gunner. He must have been hit by debris and blast overpressure from the lead vehicle's demise. But the gunner's screams were not anguish or pain; he was saying something, very loudly. It sounded like "Contact left!"

And *demise* was the proper word for the lead vehicle. Just as they were abreast of the junk vehicles piled in a neat line next to the roadway, the front end of the lead vehicle blew straight up and out from the frame, and the two Marines in the front seat, the driver and the control officer, were blown clear into pieces. It must have been a mine, remote-detonated with something as simple as a garage-door-opening fob. The large, diesel-powered truck tilted up on its rear end and fell violently back onto the roadway as a barrage of rifle fire opened up from the junk pile.

"Contact left! Turn and fire the turrets!" came the quick command from Randall into his radio. The motorcade stopped, but not because of disability. The vehicles instantly turned on a slight angle and stopped very close together, creating an improvised array of machinery and cover. The vehicles were now a consolidated line, easier to change cover and work to pin the enemy down before going for the flanks. This was the training; when the attack comes, lean into the fight. Counterattack and dominate the scene. To accomplish this, the turret gunners would deliver cover fire from their heavy weapons, while the Marines inside the vehicle would exit the vehicles in the first safe direction identified and establish cover to return fire.

Each Marine carried the M16A2 rifle. As Randall finished his broadcast of instructions to the other vehicles, he used his right hand to open the truck's door. As he moved his left hand from his microphone to the grip of his rifle, secured in a rough leather holster and facing down in the vehicle, Randall felt a sudden weight on him. The driver of his Humvee, the corn-fed corporal from Kansas, had leaped incredibly over the communication and transmission hump between the seats and was landing on Randall in an all-out race to exit the vehicle, away from the furious cacophony of rounds hitting the left side of the truck.

The driver, along with his retrieved M16 rifle and thirty pounds of gear, amounted to roughly 260 pounds landing on Randall, his left arm, and his rifle. The force continuum of this encounter resulted in Randall piling out of the passenger's side of the Humvee with his driver on top of him but no rifle. Thinking back to that moment, Randall was happy that he didn't lose his left arm in this pile, but his rifle was indeed still in its holster. Randall pushed the larger man off him and stood him up alongside another Marine, behind the engine and front axle of the truck. "Stand here, keep your cover, return fire!" Randall screamed at him over the sound of almost two dozen rifles firing into his motorcade.

Now Randall returned to the front seat of his Humvee as it sagged and chipped and started to come apart from the rifle rounds being poured into it. Randall immediately came to two observations: One was that his rifle was toast. It had cracked under the violent weight of the Marine that landed on him. As he now pulled it from its leather sheath, it was clear that the forward, threaded area of the receiver and the rear portion of the barrel and handguard were bent at an obscene angle, making the rifle unusable.

The second observation was that all the return fire was from other M16 rifles. No sound had started from the M2 machine guns in the turrets of the Humvees. When Randall looked out the rear window of his Humvee to understand why they weren't getting cover fire from the heavy machine guns, he saw a rocket-propelled grenade streak into the hood of the third vehicle, rocking it to the side and killing three of his troops firing from the passenger's side. Their screams were hushed under the thunder of the exploding rocket, and they fell back off the road, into the fairly steep drop-off on the east side that was identified by his gunner earlier. Inside his Humvee, the blast rocked Betts hard against the dashboard, and he felt his helmet crack the windshield from the inside.

Randall didn't take the time to catalog this; he had troops in contact, and he had to keep what he had left alive. When he ducked out of his Humvee and surveyed his resources, what he saw was the beginning of panic. His commo officer was screaming into his headset, trying to get the attention of Hillah base. Next to him was the major, crouching and looking eagerly at him, and his driver, who had just emptied a magazine into the direction of the gunfire coming at them, also looking at Randall as though he had some better news. The other Marine, still standing in a crouch while using the cover of the front axle and engine of the Humvee, was trying to fire into the spots where muzzle flashes could be seen.

He started with the obvious. Betts reached out to grab the commo officer's arm and made him be quiet. Then Randall leaned into the young man's face and stated, in a calm, loud voice, "Slow down, Marine. Tell them we are on Route One, three kilometers north of the cloverleaf, in contact with superior number, under small arms and RPG fire, and have numerous casualties. Request air support and immediate evac. Green smoke."

The commo officer nodded and started again, in a slower, clearer voice, and was evidently getting comeback from Hillah base. This was good news. The unrelenting focus of rifle fire on their position was not.

Randall thought for just a moment and then huddled up against the crouching major. "Sir, I need your sidearm," Randall shouted in a clear, unhurried tone. And then he waited.

The senior officer, clearly a man who deplored giving up his only weapon, stared at this staff sergeant like he was crazy.

But Betts waited him out, holding out his hand, staring intently and not changing his request.

Finally, the major relented, unsnapped his holster, and slid out his pistol. Randall simply took the gun in one hand and watched as the major reached into his vest and produced several spare magazines. Randall obliged by taking his spare M16 mags from the pockets on his vest and handing them to those with a rifle. Once the gun and the spare ammo were exchanged, then Randall leaned back toward him, and the commo officer and stated, "When I draw their fire, head straight to the east and keep running until you get some cover from here! Then pop green smoke and stay in touch with the evac crew!"

He waited for the quick confirmation from the pair before turning to the south and running in a crouch toward the back of the motorcade. As he ran behind the cover of the vehicles, he could hear shouts across the road. Evidently, these guys were organized and communicating. Once he made his way around the burning third vehicle and came to the fourth vehicle, he saw three of his troops in turmoil. One was badly injured but alive, one was emptying a first-aid kit to get out the appropriate bandages, and the third was leaning over them, hollering instructions. Nobody was returning fire, the turret held a dead gunner, and this small gaggle was getting nowhere.

Betts grabbed the hollering Marine by the arm and found that it was a female corporal. The Marine Corps had not yet allowed females into combat units, but field administration and motor-pool positions were available. Evidently, this corporal had signed on as a convoy driver and encountered a whole lot more action than she had anticipated. She looked at Randall like he was a threat but quickly shut up when she saw who it was.

Betts said, "Get your injured forward to my group, wait for the incoming to die down, and follow them to the evac point!"

The two quickly complied by heaving the injured man up, and they undertook moving north toward the others. Randall moved in a low crouch to the back bumper of the last Humvee. Kneeling behind the spare tire and wheel at the back end, he took out the pistol and laid out the spare magazines. And then he saw it. He was shocked at what the officer had surrendered to him.

Instead of a Beretta M9 pistol that was commonly issued in the field, Randall beheld an M45A1 Colt 1911 combat pistol and five extra extended magazines. Instead of forty-five rounds of 147-grain copper-jacketed 9mm ammo, Randall had sixty rounds of 230-grain ball ammo in .45 caliber. Nothing close to the M16 that he had to leave behind, but a much better firearm package than he envisioned. The pistol was a gleaming blue steel, with a USMC medallion stuck onto gorgeous pearl grips. It was a beautiful specimen of a reliable and powerful semiautomatic sidearm.

Without any further appreciation for the weapon, Randall held the revered pistol around the side of the Humvee, holding it only by the stock in his gloved left hand and aiming it roughly in the direction of the enemy fire. The only part of him that showed to the enemy was the pistol. He had taken the glove off his right hand and now stuck his index finger into the trigger guard and wagged it violently back and forth against the trigger. The barking sound of the large-caliber pistol was not much of a deterrent, but the rate of fire was noticeable. The pistol emptied its first magazine in less than three seconds, and he pulled it back in, reloaded quickly, and returned the pistol to a firing position. Once that magazine was empty, it was quickly ejected, and another went smoothly into the weapon. By the time the third magazine had emptied, the enemy was convinced that another fully automatic weapon had been brought to bear on them. The accuracy was for shit, but the heavy bullets striking the roadway and the metal frames of the junk cars convinced the Fedayeen Fighters that a new threat had emerged. Randall heard more shouts across the road as he loaded the fifth magazine; these guys were directing fire into his position.

When a captain had instructed this technique, called "bump-firing," to Randall at Marine Combat Training several weeks ago, it was made clear that this was a waste of good ammunition, but it demonstrated that any decent semiautomatic pistol could fire at a perceived rate of 420 rounds per minute. This was impressive but wasteful. Unless you were in Betts' situation.

And it was working. By the time Randall's difficult-to-locate gun came back for a fifth magazine dump, the amount of incoming rifle fire on his position was building. Betts was getting a lot of attention from the enemy, and his cover was getting chewed up fairly quickly. Shards of fiberglass and plastic from the vehicle were cutting into his face and his bare right hand, and bullet fragments were splattering all around him. His eyes were mostly protected by his goggles, but his cheeks and chin were stinging from all the flying debris. Once the fifth magazine was ejected and the final magazine was seated into this fine pistol, Randall drew around to his back side and looked down at the row of damaged vehicles he had left behind. Just beyond the heat, smoke, and flames of the third Humvee, Betts could see the small procession of Marines scrambling down the side of the road and running flat-out to the east. This was great news. Now Randall had to extricate himself from this self-created shitstorm of rifle fire. As he wiped the blood from the cuts on his face, he turned back to collect the empty magazines. That's when Randall spied movement straight across the road. He had not concerned himself with this area before, but now that he looked, he saw a wisp of blue material settling in behind the berm about twenty yards away. This was the shirt of an enemy fighter sent to address this hidden attacker.

With the last magazine loaded, Randall transitioned the pistol into his bleeding, bare right hand. From behind the spare tire of the Humvee, Betts settled into a proper kneeling position. He steadied his grip with his gloved left hand, aimed at the top of the berm, and waited. The incoming fire was ferocious, loud, and spitting dirt all around him, but Randall locked in on the blade front sight of his weapon and the movement straight across the road. The gunner seeking Betts's flank slowly rose. He saw the light outline of his target's kaffiyeh first, then the black image of the rifle. Betts eased the trigger back with a light touch, and the gun barked. The bullet exploded from the venerable handgun and went over sixty feet at just under 950 feet per second, traveled parallel to the frame of the AK-47 rifle aimed opposite, and hit the shooter just below his left cheek. The spinning bullet passed easily through his skull and brain matter and exited the back of the man's head, creating a cavity of over three inches.

As the man fell back, the incoming rifle fire seemed to intensify. Randall turned in the direction that he had seen his comrades run and was crouching even tighter to launch out. Then two things happened. First, a rifle bullet skimmed off the roadway, traveled straight under the vehicle, and caught Randall in his left ankle. As he pitched a bit forward to the pain and shock of the injury, he looked down to see that the leather upper of his Bates boot (thank God the military had found a decent boot for the troops) had held together, so there was some measure of compression against the bleeding ankle. When the second thing happened, Betts couldn't help but look up. A sound emerged, a grateful sound, a beautiful sound, an incredibly powerful sound. The sound of an M2 Browning heavy-barreled machine-gun firing 760-grain bullets in .50 caliber into the enemy position across the street.

Randall stumbled to a crouch and saw the turret of the first Humvee pouring hate into the collection of crumpled metal frames providing cover for the enemy. The Humvee gunner had been hurt, probably stunned, by the mine that took out his vehicle. But he was up now, firing armor-piercing rounds methodically into the enemy position that had been turned away from him, aiming at Betts's position at the far end of the motorcade. He had started high, going after the snipers at the higher positions in the back row that had been targeting the turret gunners. And then he swept lower into the main body of the now-suffering Iraqis who thought they had this attack covered.

Randall now ran, albeit in a stumble, in the direction of the gunner. His fire was effective, but he would run out of ammo soon at the rate he was overheating the barrel of the gun. Once he reached the first Humvee, Betts saw that he could not access the gunner through the burning interior of the vehicle that was now threatening the man's legs. Betts found that when he stopped to survey the damage done to the Humvee and the determined Marine firing back at the enemy, he was a bit woozy; his eyesight was a bit wobbly, and his head felt thick inside his helmet. Fazed but undaunted, Betts scrambled up onto the back hatch across to the gunner and shook him by the shoulders.

"Time to evac, Marine! Good job, but we gotta go!"

The young gunner turned to look up and just stared at Randall. His face showed confusion, and pain, and anger. And then Randall recognized a look of terror on the man's face. This observation was followed by a tremendous gush of forced air and shrill shrieks as 2.75-inch rockets sailed over their heads into the enemy position. The rush of the rockets and the ensuing explosions almost threw Betts off the Humvee as hot air, sand, and shrapnel pushed against him at high speed. As soon as this blast was starting to ebb, the grating whip of a USMC AH-1 SuperCobra helicopter roared over them. The twin-bladed Bell attack helicopter banked hard left over their position and circled back. But Randall knew he wasn't coming back for another pass, not yet. He was just getting out of the way for what would come next.

Randall struggled to pull the gunner through his turret and onto the roof of the burning Humvee just as another menacing presence swept the air out of the area. The electric pulsing of a triple-barreled chain gun mounted to the nose of the second SuperCobra (Randall knew they always hunted in pairs) poured 20mm depleted-uranium projectiles into what was left of the threats and continued firing as the helicopter tracked behind the enemy's position to a point one hundred yards away. This effort was rewarded with the secondary explosions of vehicles parked behind a dune that was unseen from the road. But the pilot/gunner team of the second helicopter saw them and took them away in a massive display of fire, smoke, and churned-up sand.

By the time the two attack helicopters were actively circling the area, looking for anything left to shoot, Randall and the gunner were running a three-legged race in the direction he had seen the others running. Hopefully this would be an evacuation site. With Randall's damaged ankle and the gunner's shredded legs, they looked like a two-headed monster trudging through the deep, soft sand with little hope of gaining ground. When they did finally round the first bit of dune they came upon, Randall was rewarded with a beautiful sight.

His squad of Marines had settled into a 360-degree firing position as a smoke grenade poured a thick green curtain into the air. Emerging through that green haze was a CH-53E Super Stallion helicopter (called a "shitter") with the port-side door open and a gunner manning the M134 minigun. Randall wanted to raise his arm to signal that he was coming, but he couldn't let go of the person he was carrying. The man was practically carried by Betts now, the injuries and the shock and the exertion wiping out his consciousness. Randall himself could only take a couple more steps before he stumbled and fell. The pace and urgency had carried them forward, but this welcome sight resulted in a slight loss of resilience. Randall just could not get back up.

But then he could. He felt himself rise up off the hot desert and quickly make his way over the thick sand and scrub brush to the waiting squad. Once he arrived at the door of the enormous helicopter, he found that he was not moving; something was moving him. He was pulled from someone's grasp into the bay of the helicopter, and he began to feel his clothing and his equipment being pulled and tugged from him. It was all Randall could do to reach into the pocket of his BDU tunic and pull out the 1911 pistol, dirty, bloody, scratched, and still loaded. He held it up until he felt the grateful hand of someone else relieve him of the handgun and make it safe.

"Thanks, Marine" was the last thing Betts heard before he blacked out.

CHAPTER THREE: THREE DAYS LATER, APRIL 4, 2003

Do good and throw it in the sea.

—Arab Proverb

When Betts woke up and looked around, he stayed still and built an understanding of his surroundings and his physical condition. He was alive and breathing, he was lying on his back, and he was held down by bandages and heavy blankets in a room with light-green walls and machines hooked up to him. Good start—he was in a hospital somewhere. Slowly he began to build memories of what happened. This was slow due to some amount of medication, Betts assessed. The ringing in his ears was persistent, and the sensation of numbness accompanied by a warm feeling backed up his assessment.

And then he became aware that he was slightly elevated in the bed. Sitting up like this meant that he had been awake before. The sounds of the machines were constant but not loud. Good, thought Betts, this meant that he wasn't on a ventilator. The machines he heard were simply tracking his heart rate, pulse, and respiration. The sounds outside the room were low-intensity, with some echoes. Great, he thought. This meant he was in a big hospital like the one in Ramstein, Germany.

In trying to look around, Betts became aware of the bandages on his face. Evidently, the cuts had been a bit more severe than he thought. Moving ever so slightly, he felt the heavy cast on his left leg. This was from the bullet strike on his ankle. Almost involuntarily he moved that left ankle, and was rewarded with pain that felt both sharp and dull at the same time. As he ran down the list of things he was aware of and tried to recall the things that brought him here, a male nurse opened the lone door to the room and looked at Randall. Once their eyes met, the nurse turned away quickly and called a name he did not know.

"Doctor Oldham! He's awake again!"

Betts was soon thereafter visited by two hospital employees. The first was a tall man in his fifties wearing a white lab coat and carrying a computer tablet. His expression was one of procession with no hurry. Evidently Betts waking up was not the most exciting part of his day. He was followed by a female nurse in her late forties carrying a legal pad. They approached Betts like he was keeping them from their favorite episode of *Jeopardy!*, urgent but not important.

"How are you feeling today, Sergeant?" was the first thing the doctor said. Evidently, he did not care about the answer, because as Betts tried to form an answer, the doctor spoke again.

"You really tested our mettle in here. That injury to your ankle was pretty severe for just one wound. The bullet fragment did some tissue damage and tore a few ligaments, but then, by all accounts, you went ahead and carried another injured person, one who weighs a bit more than you do, all over the desert and screwed up both the navicular and cuboid joints. It was all I could do to repair those joints and get you some semblance of use for that foot!"

Randall stared at him for just a moment to make sure this guy wasn't kidding. When no laughing ensued and the doctor just continued to stare at his tablet, Randall quietly replied, "Well, I apologize for doing my duty, thereby making your day a bit more difficult."

When the doctor jerked his eyes away from his tablet to address this snarky comment, Randall continued, "Where is the Marine that I carried? What is his condition?"

The doctor returned to his tablet and quickly answered, "He's not in this ward. We have no idea what his condition is; he's not in my care."

"Well, who the hell are you? Where the fuck am I, and how do I find out something about the condition of a man that saved several lives in the line of fire?" Randall's calm was eroding.

The nurse stepped in this time. "You watch your mouth, young man! You're lucky to have an orthopedic surgeon with this man's qualifications! He was assigned here from Cornell!" She let that hang in the air like it was a treat; then she quickly added, "And he holds the rank of colonel!"

Betts fumbled a slight salute with the arm that didn't have an IV hooked to it, and said, "Well, Colonel, could you get me a PA who can get me the answers I need about the troops that were under my command?" (Navy medics who accompanied Marines into combat were normally physicians' assistants.)

They both turned and walked calmly out of the room without another word. Betts had probably screwed up his situation here, but since he wasn't sure of where he was and what was going on, it didn't matter much. He went back to sleep.

When Betts awoke again, he quickly became aware of two things. One was that his throat was extremely dry, and the other was that he was being observed by someone in the room. When he managed to engage some measure of a swallow and focused his eyesight, he saw that he was being stared at by a Marine master sergeant. The patches on his tunic were seldom seen by a regular infantryman, and it had a tight crease like it had come straight out of dry cleaning. He had never seen the insignia in the field, but the man's pressed uniform was desert camouflage, and the ribbons on his chest indicated that he had well over fifteen years' service.

"Staff Sergeant Betts, I'm glad you're awake, because I'm tired of standing here waiting for you to acknowledge my presence!" came the barking, loud monotone that only the USMC could create.

Betts made a much better attempt to facilitate a full salute this time.

"You have survived an episode of enemy contact and accomplished many of the things expected of you in such an endeavor. You are now in the short-term ward at Landstuhl Regional Medical Center and will be transported to Walter Reed Hospital within the next seventy-two hours. Your injuries are not severe, and you will receive excellent therapeutic care while there."

The man was talking at a loud, cadence delivery. He did not falter in his delivery or his expression as he transitioned to the next part of his message,

"You have demonstrated a lack of common respect for the medical staff here, and this behavior is to be dropped immediately. Do I make myself clear to you, Staff Sergeant?"

"Yes, Master Sergeant. May I know the conditions of the troops under my command?"

"Those Marines are no longer under your command, so they are no longer your concern!"

He could care less that everyone else on the ward heard all this. The shouting and lack of decorum did not faze Betts. He had been through it at boot camp, at combat infantry training, and again at the run-up training for this deployment. This dehumanization was to be expected when a Marine shot his mouth off to a senior officer, even one as pompous as Dr. Oldham. Betts continued to stare, waiting for the senior enlisted officer to drop the "recruiting rap" and either level with him or simply storm out of the room. The master sergeant went with the former, dropping his voice to just over a whisper and bending at the waist in Betts's direction.

"The man you carried out lost both of his legs. He is still in ICU, and it's iffy at best that he survives."

At this, the master sergeant extended his hand and pressed a small item into Randall's left hand and squeezed lightly.

"But he's here, and he's getting the best care in the world because of you. You did great, son. They forwarded something you left in your BDU. You are okay, Marine." This was all he said before he turned sharply and marched out of the room. He would promptly report to Dr. Oldham that the upstart Marine in room thirty-five had been appropriately scolded for his impertinence.

Once the room was empty, Betts looked down at what the master sergeant had pressed into his palm. It was the USMC medallion from the M45 he had been using to draw enemy fire. A small but significant reminder of what he had endured. This was more important to him than any medal. Randall lay back in his bed, but just for a moment. He pushed back up and reached for the cup of water at his bedside. It was then that Betts heard the ringing in his ears. He thought it was from all the hollering he'd just had to endure, but it was not that. It was like a sinus attack, but it was more stinging in his ears. He reached down to the call button and pressed tightly.

Same day, April 4, 2003
Tennessee Regional Remote Team Report, Case 187YG5
Field Report: 04/04/03. At 0615 hours Subject rose from his bed and turned on the lights in the hallway and kitchen. Subject had a breakfast of cereal and milk, and made a partial pot of coffee. Subject proceeded to the front porch of the target residence and sat in the right-hand chair

until approximately 0830 hours. He returned to the kitchen and made a second cup of coffee.

Tech Journal: 04/04/03. At 0837 hours, the residential landline of the target residence received an overseas call. The origin of the call appears to be the military hospital near Ramstein Air Base. The call was unanswered and lasted 32 seconds. No message was left.

Field Report (cont.): 04/04/03. At 0930 hours, subject walked from the target residence to the unattached garage. Subject remained in the garage for the rest of the morning, making repeated counts of the various items in the garage. (Support Team Comment: The trash analysis reports several pages of attempted accountings of the materials in the garage, all of which are repetitive and unfinished.)

Subject returned to the target residence and watched TV until 1830 hours, then moved to the bedroom. End of Field Report.

CHAPTER FOUR: THREE WEEKS LATER, APRIL 24, 2003

Fall seven times, stand up eight.

—Japanese Proverb

Randall Betts had completed two weeks of comprehensive therapeutic treatment at Walter Reed National Military Medical Center, less than twenty miles from Washington, DC. Once he arrived from Ramstein Air Base in Germany, a small team in this prestigious hospital had overseen a rigorous protocol for assessing the extent of damage to his ankle and set out to get blood flowing to the muscles and joints that had to heal in order for Randall to walk without crutches. From a heavy cast just below the knee covering his entire lower leg, Betts had progressed to a lighter cast over just the ankle and foot.

But it had been neither easy nor friendly. The staff at Walter Reed were professional and competent, but too many casualties were being flown in from Iraq. Soldiers, sailors, Marines, even Air Force pilots were in a near-constant flow to the finest hospital on the East Coast for rehabilitation and repairs to their bodies. Lots of men and women had injuries much worse than Randall's, so he was being herded toward a quick release with an adjustable cane and an unlimited prescription for pain pills. He tried several times to get them to listen to his complaint about the ringing in his ears. The recuperation of his ankle was painful enough, but that was just joints and weight pressure. Once Betts sat down, a lot of the ankle pain went away, but the ringing in the ears and a slight dizziness were causing more anxiety every day. The sole response from the doctor was to seek a slightly more potent painkiller, followed by an appointment for an upper-body massage.

Betts called the number he had been provided when he checked out of the rehabilitation ward. He was informed that a van would retrieve him from the hospital and drive him to Andrews Air Force Base, about thirty miles south of Walter Reed. From Andrews, a military transport C-130 would carry him to Cherry Point Marine Air Station for a van ride to Camp Lejeune, North Carolina. This made sense because Betts had left his car at Lejeune before he had been flown to Andrews Air Force Base for shipping to Iraq three long months before. Camp Lejeune was headquarters of the second Marine Expeditionary Unit (2MEU), and it was where Betts had undergone several weeks of intense combat infantry training to refresh himself with the main job of the USMC.

Betts dragged himself and his C-bag to a side entrance of Walter Reed Hospital. He found a bench that was just beyond the shadow of the huge stone building, where he could feel the sunshine on him. A welcome feeling. It was then that he felt a chill. It wasn't the ringing in his ears, and it wasn't the pain medication; it was an ominous sensation that he was not alone. He looked around quickly but didn't see anyone close to him. No threats. So he looked a bit farther out, into the line of parked cars adjacent to the side entrance of the hospital. The moving cars and the uninterested pedestrians were ignored; Betts was looking for something sitting still. Something facing him. He felt that someone was watching him, and he had been proved right. He observed a man sitting in a sedan along a row of parked vehicles. Not obvious, but still able to watch the entrance. And he was watching. He was looking directly at Randall. Betts worked his hard stare to get some details about the man: white male, late thirties, face a little fleshy, so his weight would be close to two hundred. Brown hair, white shirt, and a blazer or suit coat. Betts couldn't see the color of the coat the man was wearing, so he stood slowly to get a better view. As he stood, a twelve-passenger Dodge van roared up and cut off his view of the man. The van honked twice as it stopped right in front of Betts. Startled by the van's arrival and sudden noise, Betts jerked his attention to the person driving the van. The passenger window came down, and a sergeant driving the older Dodge van said, "Staff Sergeant Betts, Randall Allen?"

"That's me" was all Betts said as he heaved his C-bag into the back seat and climbed into the front passenger seat. As he buckled his seat belt, Betts ignored the greetings from the van driver as he craned his neck to see into the parking lot. Betts looked where he had seen the sedan and the man staring at him, but they were gone.

As they pulled out of the hospital parking lot and drove toward the 495 Beltway South, Betts kept checking the side-view mirror and back window for anyone following them. When the driver inquired what was wrong, Betts just shrugged it off and kept looking forward.

After driving him south to Andrews Air Force Base, Betts was delivered to the VIP terminal, where he waited in a carpeted room filled with ornate furniture. This was where senior officials and families of returning officers would gather to welcome troops back from overseas assignments. He had never been welcomed back in his career.

The 350-mile flight to Cherry Point, North Carolina, a Marine air base adjacent to Camp Lejeune, was short, loud, and uncomfortable. The loadmaster on the C-130 transporting him had provided Betts with foam earplugs at the beginning of the flight, but they hurt his ears once they were inserted. That was strange to Betts, as he had never had trouble wearing them before.

As Betts hauled his C-bag from the plane and onto the tarmac, he observed that his walk to the terminal building was over one hundred yards. He groaned in anticipation of dragging himself and his belongings that distance. Once he was halfway to the terminal, Betts started to hear a growing roar in his ears. He stopped to avoid any further exertion, as this was certainly his ringing returning. He didn't want to be seen as a stumbling cripple falling on the cement, so he stood still and waited to catch his breath, hoping the ringing wouldn't worsen. It was then that Betts noticed the growing roar he was hearing was not coming from within him. It was an outside noise; something big and powerful was approaching, and it was a sound Betts had never heard before. As he opened his eyes and looked up, he saw two V-22 Ospreys fly over at half speed. Randall then became aware of an aviation specialist walking across the tarmac. The young man was coming from the flight building and was near Randall as he passed.

"Nice-looking aircraft," said Randall to the specialist. "But they'll never replace the Frogs."

"Frogs, sir?" was the response from the nineteen-year-old.

"CH-46s, Marine. Sea Knights. They took us everywhere."

"They still do, just a whole lot less. Have a nice day, sir," replied the specialist.

Randall didn't have the stamina or the focus to remind this young pup that he was not addressing an officer.

A van picked Betts up at the main terminal, and after a one-hour drive southwest, Betts found himself back at the administration building for Marine Corps Base Camp Lejeune. The two-story brick building seemed a little less intimidating to Betts than it had been when he was here just a few short months ago. Betts went inside and identified himself, and he was allowed to stow his bag before being shown to the administrative center in a back corner of the building.

The administrative clerks had Randall sign the paperwork needed to document his travel from the war zone and account for his lack of ability to return to Iraq. The Corps needed to know why Randall could not return to the fighting, and it took two different written reports from the orthopedic-therapy team at Walter Reed Hospital to fully account for his disability. For his part, Randall wasn't keen on returning to the hot days, freezing nights, and gritty chow from the near-constant flow of sand in the air. What he wanted was to get back to his team. As an NCO in a weapons support battalion, he oversaw an incredibly efficient group responsible for supplying the right weaponry to the frontline units. Their dedication to crossing t's and dotting i's wasn't just admin grunt work; they stayed in top physical form and regularly volunteered to go out on patrols and safety runs with the other groups. With their expertise and their motivation to take the fight to the enemy, they exemplified the military occupational specialty (MOS) of "combat arms." These were the people worth defending, worth fighting for. But Randall was certain they weren't going to rotate him back in. The clerks at Lejeune treated Betts like he was human cardboard. He wasn't being taken back in; they were going to give him some time at a local veteran affairs (VA) hospital, then make sure his prescription for Tramadol was unlimited and turn him loose. It seemed unnatural to Betts at the time, but he later came to see that it was happening to way too many people in the military.

* * *

Just as Betts was getting briefed on his next appointment at the VA hospital closest to him, a captain walked up, called him by name, and waited for a salute. When Betts saluted him, the captain gave instructions that he was to follow him, and he quickly stepped down the hall. Betts tried his best to keep up with his cane and his cast, but the only time the Marine officer slowed down was to pause at two heavy doors and input numbers on an adjacent keypad. Once he passed through the second security door, Betts found himself in a dark room filled with television monitors, world clocks, and a dozen specialists typing reports into large computer monitors at their desks.

"Right here, Staff Sergeant," came the voice of the captain. Betts squinted into the sudden reduction of lighting to see his guide holding the phone receiver for a STU-III secure phone. The line had been enabled, but the number listed on the small screen of the encryption device was one that he did not recognize. Betts took the receiver and said hello.

"Boy, where the hell have you been?" It was the voice of CIA Director Olivia Baines Johnson.

CHAPTER FIVE: SAME DAY, APRIL 24, 2003

Don't sail out farther than you can row back.

—Danish Proverb

"Good to hear from you, ma'am!" said Betts enthusiastically. This was the first acquaintance he had spoken with in over a month. DCIA Johnson had taken a sincere interest in Betts while he worked as a case officer for the counterterrorist center. Betts had provided critically important information that led to foiling a serious terrorist threat in early 1998 to the US Embassy in Addis Ababa, and he had tried to keep the threat level high against other embassies on the east coast of Africa, but his efforts had failed. Osama bin Laden took up the torch against the West and blew up the embassies in Nairobi and Dar es Salaam later that year, and Betts had taken that failure very hard. When he asked to be taken out of the field, it was DCIA Johnson who spoke to him privately and encouraged him to stay in the fight. She told him, "Your value to this country is based on your talent and instincts, and you are at your best when you are challenged." Now she was barking at him like an angry mother at her boy who had been hiding in the woods.

"Never mind that 'ma'am' crap. You were supposed to meet with me before you left!"

"They picked me up before I could see you! I called DPS and told them I couldn't make it!" said Betts weakly. (DPS was the director's protective staff)

"And then you take off into a buzz saw of a war zone, get yourself shot up, come back to the States, and just disappear! I've been calling all over Quantico, the Pentagon. Hell, I even called the duty officer at Eighth and I Street to find out something about you! I couldn't get any information about your whereabouts or your condition!"

"I would've thought the military would keep you informed, ma'am—I mean, Director Johnson," said Randall. He was standing straighter now, speaking with earnestness and apology into the phone.

Unbeknownst to Randall, several of the intelligence specialists in the crowded room had turned their heads to see this conversation, and they were openly amused at the change of demeanor in Betts. When he stumbled into the Tactical Operations Center, he was slouched and squinting. Now he was ramrod straight during the conversation, talking sheepishly into the secure phone.

"I'm leaving my office right now for a briefing on Capitol Hill. But you *will* call me tonight and fill me in. Take down these two numbers," commanded Johnson.

Betts beat on his chest for a pen. A half-dozen pens were extended from the numerous specialists watching him on the phone. "Go ahead," he said.

"The first is my personal cell phone. That goes into your head. Remember that and call me tonight, and anytime you need something! The second number is your sister Carol's cell phone. She needs to discuss family business with you."

Betts dutifully wrote down both numbers. He recognized Carol's number but didn't dare interrupt DCIA. It struck Betts as odd that DCIA Johnson knew his sister's cell-phone number, but he knew better than to ask the chief of US intelligence how she got that number.

"I have arranged for your transportation. Your car was left there at Lejeune, but I can't have you navigating Virginia traffic with a clubfoot and jet lag. A driver will be there and will take you to New River Air Station, where you will be flown to the Signature business terminal at Dulles Airport. You know how to catch a cab home from Dulles, don't you?" said Director CIA Johnson.

"Yes ma'am!" said Randall quickly.

The director of the Central Intelligence Agency then ended the secure call.

"Okay, thank you…ma'am," said Randall into an empty phone.

When he looked up, Betts was rewarded with gentle applause from the captain, who had been watching him during the call. "Man, that woman sure got you perpendicular!" The intel specialists in the room just went back to their computer screens.

Betts was guided back through the security doors into the waiting hall for the administration building. He had his C-bag returned to him, and a van quickly appeared for his hop to the small air base at Camp Lejeune. Betts was unsure if anything other than a helicopter could land at this facility, but he knew that if DCIA said to do it, it would be done.

As he buckled up and waited for the driver to get himself situated and underway, Betts looked once more across the scenic field in front of the admin building. The soothing green grass and shaded spots in this field reminded him of his real home. He was transferred in a minute to a serene, quiet hillside where nothing ever happened. Home, thought Betts.

When Betts arrived at the New River Air Station, he was amazed to see that only one fixed-wing aircraft was standing by; a white-over-blue C-37B US Air Force jet sat gleaming in the middle of dozens of flat-green helicopters. Originally a Gulfstream G500 with plenty of modifications, this business jet had a range of over five thousand miles and flew at Mach

0.90. It was beautiful and comfortable, and it had an Air Force steward waving him aboard.

His flight north to Dulles was too short. Betts pulled his bag into the Signature terminal lounge and asked the clerk to call him a cab for transportation to Falls Church. As the wait time would be short, Betts dragged himself and his bag out to the sidewalk in front of the terminal lounge and pulled in some fresh air. The cab, an older Chevy Tahoe, arrived in just a few minutes. The small, dark man driving it, an immigrant from Eritrea, leaped out and ran to the passenger's side to grab the C-bag from Randall and heaved it into the rear cargo bed.

"You shouldn't be hauling this thing around with your leg wrapped up like that!" the older man said as he motioned to Betts's cast.

"Man, I'm glad somebody noticed that," said Betts in a humorous tone. He was tired; he just wanted to get back to his apartment. He climbed into the cab, buckled himself in, and looked around the parking area quickly.

And then he noticed it; in a sedan several parking slots down from where he had been standing, Betts saw that guy again. A man who looked very much like the guy who was staring at him from the hospital parking lot was sitting forty yards away, staring at him again. Just as Betts was grabbing for the seat-belt-release button, the driver calmly asked if Betts was belted in and comfortable and then informed him of the cold bottle of water and snacks behind him on the back seat. Betts wanted to get out, wanted to hold off this trip to find out what this guy wanted with him, but the promise of a bottle of water and some chips held him in the vehicle. As he came back from the cooler with an iced-down water bottle and bag of Funyuns, Betts saw the man pull the sedan away from the parking lot.

Betts started asking himself if he was seeing things. And then the ringing in his ears returned.

The drive to Falls Church was just over one hour. The traffic around Washington was murder, but the roads eventually cleared out on the drive toward Route 7. Once they arrived at Betts's apartment on Idylwood Drive, the stretch and the clear air were helpful, but the events of the past six hours reminded him of the uneven pace of his day and his ankle pain.

Betts stepped slowly out of the front seat of the SUV, careful not to bang his cast on the doorjamb or scratch the paint with his metal cane. Once he had eased himself out of the idling beast, he stood straight and tried his best to stretch. It wasn't easy to stretch, and it didn't improve his mood much, but he was back at his apartment. And that made him happy.

Betts thanked the driver, paid him a good tip, and refused the offer to help carry his C-bag into the building.

The nine-year-old Ford sedan that had followed Betts' cab to his home eased by the apartment complex. The driver slowed slightly to see if anything else was observable, but then he continued out of the parking lot and back toward Route 7. Nothing else to be reported here, guessed the white male driver.

As the driver of the Ford sedan left the apartment complex and rejoined the rush hour traffic, a woman lowered her camera and checked the digital image she had just taken. She was pleased that she had gotten a high-resolution image of the back of the Ford sedan. It would be easier to look up the license-plate number, and perhaps the pictures of the driver might tell her something. She waited for twenty minutes to ensure that nothing else was happening before she started her car and left the far-right corner of the apartment complex parking lot.

Later That Same Day: April 24, 2003

"So what's he doing now?" came the impatient question from the section chief.

"He's just moving around inside the house, probably putting stuff away. He's been away for a few months" came the response from the junior officer. He was standing at the chief's desk, listening intently to the commentary from the field agent who was reporting the sounds coming from the discreet listening devices that had been placed in Randall Betts' apartment.

"Has he tried to call anyone?" asked the section chief.

"Nope, he's just thumping around the place. He's in the kitchen now, getting ice in a glass. He's getting a glass bottle out of the pantry," relayed the junior officer. He was repeating the words being sent over a secure radio net from the listening post nearby. The listening post consisted of two tech officers in a white panel van around the corner from Randall's apartment complex. Sitting at the edge of the shopping center off Idylwood Drive, the van attracted no attention.

"Well, he's finally getting a drink," said the section chief. This arrival of Betts was a critical part of the project given to him by his director, even though it was clumsy and top-heavy with ordinary life patterns.

"How'd you know that?" said the junior officer.

"That's the first thing I'd do if I'd gone through as much crap as this guy has," replied the chief. "Tell them to keep monitoring. And detail any phone calls he makes. Other than that, I don't need anything else tonight." With that statement, the junior officer left the section chief's office.

CHAPTER SIX: APRIL 24, 2003

It's better to light a candle than curse the darkness.

—Chinese Proverb

Betts wanted to call Director Johnson first. But he knew she'd ask if he had called his sister first, so that's what he did.

"Hey, Randy! Welcome home, my darling! How are you doing?" Carol's enthusiastic voice and upbeat tone belied any bad news she had to pass.

"Doing great, Carol. I'm back for a while, just getting my stuff put away. How is everyone there?"

"Everyone here is fine. We were so excited to get a call from your big boss! When she asked what she could do, I told her that I wanted to talk with you the minute you got back! Randy..." Carol's tone turned a bit down. "We need to talk about Dad."

"What is it? Is he okay?" Randall Betts hadn't spoken to his father since late in 2002, almost six months before. He had tried to call while he was in the hospital in Germany, but no answer. Betts didn't leave a message on his father's answer machine because...well, he really didn't know why.

"He's getting a bit senior, and we're not sure how to deal with it." Carol's use of the term "senior" was disconcerting. She was trying to say a lot with just a few words.

"Just tell me what's going on," said Randall. He felt he was trying to calm his little sister, allowing her to talk more freely.

"His energy is way down, and he seems tired whenever we call. He's had a couple of episodes of forgetfulness. Now, that's not unusual for someone in their seventies, but he's done things like forget who he's talking to when the grandchildren are on the phone with him, and we got a call from the sheriff's department near Chattanooga. Dad was wandering around a thrift store and unable to recall where he lived. We got the call because they tracked the ownership of his truck and found our address on the registration records. Kevin and I are really worried about him living by himself, and just calling the nearby neighbors every time something happens is unreliable. Is there any way you could visit for a while? You know, if you could spend a few days there, it would really cheer him up." Carol was laying it all out in one paragraph.

"Have you talked to him about this?" said Randy as he began to close his eyes and sit perfectly still. The ringing was starting again.

"You know him," said Carol. "He just blows it off and blames it on others. Kevin and I and the kids want to go see him, but we can't drop everything and drive out there."

Earl Allen Betts was a widower who remained in the house where he and his wife had raised Randall and Carol. It was a single-story-brick ranch house on four acres along a hillside in Pikeville, Tennessee. Built for the Betts family in 1954, near several stone houses originally built for workers creating dams and roadways under the Tennessee Valley Authority after the Great Depression, the little brick house stood out as a familiar but distinctive part of the community. When Randall's mother died in 1999, his dad buried her under a willow tree on the sunny side of the hill and continued to live in that house. He steadfastly refused to live elsewhere.

Randall's sister, Carol, was three years younger than him and had moved out as soon as she turned eighteen. She married and settled in Richmond,

Virginia, about ten hours away. She and her husband, Kevin, worked as registrars at the University of Richmond and Randolph-Macon College. They had a good life, and their children loved their grandfather. But most of their contact was through Skype calls and greeting cards. Randall knew this task was going to fall to him. He was the single guy with no real career (he never discussed his CIA employment with them), and now that he was back from some military misadventure, he should do his part for the family.

"I'll call and talk to him" was all Randall offered. His eyes were shut tight, and he was trying to control his breathing as he hung up from the call.

Once he caught his breath and could open his eyes, his next call to Director Johnson should have been more casual, more amiable. All it did was complicate Randall's choices.

"You finally settling in?" asked Olivia Johnson upon answering the call with no preamble or casual greeting. "Did you call your sister?"

"Yes, ma'am. She's worried about our dad living alone, and I'm not sure that—"

Randall was cut off by that quick mind and sharp tongue. "You need to go see him. Stay a while; you've got the time. And getting out there would be good for you," declared Johnson.

"I'm not sure that my military treatment will—" Betts was thinking about his upcoming appointments at the VA hospital complex in Alexandria.

"Screw all that," interjected the director. "You have a great VA medical center near Pikeville, and your ankle will heal better with some activity. Don't you *dare* worry about your leave. Whatever the military won't extend to you, the Agency will. You pack those clothes back up and get out there to see your father!" This was all false bravado on the part of the director. She wanted Randall to feel better, and avoiding guilt or worry about his dad would be the best therapy for him.

"Yes, ma'am. I'll get started. Can I ask you something?" Randall wanted to get to the heart of his call. When she responded in the affirmative, he went right to it. "Have you arranged for any surveillance on me?"

"Why would I do that? Of course not! What's going on?" was the slow but certain response from one of the most powerful people in Washington.

Randall explained the events and his observations from the last few hours. He apologized for bringing it up and attributed his possible paranoia to the slight dizziness and ringing in his ears. Randall laid out a short explanation of how he was recovering and encapsulated the various symptoms he was experiencing.

Director Johnson listened to everything he had to say, assured him again that the CIA had no surveillance assigned to him, and offered again whatever help he required. When Randall thanked her and rang off, Johnson checked her list of contacts; then she hollered loudly before making two phone calls. The first one was to the CIA Office of Security Duty Office. She had the officer on duty forward her call to the home of the chief of security. While she was waiting for the call to go through, a special agent from the director's protective staff (DPS) office ran into the room. He didn't know what was going on, but hearing the director holler from her living room made the agent scramble from the command post in her basement to see what was wrong.

"I want you to hear these phone calls," said the director of the most powerful intelligence-gathering agency in the world. "And then I want your opinion."

When the director of the CIA's security office came on the line, she ran through Betts's observations and ordered him to check and make sure the Agency had no surveillance on him, and then threatened the chief of CIA security with bureaucratic violence if he didn't have a report for her first thing in the morning. She hung up the call as the man was assuring her that the report would be ready by 0900.

The second call was of a more personal nature. The agent was still standing there, motionless and quiet. He was dressed in low-top tactical boots, khaki pants, and a dark blue polo shirt with a Force One fanny pack across his waist. The fanny pack held a pager, his badge, some twelve-inch zip ties, and a SIG Sauer P226 pistol. When the call was answered, Olivia Johnson went through some routine personal greeting conversation and then transitioned to the real reason she was calling so late at night.

"I have an employee who is going through some rough times, and I need you to look after him personally. It would be a great favor to me. He's in a remote area, so your travel to see him will be justified. He's complaining of dizzy spells and ears ringing, and he's recovering from a bullet in his ankle, along with some battle trauma. If you have to stay longer than the VA permits, call me. You'll have whatever support you need. Thank you, Marilyn." With that, Johnson hung up and looked at the agent.

"It sounds to me like the guy picked up on something, but it doesn't sound right," said the agent. "Ordinarily, ma'am, if we have somebody under surveillance that tight—we call it 'not to lose'—then we'd have two agents in the car. That's in case the target goes into a building, so we have someone who can jump out and follow them. What this guy's describing is amateur hour, and that is troubling when you consider the area he's talking about, from Baltimore to Dulles Airport." This agent was not the leader of her protection detail, but he was a reliable, experienced agent. His name was Mark Trout, and he knew Randall Betts.

"What if I told you the guy reporting this is Randy Betts?" asked the director.

Trout's eyes widened. "Holy shit! You're kidding me!" Then he remembered who he was talking to. "Oh! I apologize, ma'am! I'm sorry for the language, but if Randall Betts says somebody's following him, you better believe it. Request permission to go out there and look in on him, ma'am!" Senior Special Agent Mark Trout had met Betts in Ethiopia as they raced across the Horn of Africa to foil a serious terrorist threat. Since that time, Trout had heard about Betts's numerous overseas deployments and effective operations against al-Qaeda, Hezbollah, any terrorist organization threatening the United States. Betts had built a solid reputation as a straight shooter who mixed his military background and his case officer training to provide valuable information while trying to prevent as much carnage as he could.

"You're fine right here, Mark. Request noted and denied. Betts can take care of himself, but thank you..." And with that, she excused Senior Special Agent Trout and returned to her classified briefing materials.

The president and his staff had just won a second term in the White House, and CIA Director Johnson was a convenient target for realigning the president's foreign-policy team. Johnson had not demonstrated sincere support for the invasion of Iraq, and therefore she was no longer considered to be a trusted part of the team. In an effort to show the voters that he was keeping the sword sharp, he would happily accept Johnson's resignation and nominate someone more in line with the White House's agenda. It was all politics and nothing to do with reality, Johnson knew. But with her remaining time, she was going to make sure the intelligence community was being aimed in a positive and productive direction. Critical to that endeavor would be delivering the enemies of the United States to justice. Randall Betts was important, but he was one employee among seventeen thousand who were working to keep the country safe. She knew that Marilyn Emerson would be good to Randall; now she needed to focus on the matters of espionage, counterintelligence, and counterterrorism.

CHAPTER SEVEN: APRIL 25, 2003

My father used to say, "Don't raise your voice.

Improve your argument."

—Archbishop Desmond Tutu

The section chief placed the updated file on his boss's desk and stood back. This duty, delivering the daily surveillance reports on the Betts family, was becoming tiresome and unnerving. His boss wanted daily updates delivered personally with no digital trail, and the various collection teams and their activities rivaled any project he had faced before. Terrorist financiers overseas weren't getting as much attention as the Betts family right here in the United States. But the order had come down from the man in charge: collect everything on Earl Betts, including on his son and daughter, and handle the project as a matter of national security. Only the section chief's boss was to be kept apprised of this collection effort, and as his boss was a senior member of the president's cabinet, nobody questioned the orders.

"Tell me what's in that file," said Keith Polyander, the director of the National Security Agency. His office, on the top floor of the National Security Agency headquarters at Fort Meade, Maryland, overlooked an expanse of trees and security fences that helped shield the NSA from the prying eyes of enemies, the general public, and the rest of the US government. Although the revised diagrams listed it as one part of the US intelligence community, the NSA was an entity unto itself, and Polyander relished the power and perspective of his empire.

"Nothing new with the daughter and her family," said the section chief. "The target's son made two phone calls last night. One was to his sister, and one was to a phone number we didn't recognize."

Director Polyander raised his eyebrow at this; since when did an American citizen have a phone number that the NSA did not recognize?

"With the voice on the line and the gist of the conversation, we surmise that it was Olivia Johnson," continued the section chief. "They spoke for three minutes, mostly about his health; she encouraged him to visit his father. And then he asked a bad question." He let that hang in the air to ensure his boss was listening.

"What was the bad question?" asked Director Polyander.

"He asked her if she assigned any surveillance on him. When she said no, he detailed a couple of sightings of a similar man in a similar vehicle that were separated by time, distance, and change of direction," responded the section chief. He was hopeful that this revelation, that the CIA-trained Marine had detected their vehicular surveillance, would bring a quicker end to this project.

"Shit," said Director Polyander; then he continued. "Take that man off the project and assign him to midnight-shift desk duty. I don't want anyone talking to him. Find me a female agent who knows what she's doing and put her in a different vehicle. Make it one of those huge SUVs that housewives drive around in."

The section chief was shocked at this, but he didn't show it. Any appearance of arguing with Director Polyander or expressing displeasure at his wishes had resulted in being posted to Antarctica or the Black Sea.

"Now, what about the target? Earl Betts? This is what I care about, not some paranoid cripple," said the director.

"He's been doing the same, gets up in the morning, drinks two cups of coffee, then goes out to the garage and spends hours trying to count his supplies," said the section chief, hoping that this meeting was coming to an end.

"That's it?" demanded the director.

"Yessir. He used to drive into town occasionally, but since we sent the police after him in that local thrift shop, he has stayed pretty much at home!" answered the section chief.

"Awright, now here's what you're going to do..." said the director as he pulled a sheet of paper out of the top drawer of his desk.

The section chief's stomach turned sour. He knew that a renewed list of listening post assignments and surveillance vehicles was being prepared, along with more advanced surveillance equipment being used to collect intelligence on the Betts family. The director was capable of changing the orbit of satellites circling the earth, and his affinity for Earl Betts, a man who retired over fourteen years ago, was disturbing, if not illegal.

CHAPTER EIGHT: APRIL 29, 2003

To be willing is only half the task.

—Armenian Proverb

Upon doing the math, Randall surmised that it was easier to rent a car for driving to his dad's house. To get from Fairfax, Virginia, to Camp Lejeune, North Carolina, to retrieve his twelve-year-old VW Passat, Betts would have to arrange for more "Space-A" flying, or take a bus or train, or ask someone in the office to drive him there. As none of these options sounded easy or unimposing, Randall simply used his frequent-flyer miles and rented a Jeep Liberty for two weeks. The small, capable four-wheel-drive vehicle would get him where he needed to go and probably got better gas mileage than his Passat. He called a cab to deliver him to the rental office in Falls Church, then brought the Jeep home.

At 0700 hours the next morning, Betts locked his apartment door behind him, threw the last bag into the back of the Jeep, and headed out to Interstate 66 for the first leg of a ten-hour drive to the Sequatchie Valley of Tennessee.

As he pulled from the apartment complex, a female in a pearl-white Lexus SUV radioed that Betts was departing for his drive west, and she confirmed that the license-plate number corresponded with the one listed on the car-rental agreement Betts had signed the day before. The female

NSA surveillance asset was informed over the secure radio that her part in this "special project" was ended, and she could return to Fort Meade.

At the far-right corner of the apartment complex parking lot, where she had been parking for the last four days, a different woman took several high-resolution pictures of the departing Lexus SUV, along with some good shots of the female driver talking on a handheld radio. What an amateur, she thought.

The woman taking pictures and filing detailed reports on the surveillance of Randall Betts was Alexandra Stallings, a special agent with eight years' service assigned to the Investigations Division of the Office of the Inspector General for the National Security Agency. Her job, in addition to ensuring whistleblower protection and law-enforcement collaboration, was investigating possible mismanagement of NSA resources. This effort to surveil Randall Betts was one that had not been authorized by the Office of the General Counsel, and anytime resources were utilized for domestic surveillance without a warrant, the OGC had to approve it.

Stallings had been assigned this case directly by the two-star in charge of the Investigations Division and told to keep it close to her vest. It could have been simple criminal use of NSA resources (that had happened in the past), or it could be a result of a presidential finding that instructed the NSA to conduct surveillance on someone in the intelligence community. As neither of these possibilities were apparent, Stallings was checking deeper into Betts's background to see what all the hush-hush was about.

The phone in her car rang, and Stallings answered it by tapping the small device in her right ear.

"This thing is really stupid," said the administrative specialist to Stallings. He had been tasked with looking into how the team used to surveil Randall Betts was being funded, and Stallings had been waiting for him to call since yesterday. His calling before breakfast was proof that something was not right.

"What is it?" asked Stallings. With the departure of the two vehicles, Betts and the female surveillant, she could sit still for a while.

"The Ford sedan you reported is a rental. It comes from a Rent-A-Wreck company outside of Baltimore. The account used to pay for the rental is a discretionary account from the executive staff. That's an account covered by black ops funds, totally untraceable."

"So somebody from the top floor paid for this car?" Stallings knew this was coming. She had guessed that some top-level member of the NSA had authorized this, and the rental coming from an account that could not be tracked was something she had counted on. What she was told next was something she had not.

"Yeah, but it doesn't start or stop there. This car was one of a dozen vehicles arranged by this company. When it seemed strange that such a small shop had a dozen cars to rent, I checked further. Turns out this company is linked financially to several other lots, and the vehicles rented out of this discretionary account are from all over the place. Besides the two cars rented out in Baltimore, I found records of four cars rented out of Richmond, Virginia, and six vehicles, including two work vans, rented out of Chattanooga, Tennessee."

Work vans normally meant that technical surveillance was being conducted. Stallings was getting uneasy with this information, as it was not just a senior military officer checking up on the boyfriend of their daughter. This was something bigger, and possibly more nefarious.

"What did you come up with on their target? Who is Randall Betts?" asked Stallings next. Her office had the capability to conduct full-scope background investigations of American citizens without consent or consulting with any other organization, but only if they were connected to an intelligence operation or a possible criminal act against the NSA. She had to tread lightly on this request to the admin staff. She was asking questions without a warrant or the express approval of her chain of command, but this operation, conducting physical surveillance of a US citizen without prior approval of OGC, was creating more questions than answers.

"Betts is a noncom currently assigned to the Marine Corps at Camp Lejeune. He was injured during combat actions in Iraq and has been placed on medical leave. He's just a guy with no arrest record and a cast on his leg, but there are two things you need to know..."

Stallings held her breath as she ran through the myriad notifications she would have to file for this case.

"He's also a CIA case officer, and his father is retired from NSA, currently living in Pikeville, Tennessee, fifty miles north of Chattanooga."

"Three things," demanded Stallings suddenly as she started her Audi RS5 and raced out of the parking lot. "First, write up what you found so far on a legal pad and walk it into the Investigations Division's office. Nothing electronic, and erase any checks you've made on this. Second: Text me the phone number for Marjorie Jenson; she's the chief of staff for CIA Director Olivia Johnson. Third: Find the address for Betts's father but don't send it to me. I'll retrieve it another way. And yeah, include that address on the ID report on that legal pad. I want the chief of the Investigations Division to have all that info."

Stallings was going to go dark on this, in that she was going to push hard on the case of who was surveilling Randall Betts and his father. And she might have to make some bumps doing it. While she trusted the two-star general in charge of the Investigations Division, she didn't want any advice on how to proceed or whom not to talk to. This would be her case, and she was going to get a better understanding or slam it to the earth. Or both.

The traffic on Route 7 getting to Interstate 66 was thick, but once she pointed her sleek two-door coupe west toward Front Royal, Virginia, the traffic thinned, and she gunned it. The RS5 coupe had all-wheel drive with a four-cylinder engine, but with a beefed-up turbocharger and sports suspension, the car moved smoothly past eighty miles per hour and felt like it was gliding over the concrete interstate. Stallings was hoping to get to Pikeville in a hurry. She presumed that Randall had packed his Jeep for a trip to see his dad, but she couldn't be sure. What she was sure about was that Randall's father was the key to all this, and she needed to find out why.

Later That Day, April 29, 2003

Earl Betts had retrieved the last beer from his small refrigerator under the workbench in the garage and opened it quietly as he undertook his count. He had learned early in his married life that loudly popping open beer cans or gulping beer from those cans or belching loudly as the cans went into the trash were grounds for a sharp rebuke from his beloved spouse. Louise Betts did not care about him drinking beer, but she had no use for loud noises or boorish behavior. As she was raised in a small town in Indiana, her parents kept a quiet household where the sole occasion to raise one's voice or play loud music was at church on Sunday. When she met Earl Betts at Purdue University, he was a thoughtful, shy boy seeking a technical engineering degree on the GI Bill. His love of radio engineering and digital circuitry kept him in a quiet environment, and she loved that. When they married and raised two children on their little four acres, Louise allowed the children to be as noisy and active as they needed to be. But her husband always seemed to enjoy the quiet of the country and the amazing view of the sky. So she quickly made it clear that unnecessary noise and alarming sounds were to be avoided once the kids got into their teens. Earl disappeared several times for military deployments, sometimes for months at a time, and keeping the house quiet was a routine that Louise preferred.

Now that she was gone, the kids had moved out, and Earl was retired and on his own, he could make all the noise he wanted. But he didn't. He opened the cans of beer quietly, he avoided the use of the blender in the kitchen, and he kept the transmissions on his ham radio to almost silent. Maybe it was force of habit, maybe it was to ensure that none of the local wildlife could sneak up on him, or maybe it was because that's the way Louise wanted it. Earl preserved a quiet, serene life, which included very little contact with the persistent noise of town, and the task of compiling a count of his inventory.

Earl had made the daily trip to the unattached garage for the count. His walk to the garage was not the most strenuous thing he would do all day, but it was the effort that he enjoyed the most. His stroll to the garage, a thirty-yard trek on grass kept short, allowed Earl to look over at the willow tree that swayed gently over the grave of his beloved Louise. She had always enjoyed sitting on the bench next to the tree while it was growing, even though Earl thought it a waste of time. She soaked in the sun and the view of the valley, and she always insisted that her husband sit with her. Now she was buried there, and the bench had rotted away. So Earl enjoyed the simple view of the willow, now almost forty feet high, with branches that hung very near the ground, as it gracefully shaded Louise. Earl often thought that he was looking forward to being buried next to her under that tree.

He walked a bit unsteadily from the workbench area to the vehicle bays of the garage, turned on the light, and gathered his legal pad and pen that were hanging from the wall. Earl looked over the boxes stacked on the shelves along the walls of the empty two-car structure. Earl began on one end, as he had done almost every day for the past few months, writing the date along the top of the page. He then undertook listing the number of each box and its contents. Then he would note the location of the box with respect to the other materials and move on to the next line, the next box. As long as he had no interruptions, he could finish his list tonight.

It had grown dark, and Earl was three-quarters of the way through his count: two full pages listing each box, its serial number on the front, and its location. The single light bulb hanging from the ceiling of the garage was enough to allow him to finish his count. And then a distraction came. Additional lights began to illuminate the garage, even through the blacked-out windows. The enhanced light in the garage startled Earl, and he looked again at the numerous boxes arrayed on the shelves. Which ones had been counted, and which ones hadn't? Earl was now unsure. He looked down at the legal pad and saw that he had made dozens of entries over two full pages, but now he was unsure where he had left off. These extra lights threw off his count. Frustrated, he tore off the full pages of listings and threw them into the trash can under the workbench. He hung the legal pad and his pen back onto the wall and headed out of the garage.

Just as it had happened for the last few months, Earl Betts had lost his count, thrown away his list of the boxes, and walked out of the garage. He'd start the count again tomorrow, maybe without a distraction.

The distraction tonight was different. This was a pair of headlights coming up the driveway toward the house. Earl glanced quickly at the willow tree ("Don't worry, dear; I'll look into it") and walked to the house where the headlights were aiming. Earl could discern that the vehicle holding the headlights was a small Jeep, and when it got to the house and turned off the headlights, he could see that it was his son, Randy, driving. Randall eased himself out of the Jeep and reached in the back for his cane. As he closed the door and stepped forward, he quietly said, "Hey, Pop."

Earl Betts stood still, adopted a look of complete confusion and dismay, and responded, "Who's there? Who are you and what do you want?"

Randall stopped and said, "Dad, it's me, Randall."

The elder Betts just stared, and kept staring. He kept that vacant, open-mouthed stare as long as he could. When he couldn't stand it further, he broke into a laugh and walked over to hug his son.

As he held his treasured boy tight in his grip, he shouted into the air over Randall's shoulder, "Is that what your worrywart sister told you about me? I'm just some tottering old codger falling apart on the mountain?"

Randall's emotions just bled out. He held on tight to his dad because he didn't want him to see the tears and the snot and the quivering mouth that announced how happy he was to see his dad and be home again. Even without the fake dismay his dad had exhibited, Earl Betts looked a lot older than Randall had remembered.

"She said you were terrorizing the neighbors and chasing the Chattanooga deputies around," said Randall as he turned to get his bags and hide his face.

"Here, I'll get those. You go inside and get yourself a beer and a bathroom. I know you've been traveling all day." Earl said this as he eased past his boy and ushered him toward the front door.

Randall used the effort of slinging the cane in front of him to agree with his father as he lowered his head and went into the house and into the bathroom next to the kitchen. He didn't need to pee; he needed to blow his nose. Earl Betts grabbed the one hard-side suitcase and the two canvas bags and heaved them into the house before dragging them into the second bedroom.

As the two Betts men relaxed and talked and shared stories, two men in a van a half mile away recorded the conversation and noted the time and date. This would be important for the director, as the next phase of this project was about to start. The driver of the van started up his laptop and pasted the audio of Randall's arrival into an encrypted email to an office at Fort Meade, along with the ensuing conversations between father and son, hoping for any admissions made by the father.

CHAPTER NINE: MAY 1, 2003

Still waters run deep.

—Latin Proverb

Randall loaded his cane and his father into the Jeep Liberty early the next morning for a trip to the hardware store. Some of the hinges on the kitchen cabinets were loose, and the need to either replace the hinges or ream out the holes and reset the screws that held the hinges had to be accomplished. Once the elder Betts was secured in the vehicle, the younger Betts walked around to his side and stopped. Randall Betts looked up from the driveway and was suddenly overwhelmed. He found himself staring beyond the house and the driveway and the garage, into the hills and the sky above them. For the first time that Randall could recall in his adult life, he was overwhelmed with a feeling of external beauty and internal peace. It came so suddenly that Randall couldn't comprehend what he was experiencing, but it washed over him like a bath of gladsomeness and quiet acceptance of life. For once he could actually see the sweeping panorama of the valley for what it was, the deep-green hills and lightly waving grass beneath a blazing azure-blue sky with billowing clouds. The breeze was just cooler than the air, and the sound of the weeping willow branches in the backyard was an enchanting soundtrack to the gorgeous tapestry that suddenly lay in front of him. Randall had been in and out of this house and all over this property most of his young life, and he had never noticed how stunning and peaceful this land appeared. He took a moment to take this in, but then he tried to make sense of it; was it because he had found himself so welcomed by his dad? Was it the ghost of his mom putting her hand on his shoulder to make him look at the landscape, really look at it, like she used to? Maybe it was both. He didn't want to be critical or analytical of what he was experiencing, but he couldn't remember feeling this way in a long time. The fact was that this feeling took away all the ringing, all the distractions, all the worry, all the pain. For a moment. He climbed into the Jeep with a renewed feeling of joy. He didn't tell his father about it.

As the two men headed down the mountain from the house, a sharp curve revealed an unfamiliar sight: a drivable car parked in front of a stone house. The stone houses in this area were all abandoned, and any vehicles parked near them were wrecks or mechanically unsound hulks that had been left behind.

This vehicle was indeed drivable; it was a nearly new Ford Explorer, shiny and light-blue. Randall thought it was another reporter doing a story about the stone houses. Earl thought it was a revenuer, someone from the county clerk's office trying to figure out the value of the property for taxing the property owner. Both men craned their necks when they saw an attractive, tall blonde looking intently into the stone structure that was nearly one hundred years old.

* * *

Once Randall gathered the various hinges and screws and bits for his kitchen rehab, he piled them onto the counter. The hardware store clerk, a bulky twentysomething who had evidently been piling bags of mulch all morning, sniffed loudly and wiped his hands before picking up each item and holding it to the reader so that the register could list the price.

When he got close to the end of his scanning, Randall asked, "Do you give a military discount?" Suddenly exasperated, the clerk dropped his shoulders as he sighed and reached for the store intercom. He called for a manager, so Randall asked, "Is there a problem?"

"You gotta ask for the discount before I start scanning," said the clerk in a tone that was both dismissive and parochial. "Now I gotta void all the stuff I rung up and start over! Gotta have a manager do that!"

"Well then, how about my store card; will that get us a discount?" Earl Betts had come up beside his son with a logo-stamped card slightly smaller than a credit card.

"Naw, that card just tracks your purchases here; it doesn't give a discount," said the clerk. He wasn't looking at either of the men, just staring at the back, awaiting a manager.

"Then never mind. Just finish ringing it up," said Randall. He wasn't in a hurry; he just wanted to end this transaction.

"Yeah, it's not much of a discount anyway, and it's only for active-duty military," said the clerk, happily scanning the rest of the hardware. Betts had the ID necessary to prove that he was still on active duty, but he decided against any further conversation with this rude punk. Slowly, Betts began to feel the joy he had experienced before leak out of him during the drive home.

* * *

When they returned from the hardware store, the blue Explorer had moved. It was now parked in the driveway of the Betts' house. The woman they had seen before was not in the vehicle, and she was not visible at the front of the house. Randall looked back down the road toward the stone house where they had seen her before, but no joy.

Earl Betts got out of the Jeep and made his way up to the front door. It was still locked, so she hadn't broken in. He walked around to the left side of the house and started toward the garage. He had passed the rear end of the house and was still moving toward the garage when he instinctively looked to his right and stopped dead in his tracks. His interrupted movement to the garage showed that Earl Betts was a bit unsteady on his feet.

The willow tree that he always looked to was still swaying over Louise's grave. At the grave site itself, the tall, attractive blonde woman was bending down, reading the inscription on Louise's stone.

"Excuse me, lady. Can I help you?" asked Earl in his most impatient voice.

"This inscription. It's beautiful," replied the stranger.

"It's none of your business," answered Earl. He had no use for uninvited guests, regardless of how attractive they were.

"Sorry," she said quickly as she rose to her feet and extended her hand. "I'm Marilyn Emerson."

"And?" was all that Earl said. He never took her hand; he stood still and stared at her.

"Mr. Betts, I'm here on behalf of the veterans affairs system," she started, but Earl cut her off.

"They send you here to march all over my property and gawk at my wife's grave?" Earl's tone was level, but his stare had become slightly malevolent. "Identify and explain your objective."

"Him," said Emerson as she pointed past Earl toward the sight of Randall Betts as he rounded the back corner of the house.

Earl looked over his shoulder at his son's hobbling approach and turned back to Emerson. He said nothing; he just stared as Randall walked up and repeated the earlier question about whether or not she needed help.

Not a good start, thought Emerson to herself. "Mr. Betts, I apologize for intruding on your property and your wife's resting place. I rang the bell when I got here, and when I received no answer, I walked around the back to see if you were back here. That tree was so inviting, I had to visit it; my grandfather had a weeping willow on his property, and it really took me back. Then I saw the stone and the inscription. Even though I heard you guys roll up, I was just entranced by the message on your wife's stone. Please forgive me for prying."

"Copy all, RTB for debrief" was the sudden, loud statement out of Earl Betts. He stood completely still and stared away from Emerson, toward the top of the hill behind the property.

Both Randall and Emerson stared at the elder Betts for a moment before Randall stepped up and shook her hand.

"How do you know who I am?" said the younger Betts as he shook his dad out of a momentary stupor.

"Randall, I was dispatched here at the request of a mutual friend. Olivia Johnson knows that when a vet who requires outpatient treatment lives more than eighty miles from a VA facility, a field-care rep can be dispatched for that treatment."

"The director sent you? Do you work in the Chattanooga area?"

"Not really. I'm a field-care rep, but my normal area as caregiver is western Maryland," she explained.

As the three people talked and shook hands, two men sat in a fifteen-year-old sedan and took pictures of the scene with a digital SLR using a 200mm lens. As the woman and the Betts men talked and walked toward the front door, the pictures showed the faces a bit better. When the three of them turned and walked into the house, the men took pictures of this as well.

"Looks like they made a new friend," said one man to the other.

"Yeah," his partner replied. "Get a good shot of the license plate of the Explorer. The boss will want to know who this woman is and why she's the first non-family visitor in over three months."

This non-family visitor might complicate the next phase of the operation, the two men knew. Kidnapping and/or murder were not out of the realm of action for these men, and they had no problem killing a woman if it came to that. It was just the numbers: surprising and controlling three people was a bit stickier than two, and these men did not have any extra personnel. They had been sent as a two-man team, no backup or connection to any local resources, and they were very good at what was needed. The element of speed and surprise of action normally worked when they had all the advantage, but this newcomer made the plan a bit thicker, a bit more expensive for the man paying them.

Once they electronically forwarded the pictures they'd taken to the phone number provided to them, they included a note explaining that the presence of a third person made the home intrusion a bit costlier. The men discussed the next step and how to proceed.

Their plan of action and directives were clear: isolate, interrogate, and dispose of the elder Betts and his son, and make it appear to be a random act of violence or a murder-suicide. The rural area where they lived was perfect for this scheme, and the timetable was short. It had to be done now. The arrival of this woman was not an obstacle, and since she didn't carry a badge, she was just a civilian. The short response from the man who hired them was "Time is short, get it done."

"She didn't carry in a suitcase, just her purse. Maybe she'll leave soon," said the first man, eager to avoid a messier situation than already expected.

"It's perfect having her there when we do it," said the second man. "We can make this look like a fight about the woman. You know, the older guy refuses to accept the woman into the house, and the son flips out and kills everybody. He's already had PTSD issues in the hospital, so this will fit the narrative real well." He had been provided with a full report on Randall Betts' war wounds and disrespectful behavior at Ramstein. Whoever these people were who hired them, they had access to a lot of good information.

"You wanna wait and see the comeback on the license plate? Maybe she's somebody important," said the first man. He didn't want to delay this action; he just wanted to be sure of whom he was going to have to kill.

"We were told to get this done, and now. No use in waiting so they can get comfortable. We'll catch them early in whatever conversation they're having and find out all we can from the old man. Let's go."

The two men opened the doors of their car and moved with a smoothness that kept the sound of their approach very quiet. They had crept up to lots of places in the past, and they knew how to work together and walk carefully. Their gait looked a bit like slow motion, but they cleared the hundred yards from their parked location downhill to the house in less than a minute. Easing up onto the front porch, they could hear some conversation inside. No break or silence in the conversation was apparent once they stood at the front door, so the first man balanced himself hard on his right foot and smashed in the door with his left.

As the front door crashed open, the two men rushed into the house with their silenced pistols up, and took aim at the *four* people in the room.

PART TWO

CHAPTER TEN: MAY 1, 2003

The work praises the man.

—Irish proverb

The two Betts men and the VA care rep walked casually into the house, talking and smiling. Once they were inside and closed the front door, they froze and stopped talking.

A woman was standing at the living-room fireplace. She looked to be in her late thirties, with brown hair and sharp gray eyes that looked as though they had their own light. She appeared to be slender; she wore black shoes, dark-gray slacks, and a beige overcoat made for the rain, and she was completely unapologetic as the three of them stared at her and began to formulate a challenge.

"Randall Betts, Earl Betts, ma'am," said Alexandra, and she nodded at each. "My name is Alexandra Stallings. I'm an agent of the Investigations Division out of Fort Meade, and I have been trying to make sense of why you men are being surveilled by my agency."

"You mean it's not just me?" said Randall.

"How am I involved in this?" said Marilyn.

"What the hell are you doing in my house?" said Earl.

As she raised her hands to explain why she was there and share the extent of what she knew, Earl Betts started the same routine he had exhibited in the backyard. He stood stiffly and uttered loud sentences that were clearly English but completely undecipherable.

"Anaconda One-Zero, Anaconda One-Zero, you have traffic from Cobra One-Two. Your team should proceed south to LZ Gulf and await further!"

He rattled off several such statements to the amazement of everyone else. Finally, Marilyn asked, "What is happening to him?"

"He's under some stress, some kind of duress, I think" was the only explanation Randall had.

"He is remembering radio traffic from his time in Vietnam" was the cool answer from Stallings. "He was a signals intelligence officer working a listening post along the Vietnamese border, and much of the radio traffic from his time there is coming back to him."

"After thirty-five years?" asked Randall. He was still dizzy from all the new people and situations being presented.

"He has an echoic memory" was the simple statement from Stallings. She waited to see if anyone knew what she was talking about before she continued. "You've heard of photographic memory? Well, Earl Betts remembers every radio broadcast and conversation he's had. I saw that listed in his field records. It's what made him so crucial to reporting the results of the signal intercepts, not to mention the reconnaissance teams working the bush, and it might explain why there is such interest in him."

Just as Earl started to waver and blink as he came out of his trancelike state, Randall was extending his hands to start asking how the hell this woman knew these things and who she was.

It was then that the door crashed in, and two men rushed into the room with silenced pistols raised. The first man moved quickly to Earl Betts and took him by the arm; the second man brought his pistol into sighting at Marilyn and began the trigger pull when he was suddenly surprised by the *fourth* person in the room. He had been expecting three people and was caught off-guard by the unexpected female.

That slight look of surprise was all Stallings needed as she pulled back her raincoat and drew her GLOCK Model 19 from an open-top hip holster. Alexandra brought her sidearm level with the floor as she raised the pistol to join with her supporting hand and started depressing the trigger before she brought the pistol straight out. The draw, aim, and fire of Alexandra's pistol took just over a second, and the second man fell dead with a 9mm hollow-point round striking the dead center of his upper chest.

Stallings then swung to the first man as Randall grabbed Marilyn, and they fell to the living-room floor. Earl Betts was being pulled by a strong, practiced arm that aimed him toward the open door. Stallings saw that the two heads-Earl Betts's and the one of the man pulling him outside-were too close together. Pulling Earl Betts along and trying to keep him between him and the armed female prevented his ability to get his gun up easily. Stallings settled for a leg shot and caught the first man's leg just above the left knee with a single shot that sent the man screaming to the floor. He still held his silenced pistol and was maneuvering it for an effective shot when Stallings put her third round of the night into his head. The shattering noise of the GLOCK pistol and the slight percussion of the rounds being fired made the kitchen seem smaller and smoky.

Earl Betts just turned and looked at the man whose leg and head bore bloody wounds and started another broadcast: "Spad support inbound! Cobra Oh-One reports heavy losses in sector three seven! All teams check in immediately! Say again close air support is imminent! RTB and report to Alaska One-One on ARC-ten net!" He was hollering at this point, and it took Randall to shake him a bit to get him to cool down.

Marilyn quickly attended to Randall, as he was her first priority. Once Randall responded that he was okay, Marilyn took Earl Betts by his arm and led him to a chair at the kitchen table. The main room of the house was broad and open; the furniture and appliances indicated where the dining/living area stopped and the kitchen started. Marilyn fished quickly through the cabinets and found glasses for water. She filled them from the kitchen sink and urged both men to take some sips. The smells of gunpowder and smoke were heavy in the air. Marilyn moved to open the front door, but she was quickly prevented from exposing them further by the sudden movement of the female carrying the GLOCK.

Stallings had moved quickly to the two men and ascertained their demise. No breathing, just the slight writhing and bloodletting of a dying person. Once she had prevented Marilyn from opening the front door, she holstered her pistol and began searching through the dead men's clothes. Some cash, some receipts for local fast-food restaurants, and a set of car keys. Spare magazines for the pistols they carried. That was it. Once she was satisfied that nothing else was to be collected, she stuffed the receipts, keys, pistol mags and cash back into the men's pockets and opened her phone. She called a number from her phone's memory.

"You're not calling the police?" said Randall. He surmised that Agent Stallings would have NSA offices in her phone's memory, not local law enforcement.

"I'll get my boss updated; then they can make all the calls they want," said Alexandra.

Sure enough, a 911 operator called the Betts house fifteen minutes later and confirmed that a call had come from the home's landline number with a request for an ambulance and sheriff's deputy. The NSA could disguise their calls and be very effective at keeping their people free from discovery.

While they were waiting for the authorities to arrive, Alexandra took a minute to ensure that everyone was ready to give the same story.

"The truth is best; we're just going to adjust it to avoid too much scrutiny," said Stallings.

"You mean lie to the police?" said Marilyn. She was the least experienced with this kind of situation.

"The four of us were talking in the house, just getting to know each other, and two strangers busted in with guns. The sole diversion from the complete truth is that I work with the local veterans affairs office and was accompanying you"—she pointed at Marilyn—"on this initial survey visit. Oh, and this..." said Alexandra as she bent down and carefully screwed the silencers off the two pistols. She used a tissue to keep her fingerprints from each pistol and pocketed the silencers when she was done.

"So who were these guys?" said Randall as he took a second sip of tap water and regarded his father. Randall was uncertain about any of this, and his dad's erratic callouts were disconcerting as well.

"Damn fine question," said Stallings. "I had become suspicious of this whole thing about surveilling Earl Betts and his family, but when I got here and discovered these two guys, who were clearly not technical guys and not surveilling you, I got real nervous."

"Why are they surveilling me? And what does my family have to do with it?" Earl Betts was lucid now, and his voice held none of the loud radio traffic he had blurted earlier.

"Mr. Betts," began Alexandra, "you worked signal intelligence operations and wiretap sites all along the Cambodian and Laotian border of Vietnam during the 1960s for the NSA. Your assigned unit, the Military Assistance Command Vietnam Studies and Observations Group, had the highest casualty rate of any military group during the war in Vietnam. MACV-SOG attributed many of those casualties to enemy engagement. But some of those casualties, in which American and allied soldiers were killed, were believed to be due to leaks. Your commanders canceled some trips due to the apparent presence of North Vietnamese Army (NVA) troops at your landing zones. Someone was telling the NVA about troop strength, planned operations, base-camp locations, lots of things that led to compromising some of the most closely held actions conducted during the war."

"Command presumed it was the South Vietnamese malcontents. The gooks had all kinds of spies!" said Earl Betts. He had gone back to staring into the distance as Stallings spoke. As he sat at his dining room table with a glass of water in his hand, Earl suddenly felt tired and confused, and old.

Randall Betts was simply astounded. He knew that his dad had worked for the Army during Vietnam, and he remembered some of the harrowing stories about the jungle and the Ho Chi Minh Trail, but he was clueless about the NSA connection. Randall's dad was a radio whiz and still kept his ham-radio license, but he never suspected that his father operated a listening post in enemy territory.

"What I'm about to tell him is at a higher classification, so none of this leaves this room," warned Stallings as she pointed at Randall and Marilyn. Then she continued, "Our analysts were convinced that the leaks were not all by the South Vietnamese. Chinese communications from that region reported in-depth briefings about the personnel and backgrounds of special-operations officers assigned to MACV-SOG. This couldn't have come from anywhere but the American side. When Earl's third tour was done in 1969, his work history and travel patterns were heavily scrutinized. Your father worked on some of the most sensitive listening platforms and wiretap sites ever created for this conflict, and it was clear by the time he got home that he was not the source of the compromised information."

Stallings shifted her gaze to the driveway as several sets of lights were moving toward the house. As a wrap-up, the NSA agent said "Your service record remains exemplary Mr. Betts, and we think that's the reason you're being targeted." Then she headed to the door to greet the sheriffs and first responders.

Earl Betts just sat there and smiled. He knew his work was something special. It was nice to finally hear somebody say that. That's why he was counting those boxes these past few months. His pride in his work compelled him to help find the traitorous son of a bitch whom he had been warned about. "We always knew we had a rat in our ranks," said Earl quietly, almost to himself.

* * *

The investigation at the Betts house was fairly quick. The story told by everyone was a bit strange, as very few home invasions happened in this area. The facts, however, could not be argued: two dead guys on the floor with guns and no ID, and everyone's identity checked out. Alexandra's call to her boss guaranteed that a valid employment record was inserted into the VA database, along with an exemption noting that Alexandra held a valid concealed-carry permit in Virginia, along with details about the firearm she carried. Ironclad identity check.

After the sheriff's deputies and the requisite responders left, the group relaxed and talked a bit more. Stallings knew a lot about Earl Betts from her NSA retiree files, but she refrained from saying anything further, as she was intrigued by his son, Randall. The CIA case officer turned on the "shaken-up son" role to the ambulance crew very well, and his story about his injuries from his recent military service carried a lot of weight with the deputies. She felt that Earl Betts was in capable hands, and she needed to get back to her office at Fort Meade and start getting a handle on why Betts was being targeted. Monitoring and watching an NSA target was one thing, but this armed assault seemed to be aimed at kidnapping Earl and killing everyone else, and that made no sense. She would return to the Investigations Division and start getting whatever this thing was to unravel.

The other thing she wanted to do when she got back was buy lunch for her old friend Marjorie Jenson. Stallings had lost touch with her after college, and only by Christmas cards was she aware that Marge had climbed the ladder at the Pentagon and then CIA and was now an executive assistant to CIA Director Johnson. Very impressive career, but the reason she wanted to meet with Marge would be to find out all she could about Randall Betts.

Marilyn Emerson was also interested in knowing more about Randall Betts, but she knew all she needed to know about his job at the CIA. CIA Director Olivia Johnson told Marilyn that Randall was a case officer who had been injured on military leave, and the effects from his injury included more than just a busted ankle. The post-traumatic stress indicators that Johnson told her about would take some time to address, and while Randall was not unattractive, he posed a bit of a challenge to "unroll." Randall Betts was a bit older than some of the kids who survived injuries, and that meant that getting him to trust her would require some "interview manipulation." In addition, Betts was clearly concerned about his dad.

As Marilyn thought about this, she happened to glance over the table as Earl Betts made his way to the kitchen cabinets to bring out some ceramic cups ("While we're doing all this talking, we might as well have a cup of coffee!"). That's when she noticed that the elder Betts was favoring his right arm. The way he carried himself indicated that he was used to holding the right arm close and turning his shoulders to make his left arm do the work.

"Mr. Betts, were you injured when that guy grabbed you?" asked Marilyn. Her question hung in the air as everyone turned to hear Earl's reply.

"Nope, I'm fine," said Earl as he looked down and away. He was trying to evade any further interest.

"You're holding that right arm a bit tight. Is it okay?" said Marilyn as she started to rise from her chair.

"I told you I'm fine! Why are you so nosy about me? Didn't you say you were here for my boy?"

Earl's sharp rebuke caught everyone by a bit of a surprise; the shuffling old guy had snapped at Marilyn, and Randall quickly assessed that it was because she had been looking at his mom's grave earlier.

"Hey, Pop, let her have a look. She's a nurse, and nobody else got grabbed like you did by the guy," said Randall in a calming voice.

Earl Betts relented and rolled back the sleeve of his flannel shirt. What Marilyn saw was more than worrisome; it was serious. Earl Betts had a reddish-purple area over a clearly swollen portion, about seven inches long, around his right elbow. The center of the colored area held a scabby circle about the size of a quarter. The scab was dry and white. The whole area looked like some sort of infection under the skin.

"How long have you had this?" said Marilyn as Randall and Stallings moved to peek at Earl's elbow.

"I don't know," said Earl. "I must've bumped it or pulled a muscle in my elbow. I just put some liniment on it at night. It's just part of getting old."

"Do you have any more areas like this on your body?" Marilyn was now in full investigation mode. This was no sign of aging or arthritis. This was possibly malignant.

"No! And you're not checking me over!" said Earl as he pulled back his arm and rolled down his sleeve. The inspection was over.

Randall moved in to calm his dad and assure him that everything was okay, but Marilyn suddenly raised her hand and placed it on Randall's chest. She stopped him from moving any further and kept her gaze locked on the elder Betts.

"Mr. Betts, you have a tumorous lesion that could be serious, possibly fatal. I'm going to get you an appointment at the VA center in Chattanooga for an MRI, and you are going to have it done."

Marilyn's tone had changed from curious and helpful to demanding and final. Stallings was impressed how this VA field nurse had turned pit bull, and she had to agree; the area on his arm looked horrendous.

Earl Betts, for all his bluster and mistrust for this intrusive woman, just dipped his head and agreed. He knew that spot on his elbow had grown from a bruise to something that looked bad, and maybe it was time to get it checked.

Randall kept his place and admired the calm and confidence exuded by Marilyn Emerson. She was someone Randall could trust. Although he was concerned about his dad and this threat to his health, he was looking forward to spending more time with this therapist.

CHAPTER ELEVEN: MAY 2, 2023

A spoon does not know the taste of soup,

nor a learned fool the taste of wisdom.

—Welsh Proverb

The section chief walked with faked calm to the director's office. He looked calm in his gait and his demeanor, but inside he was scared to death. He knew this "final solution" the director wanted was a huge gamble, and the chance of success was very low. But it had failed spectacularly, and now he had to face the wrath of the man who gave the orders.

As he walked into the director's office, he was waved to a seat by a smiling man talking on a phone, and the man did not resemble the director whom he had briefed just two days ago.

"No sir Senator! That date is fine! What time is the briefing? Great, I'll set that up with my admin staff, and we shall arrive thirty minutes early! Thank you, Senator!" The director hung up the phone, and his smile, amazingly, did not leave his face.

"Sir, I have reports from the 'mountain' staff." This code word had been chosen to address the surveillance operation against Earl Betts's house. The surveillance op against Randall's apartment in Falls Church was simply called "church," and the surveillance on Randall's sister in the West End of Richmond was called "Regency" due to the name of the indoor mall close by.

"Old news," said the director. "I shut down the car lots and told our employees to leave the vehicles at donation lots nearby. The church and Regency equipment has been removed and is being sanitized right now."

The section chief was surprised at this. He was unaware that his boss had any connection to the crews who were surveilling these locations, let alone that he had taken steps that quickly to extricate the NSA from anything related to them.

"So you know about the shooting," said the section chief.

"It made the local news at six this morning on the NBC affiliate in Chattanooga," said the director. "Two out-of-state criminals cased some old guy's house in a remote area and busted in to find that he had house-guests, and one of them was a VA rep with a concealed-carry permit. She shot them while they were interrogating the old guy about where he kept his loot! Great story, and it has nothing to do with us!"

The section chief was relieved. Relieved that his boss already knew about the deaths of two criminals who had been hired through a cutout to kill Randall and interrogate Earl Betts. They had been paid well and instructed to find out where Earl had stashed the property he had stolen from NSA, and then to dispose of both of the Betts men.

What still worried the section chief was that the men they had hired were real professionals. They had no discernible background and lived off the grid, and they were consummate killers. How did some health-care worker with a pistol, probably some five-shot revolver in a purse, get a clear bead on them before she was shot? This was interesting, and the section chief reminded himself to obtain the police report and autopsy results when they were posted on the county's police records.

"The guys in the LP reported that the female VA rep that shot the guys may not be a real VA rep. She made some remarks when they walked into the house that the team couldn't quite hear over all the background noise. After she shot those guys, she made a call on her cell phone. They only heard one side of the conversation, and she seemed to be talking with some senior military guy about what happened and got him to make the 911 call. Kinda strange," said the section chief. This case was becoming more bizarre than complex.

"So she got some wonk at the VA to make the call. She was probably in shock and too scared to do it herself. Typical woman. They want the authority but don't want the responsibility," said Director Polyander. He had little use for anyone who wanted to work in the field but got weak in the knees when a tough decision had to be made, and females at NSA were good as furniture, not as field operatives.

"What do we do now?" asked the section chief.

"The only vehicle I've kept on the job is the LP van on the mountain. Keep them going and report to me anything they come up with. Line up another 'contractor.' This one a woman. Get her to come to the house posing as one of the regional health-care folks. Get her to do the job quick, maybe drug the boy and take her time with the old man. I don't care how she does it, but I want to know where Betts put that stuff, and I want him ended. Is that clear enough?"

The section chief nodded, then got up to leave, but before he could get out of the director's office, he heard, "And get everything ready for a briefing to the Senate Intelligence Committee on our proposal to use facial-recognition software in those skill-game machines."

The section chief nodded and continued out of the office. This was going to be as dicey as getting a female hitter to go after the Betts men: convincing Congress to approve spyware for businesses to use in their one-armed bandits was just as dangerous as the "mountain" op. The difference was that getting USG money for spyware to be installed in skill-game machines; the "almost-like-gambling" equipment would pay for itself in less than two years. These devices were popping up at truck stops, gas stations, and roadside diners. They were becoming very popular, and the makers of the machines wanted to gather more information about the people using the machines. That information would be valuable to an industry that tracked the public's taste for recreation. The casinos were already using facial-recognition software more advanced that what the USG was fielding, and the metadata from the surveillance conducted in places like Las Vegas and Atlantic City was making a lot of money. This surveillance op against the Betts family, the used car lots and the cameras and the microphones and the employees' salaries, had just exceeded $5 million, and it wasn't over yet.

CHAPTER TWELVE: MAY 3, 2003

One good way to test your memory is to try to remember the things that worried you yesterday.

—Toronto Star (October 1954)

Randall Betts made sure that his father had enough coffee today. The morning after all the new people left and the carnage in his front room was cleaned up, he made a full pot. Randall wanted to make sure his father didn't complain about the coffee supply being inadequate.

This morning, Randall had awakened from an incredibly restful night's sleep to make a twelve-cup pot of coffee. The great sleep he had may have been due to the pills left for him by Marilyn, but he attributed it to his ability to relax now that the bad guys were gone, the NSA agent was gone, and his dad was not blurting any more radio traffic. Randall felt like life was becoming "normal," thereby allowing him to rest. The ringing in his ears seemed to be receding, and his anxiety seemed to dwindle. This reduction in symptoms could be deceiving, Randall knew. Oftentimes PTSD patients would "think" they were getting better when actually they were just getting used to the disastrous effects on them.

Earl Betts came into the kitchen area and grabbed his mug out of the cupboard. He filled the mug and sipped as he looked out the back window of the house to see the weeping willow tree where his wife was buried and the garage where his boxes were arrayed. Today, thought Earl, today he could get the count right.

"How's it going for you today, Pop?" said Randall as he joined his father to look out the back window.

"I'm sorry, son" was all Earl said.

"Pop? Sorry for what?" asked Betts as he turned his body and shifted his hated cast to face his dad.

"Making all that noise. Your mom always loved a quiet house. And here I was, hollering all that radio stuff. I can't help it; when I get frustrated or rushed or upset, that stuff just flies outta me!" It was clear that Earl was thinking about something else as he spoke about his reaction to anxiety.

"Well, you didn't make nearly the noise that the security girl made when she shot those guys," countered Betts. He saw the faraway look in his father's eyes, and he came face-to-face with two things. One was that his dad was right; his mother always insisted on a quiet house, and he had forgotten that.

The other thing Betts had to face was that his dad looked pale, tired, and worn. First thing in the morning, freshly dressed and gulping a healthy cup of coffee, Earl Betts looked worn out and smaller. Randall couldn't get past the impression that his dad looked sickly.

"Tell you the truth, I never heard a shot. I just froze, right where that fella died, and all I could do was recall a transmission from one of the recon teams that had been shot up and..." Earl Betts let that recollection fall away.

"It's funny how your hearing shuts down when you're under stress," said Betts, as he recalled never hearing the shot when he killed the sniper across the street. It was like the big .45 handgun never made a sound.

"Well, let's not let that keep us from our work," said Earl as he put down his cup and headed to the front-door closet.

"Work? What do we need to do?" said Betts. He was confused by his dad's sudden burst of effort.

"Get that count done today." was all that Earl said as he snatched his favorite windbreaker from the closet and put it on as he proceeded for the back door.

"Count? What count are you talking about?" Betts pulled his light jacket off the back of the dining room chair and carried it with him out the door after his father.

Earl didn't answer him. He just kept walking toward the garage in the backyard while he looked to his right and mumbled something in the direction of the weeping willow tree. "I'm doing it, Louise. Don't worry. Me and Randall will get it done today."

With Earl's unsteady gait and his son dragging his ankle cast, they both arrived at the garage at the same time. The two car-size doors were down, so the sole access was the regular entry door to the workbench area. Once inside, Earl turned on the lights, as no natural light came in through the garage doors. They had been spray-painted black. Earl grabbed the legal pad held by a clipboard hung on the wall and retrieved the Bic pen hanging by a length of twine from the same nail that held the clipboard. Betts followed his dad as he made his way over to the car side of the garage, and for the first time noticed that the garage door windows had been painted black. He couldn't remember the windows ever being covered like that. As he stepped into the car side, Randall saw something that gave him both pause and confusion.

Arrayed in the two-car area were almost a dozen shelves running along the length of the back wall. The shelves looked to be about a foot deep, and they were spaced almost a foot apart, and they were covered with small cardboard boxes of various sizes and colors. The bottom shelf was just off the garage floor, and the top shelf was high enough that you needed a ladder to get to it. The boxes were neatly arranged next to each other and organized in such a way that boxes of the same color were stacked together on the shelves, and there had to be hundreds of them.

"Let's get to it," said Earl as he wrote the date on the top of the page.

"Dad, how long have these boxes been in here? I don't remember them being here," said Betts.

"An old colleague sent them to me. They were something he had kept for years after I left 'Nam, and he shipped them here a couple of years ago for safekeeping!" said Earl as he stepped to the far-left end and undertook counting the boxes.

"Why did he keep them?" asked Betts, clearly awed by the boxes, the elaborate shelving, and the daunting task his father was undertaking.

"Creep didn't tell me. Just said they were important to proving who the traitor was, and once the dust settled, he'd explain everything" was Earl's response.

"Who?" Betts was getting lucid answers from his dad, but none of it made sense.

"Old AC-119 pilot who worked with us out of Da Nang. He flew some crazy kind of brave operations to give us ground support. The bird he flew was initially called 'Creeper' because it was quiet and deadly, so we always called him Creep," said Earl. He was methodically counting and documenting each box.

"AC-119, was that 'Puff the Magic Dragon?'" asked Betts. He had known about the converted cargo planes with GAU rotating-barrel heavy machine guns that were used to dominate ground fighting. These were formidable aircraft that were legendary for their firepower.

"Naw, these things were more agile. These were Fairchild planes that used to be flying boxcars. We could use them for psyops stuff, like dropping leaflets to tell the NVA that there was a better way, but puttin' guns on them was more effective. The military called them 'Stingers,' put .30-caliber miniguns and 20mm six-barrel cannons in them and they could fly faster and lower than Puff. And Creep was the best. Anytime a recon team under fire got the shiny that Creep was inbound, they were really happy." Earl Betts seemed to be under the spell of his radio calls again.

"Shiny? You said something about a traitor? What are you talking about?" Betts was standing next to his father and reached out to pick a box from the shelf.

"Careful with that!" was the quick and emphatic statement from Earl as he stopped counting to grab his son's hand. "Now, see? You've made me start over."

Earl placed the box Randall had removed back to its exact place on the shelf as he moved almost mechanically to the left-hand end of the shelves and ripped the top sheet off the legal pad. He started the count all over again and eventually formed a reply to his son's query.

"I worked for the Army Security Agency at first, and later transferred to NSA. They were working with a hybrid collection of recon teams that had a few US special ops guys and a team of South Vietnamese or Cambodian troops who would work the Cambodian-Laotian border and give Charlie hell. This was the mission of the group blurted out by that NSA agent, 'Military Assistance Command Vietnam, Studies and Observations Group'; I was the listening post for the MACV-SOG recon teams that went into the bush after Charlie—the NVA—and these teams relied on me whenever they got into a scrape. The CIA had an OV-10 plane flying around to coordinate their missions, but lots of times those Agency guys were elsewhere trying to get their own intercepts. The recon teams got into a lot of scrapes. When they would report contact with the enemy and request extra firepower or evac, it was up to me to locate the air assets available and vector them into the right area. When I would send a signal from my ground station to the air asset—a Kingbee ARVN helicopter, a ground-support plane, even a B-52 bomber—that signal was called a 'shiny.' Lots of times I was the only way to get help into some of these areas because they were so remote. But Creep always answered the call. He even came in when all they needed was an evac helo. He would stay on station to make sure they got out all right. I tell ya, son, they don't have the medals to recognize what those boys went through. They volunteered to go through hell and fight the devil himself." This was the most Earl Betts had spoken since his wife died, and he stood still to recount the story.

"And why did he send you all these boxes?" asked Betts. He was impressed with his father's service, as he had heard about the vaunted MACV-SOG recon teams in classified briefings at the CIA, but never knew his dad was part of this effort.

"Almost all of the missions into the bush for the recon teams resulted in casualties from contact with Charlie. A lot of these fights were simply due to being in the wrong place at the right time—the reason they were sent out. But some of the battles they endured were clearly the result of Charlie being tipped off. Somebody was telling the enemy about planned missions. We always suspected the South Vietnamese troops of this, but Creep was convinced that someone on the American side was giving them information too. The crap that the NSA chick blabbed in my living room—stuff that she had no business discussing—confirmed what Creep had always suspected. We had a traitor in the American lines!"

Earl wasn't finished talking, but he resumed his careful count as he finished his answer.

"Anyway, Creep stayed on after most of the military withdrew from Vietnam in '73. He took a job with the South Vietnamese Air Force flying the same AC-119 he had flown for the US. He was convinced that he was on the trail of the traitorous GI who sold us out. When everything went to shit in '75 and the NVA rolled into Saigon, he loaded up his plane with all the evidence he had collected to prove that some American was working with the North Vietnamese government and flew it out of the country. He landed in Bangkok, rented an old hangar at the end of an abandoned portion of a US airstrip, and set up a bar in Patpong. He ran that place for years!" Earl Betts explained.

Before Betts could prod for a better answer, his father started again. "That was the last I'd heard from him. He was making a fortune and having a ball running a nice, quiet place in the rowdiest part of the city. He wrote to me and said he was trying to get the evidence against the traitor out of the country, but he was being hung up every time he tried. I just lost contact with him. Then, one day, a couple of months after your mom died, I started getting strange notes in the mail. Frantic-sounding, fragmentary notes about watching my back and remembering things about certain places in Vietnam. Hell, I'd forgotten about some of those places, but the notes jarred me back, and I knew it was Creep. I just couldn't figure out what they were all about."

Earl had stopped his count. The yellow legal pad in his left hand and the Bic pen in his right hung loosely at his side. He was staring at the shelves now, almost in a trance.

Randall heard a vehicle come up the driveway outside, and he wanted to see who it was, but his father was still talking, so he stayed by his side.

Earl continued, "So two years ago, all this stuff just showed up. It was tightly wrapped in waterproof plastic onto a pallet. Thank heavens the truck that delivered it had a forklift to put it into the garage. But they dropped it here and left. No signature, no bill of lading, nothing but a note taped to the side. It read something like 'Here is the proof. Don't call anyone or send an email. Just make sure everything is here, and get that son of a bitch arrested.'"

"So that's why you are counting everything? Why haven't you done that before now?" said Betts as he headed for the entry door on the side to see who was visiting.

"I've tried almost every day since then. Just can't finish the count," said Earl weakly.

Randall stopped at the door and stared at his father. Had he really been counting these hundreds of boxes for two years? It seemed like a surmountable task; it just took some concentrating. Then Randall looked at the trash can just under the workbench, and he froze. What he saw truly shook him. The realization of how his father's life had become so vacant and lonely and discarded.

The fifty-five-gallon trash can was filled to the brim with yellow sheets. Every sheet, presumably the color and length of a legal pad, was filled with notes about the boxes. They had been meticulously cataloged and numbered, yet the sheets were unfinished. Something, every time he undertook to count the boxes, interrupted him, and he had to start all over. This was an indication of obsessive-compulsive behavior, Randall knew. He was just now understanding that his dad was in a sort of prison, mandated to protect and account for the evidence that he had been entrusted with, locked into a routine that kept him from a productive, healthy life.

Randall was shaken from this realization by a soft, warm voice behind him. The dichotomy of a horrible discovery and a woman's friendly greeting at the same time made Randall react in an almost feral manner. He bent slightly, making his core somewhat smaller, as he spun in a surprisingly quick turn to face the source of the female voice. His face registered confusion, panic, and anger. He had discovered some alarming and confusing things about his father, and the interruption by this melodic greeting stirred something in him that resembled an animal ready to fight.

"Hey, Randall! Are you okay?" said Marilyn Emerson as she approached the garage. Marilyn noted from the strange look on his face and his body language that he looked ready to pounce on an intruder. But she wasn't shocked by this; she had seen it many times with veterans who were dealing with several challenges at once. She knew the military conditioning that prepared troops for battle left them with aggressive responses to unfamiliar challenges. Getting used to "regular" life back home after prolonged exposure to combat conditions could trigger an angry or unexpected response to anything. What hit these vets even worse than the feral reaction was the sudden return to real life, the shame and embarrassment of being surprised, along with the regret of their response. This took a heavier toll on some of these vets than stress. The "fight" syndrome served to isolate and marginalize these people from the ones who loved and cared about them. Thus, a spiral of rejection and miscued communication made the combat vet a mixed bag of emotional confusion and denial.

She was somewhat happy to see this in Randall Betts, as it would give her a behavioral point to help him understand, and hopefully defuse, what he was facing.

"Marilyn!" said Betts as he relaxed and stood straighter. He was quickly elated to see the attractive field rep with her blond curls and her deep-blue eyes. "How are you doing? Have you come to check up on me?"

"Actually," said Marilyn as she stepped past Betts and made sure she didn't trip over his ankle cast, "I'm here to notify your dad of his MRI appointment. Mr. Betts, I've gotten you a test scheduled for 1100 on Cinco de Mayo; that's two days away. Will that be okay?"

Earl was standing still and said nothing at first. He had turned to see Marilyn as she entered the garage, but he was looking in her direction without looking at her. His face was empty and distant.

"Wow, getting one of those this quick is impressive," said Betts as he passed by Marilyn and approached his dad. "Isn't that great, Pop?"

"Great, yeah" was all Earl said.

Marilyn then said, "And you'll drive him to the clinic, Randall. I have arranged for a specialist to look at that awful, dirty clump on the end of your leg." She gestured toward his ankle. "I think that thing needs to come off."

"I hope you're talking about just the cast," said Betts.

The resulting laughter from everyone in the garage helped the Betts men shake their emotional stupor.

Once the laughter ended, and before the rest of their conversation began, Marilyn became aware of something else. It was faint, but it carried a distant alert that made Marilyn pause. There was a scent hanging in the air, a very minute whiff of something she had studied before. It was some kind of musty, chemical, almost metallic smell that she couldn't recall right away. Then she looked at the back wall of the garage, just beyond Earl Betts.

"Mr. Betts, you have quite a supply of radio gear here," she announced.

CHAPTER THIRTEEN: MAY 4, 2003

What you see in yourself is what you see in the world.

—Afghan Proverb

"Why am I getting this report now? Why wasn't this presented to me yesterday?" demanded Director Polyander. His cold anger could be felt, as though he were squeezing the life out of the printed pages in front of him.

"You spent most of your morning preparing for your testimony on Capitol Hill, and the guys in the van were trying to get something from the conversation inside the garage," replied the section chief. He was trying to calm his boss down, but the blind obsession with the "mountain" op was relentless.

"Why? Don't they have microphones in the garage?" The director looked incredulous at this question.

"He's never met with anyone in the garage, so it was never considered to be part of the op!"

"But he spends hours each day in there! You mean to tell me we've never looked inside the garage?" asked the director. He looked off now, suddenly aware that he had not covered all the bases needed to bring this threat against him to an end. Polyander had spent all this time and resources trying to find the contraband that had been stolen from him, and he was just now realizing that it was probably in the garage.

Before the section chief could offer a further explanation about the angle of the signals between the garage and the mobile LP, the director cut him off with more instructions.

"Never mind that. Get that female professional that you hired to go after Betts. Tell her the salary just doubled, because we need two things: I want her to do away with Earl Betts, but I need her to burn down his garage too. Maybe she can do both at one time! Yeah! That's it. Tell her to make sure Earl Betts burns up in his garage. That way, the chemicals won't be discovered!"

* * *

Thirty miles away from Director Polyander's office—more precisely, one hour's drive away—NSA security officer Alexandra Stallings was waiting for her former roommate at Bryn Mawr College. As Marjorie Jenson walked into the dining room of the Old Ebbitt Grill on Fifteenth Street in Washington, DC, Stallings stood and hugged her energetically. It had been years since they had seen each other, and the progression of family and career had been good to both women. Stallings had been fascinated with getting her law degree, and that led her to a career with no husband or children but plenty of action and technical expertise rather than making deals behind a desk. Jenson desperately wanted a desk and a family. Her dedication to the Johnson family had granted her untold opportunities in service to her country, all while raising a family as mother of three and administrative support for her husband, a town council leader in Rockville. Between these two young women, over thirty years of decorated service to the US government in one form or another had resulted. And more was to be done.

"I can't tell you how much I appreciate you taking time to meet with me," said Stallings once the pleasantries and updates were exchanged.

"Any time I can make to see you is worth it, Alex. You asked me some questions when you called, and the fact that you used the secure phone to ask means that this is business," said Jenson.

Stallings wanted to lay out a simple request and allow her old roommate the ability to fill in some blanks. "Marge, Randall Betts may be in trouble because of something in his father's past. I'm still trying to work out the details, but I just wanted to know if Randall Betts had anything that would result in a threat to him and his family."

"His father's past? Is he one of ours?"

"Nope, his dad worked for us. He did a bunch of things in Vietnam and retired after a positive, decorated career. He's been living a quiet existence since 1989, as far as I can see, but all of a sudden, his boy comes back from Iraq, and I'm finding that he and his dad, and maybe his sister in Richmond, are under surveillance. And to tell you the truth, the surveillance is probably being done by us!" admitted Stallings. She chose not to disclose anything about the armed team that she had neutralized.

Marge considered all this and formulated the things she wanted to pass along since Alex had asked. "Randy Betts has been a solid, successful officer who got pulled out of an important HQ office to serve in Iraq. He got hurt saving a man's life under fire, and the director has granted him an extended leave of absence while he recovers. She believes that staying with his dad in Tennessee is the best thing for both of them. She told him to take off and spend time with his dad. Director Johnson really thinks a lot of Randall Betts; she even got him the star!"

"The star? You mean a promotion?" Stallings was used to dealing with the military, not CIA.

"No, the Intelligence Star. It's a very special award given for valor, and Randy took some pretty mean risks to stop a terrorist bombing. He's the real deal, Alex," said Marge.

"Okay," said Stallings, "that helps me understand. Thank you, Marge. How's your boss doing?"

"She's getting scapegoated out of the job. Olivia Johnson wasn't as vocal in supporting the invasion of Iraq as some of the other members of the president's cabinet, and that may have soured his opinion of her. The president wants a new crew, and they'll be cutting her loose like she's done something wrong. I tell you, Alex, the politics in this town makes me crazy!"

Stallings smiled. "Marge, the politics *is* this town."

"Amen to that," said Jenson as she picked up the menu to find something for lunch.

When the lunch was over and the two friends were finished talking, they stood, hugged, and walked to the front door together. As they passed the first table in the room, Jenson was updating Stallings on her husband's health, and the man sitting at the table took note. He had been at this table thirty minutes before Marjorie Jenson arrived, and once she came in and hugged the brunette who had gotten there before her, the man had taken dozens of pictures on his cell phone. He tried to make some sense of the conversation, but all he captured was the name of Randall Betts and the word "surveillance." This was enough to compile a report to the counterespionage section at the CIA. He finished some notes on a small notepad, paid his bill, and left for a twenty-minute drive to Langley. Whoever this woman was, she was getting intelligence information from Marjorie Jenson, the executive assistant to DCIA Johnson, and that would result in serious charges against the director's office. If they could get a facial-recognition identification of this brunette, his report would be welcomed by the White House staffer who asked the counterespionage deputy chief to find some dirt on Olivia Johnson. With this report, it would make her removal more palatable to the American people, and the president would look like a watchful avenger. This would be great.

That afternoon, Alexandra returned to Fort Meade and sat in her small office. She thought back to what Marge Jenson had told her and checked over her notes. She reviewed the handwritten notes from the research done by the admin staff who uncovered details about the NSA employees involved with the surveillance of the Betts family and the vehicles they used. Then she thought about meeting Earl Betts, the stalwart retired sigint officer with an echoic memory and the key to this whole mess.

Her use of a firearm had been a serious breach of NSA policy, so laying out the facts as they pertain to this case and the deployment of deadly force would be necessary. Finally, she came to the thought about Randall Betts. Then she found that she had been thinking about him a lot.

She spent the next hour compiling all the details she had gathered into a set of bullet points on clean pages of printer paper and proofread what she had written. Once she had recapped the details and arranged them in an understandable and effective order, she took the underlying sheets of printer paper and ran them into a shredder. Nothing of these notes needed to be discovered, not even by other NSA security people. She took the single sheet of notes and headed to the office of the chief of the Investigations Division. She had been working this thing up, and it was time to get this bag of shit exposed so that it could be hidden properly. The irony of that thought did not make Stallings smile as she walked on. Operations such as these, regardless of the criminality involved, were conducted for a reason. Whether it was a matter of national security or not, Alexandra understood that whoever in the NSA was doing this criminal thing would be quietly informed of their indiscretion, eased out of their office, and then wait for a judge who was cleared for classified information to make a decision on whether or not to prosecute the charges. There would be no "perp walk" or observable arrest made; it would create too much public scrutiny for the NSA. And that was part of the job of the inspector general's office: to avert discredit and negative publicity for one of the most powerful agencies in the federal government. This was the way it was.

When Stallings arrived at her boss's office, she was quickly ushered in and told to sit.

"What do you have?" was the first question out of the chief of ID for the NSA.

"I have a fairly complete report of illegal spying and possibly the attempted murder of an NSA retiree related to a case from the Vietnam War days" was the answer from Stallings.

"Higher-up?" asked the chief. His query was based on politics rather than prosecution. He knew, like Stallings did, that when senior officers stunk, then the entire room could adopt a poisonous atmosphere. It would take a lot of nerve to make accusations at cabinet-level officials, especially those outside the Pentagon. The military had a complete array of careful choices to deal with the improper acts of a military officer, but in the civilian world of political connections and media manipulation, it would be tricky to make something really stick.

"Yes sir," answered Stallings. "The money that's funding this operation is coming from the director's discretionary fund."

The chief stared for a moment, then politely asked, "Are you saying that Director Polyander is behind this?" He was starting to get hives from this meeting. Polyander wasn't just an impatient taskmaster; he was vicious with anyone that opposed his point of view. He was quietly undertaking efforts to open up to the non government sector, seeking associations with research firms and corporate entities that might be developing their own technical surveillance capabilities. By offering NSA insights and advice, he would be possibly trading the Agency's most precious technology in exchange for non secure products that could result in a threat to the United States and its economy. The investigations division chief knew this but could not voice a concern. Polyander had the ear of the US president, and that power was too great. Maybe his best bet was to let Stallings play this thing out and associate her "findings" with the inspector general. That way, the IG and Stallings could take any heat Polyander and his sycophantic political connections would apply.

"This may be better suited to the inspector general's office. I want you to have all the horsepower you'll need to make this case go forward," said the ID chief. He spoke like a patriarch, like he was trying to protect Stallings. In truth, he was passing this crappy case up the line to avoid any negative scrutiny on himself.

Later That Evening: May 4, 2003
Earl Betts's Residence, Pikeville, Tennessee

1. *Describe a major change that occurred in a job that you held. What specifically did you do to adapt to this change?*

2. *Tell us about a situation in which you had to adjust to changes over which you had no control. How did you handle it?*

3. *Tell us about a time that you had to change your plans at the last minute. What was the final outcome?*

4. *What do you do when priorities change quickly? Give one example of when this happened.*

Marilyn looked at this list of questions and quickly shuffled the sheet containing them to the back of her notebook. As a trained field rep for the VA, she had very specific guidelines in getting veterans to talk about themselves, their challenges, and their strengths. Most of the analysis of these vets, primarily the ones returning from combat duty, involved engaging them with a list of questions that would help expose any limitations or self-doubt. It wasn't about telling them how to fix their lives; it was about them coming to realize the fixes themselves. Additionally, she could get a better understanding of the demons and divination that might be keeping these warriors from succeeding in civilian life.

But this wouldn't work with Randall Betts. As she sat across the table from him in his dad's house, Marilyn considered Betts to be a trained spotter of manipulation techniques. His work at the CIA would allow him to spot a "guided" conversation easily, so she had to compose questions other than the simplistic ones devised by the VA.

Earl Betts had gone to bed, and Randall found himself willing to talk more with this amazing woman. She was so open and honest, along with her desire to help Randall deal with the anxiety in his life. So they sat at the table, each with a bottle of near beer that Randall had purchased to keep the conversation going, while Marilyn busied herself to prepare a list of topics to discuss.

Because of his background, as well as her understanding of the elder Betts, Marilyn had to make her approach to Randall on a much more careful plane. She had dealt with veterans who were certain that they were God's gifts to society, and she had talked with men whose souls were as deep and dark as any scary movie. In a broad variety of people changed by traumatic stress, she had managed to find the keys and pathways to allow them to find peace and understanding in their lives. But Betts was different. He was dealing with more than the shock of combat. He had been wounded, then pulled from his people, dumped back into civilian life, and then braced with the health challenges facing his father. This was like stretching a rubber band in several directions, and changing the direction constantly. Betts was trained as both case officer and killer, and his relationship with dopamine, the drug induced when the brain feels pleasure, was scrambled at best.

"What are you thinking about?" asked Betts finally.

"We have done some preliminary work in guiding you to a better understanding of the things that stress you, but I'm thinking about how to conflate those things with your current environment," said Marilyn. She was being totally honest about this, but she still sounded like some dissociated shrink.

"You mean the ringing in my ears from people trying to kill me and my dad, or the uncertainty of my dad's mental health?" Betts was only half kidding, and Marilyn had to tread lightly here.

"They wanted to kill me, too, okay? And we're getting excellent care for your dad. We have a lot of unknowns right now, but the answers will come—"

Betts cut her off by leaning forward in his chair and tilting his head as he kept his voice low with a slow enunciation of the words. "Did you see the trash can full of yellow sheets? He's in an obsessive-compulsive loop that traps him here! Whatever those fucking boxes are all about, it's driving him insane!"

"No, Randall, it's all he's had in front of him for the past two years! A man like that, a man like you, he has to have an objective. And as so much of his world has eased away from him, he has to find a goal that gives him purpose! It's why the fastest rising demographic of suicides in this country is the fifty-four-to-seventy-year-olds. They find themselves with no kids, retired, trying to find their way in a rapidly changing world. Your dad is no different. He just needs an objective, something he can overcome. Your presence here is probably the best thing that's happened to him in a while. He needs you, Randy, and quite frankly, you need him!" replied Marilyn.

Betts considered what she said for a moment, and then he calmed down and smiled. "A wise man once told me, 'What you see in yourself is what you see in the world.'"

With that statement, Marilyn understood why she was being so careful with Randall Betts. Why she was having to reorient her observations and guidance for dealing with his anxiety. It was why she was so careful in her approach to his care. She was falling for the guy. Betts was strong, caring, and self-aware. She wanted to reach across that table and touch his arm. Just a light touch, a tender touch, to convey to him how much she was beginning to care for him. More, perhaps, than what was appropriate in her current role.

Marilyn Emerson had built a career of helping damaged soldiers find their way back. She had eschewed the routine yearning to "fix" men who were off-course, something many women unconsciously sought in their life. This was her job, not her search for a mate. And here, she had found a man who had serious challenges in his life, one who was faced with physical and emotional rehabilitation. And this one didn't need her help. That made him so attractive.

Marilyn had to quickly draw back her wandering thoughts of being in his arms and focus on the job at hand. This was becoming surprisingly difficult. His strong exterior was causing her to be weak with attraction. "Focus, Marilyn, focus."

Their talk went long into the night.

CHAPTER FOURTEEN: TWO DAYS LATER, MAY 6, 2003

Life can only be understood backwards,

but it must be lived forwards.

—Søren Kierkegaard

Randall Betts woke up late in the morning. His dad had gotten up and was bumping around in the kitchen, trying to get Randall to awaken, but it didn't work. Randall had lain awake much of the night, thinking about a myriad of things, and once he fell back to sleep, it was tough to get him up.

The things keeping Randall awake were a combination of good things and painful things. On the good side, Marilyn was effective in her efforts to get him to face the anxiety and distractions he was feeling. These interviews with Marilyn made Randall look forward more and more to each one, and Randall had to admit that he found himself attracted to her.

The painful thing was that his dad was growing old and weak in front of his eyes. While the time he spent with his dad was great, Earl's surrender to aging was grating on his son. His dad was not that old, just under seventy-five, but the days just seemed to take more and more from him.

Then he remembered, and he leaped out of the bed. Now he understood why his dad was making so much noise perking one pot of coffee; they were going to find the man called "Creep" today.

"Hey, Pop, sorry I overslept. Are you ready for us to hit the road?" said Betts as he stumbled into the kitchen while buckling his jeans. Surprisingly, Betts looked at a new man, a man of action and preparedness, a man of dedication and determination, a man ready to face the day.

Earl Betts stood on the far side of the dining room table from Randall, facing the door. He had on his best shirt and a rakish brown-leather jacket that looked like something a World War II ace would wear. He stood straight and tall as he peered over in the direction of his haggard-looking son. Betts was embarrassed at his appearance; he must have looked like some vagrant stumbling into the kitchen. Earl was staring at his son with a "Let's go!" look on his face. Then Randall noticed on the table, two shiny steel cups had been prepared with hot coffee, and one of them was being brought into his father's anxious hand.

"Do you think that little Jeep of yours will get us all the way to Atlanta?" was all Earl said.

* * *

At the same time Earl and Randall Betts were climbing into the rented Jeep for the 120-mile drive from Pikeville, Tennessee, to the VA hospital in Atlanta, Olivia Johnson was checking her wall clock.

The clock on the wall, positioned just below the framed picture of her and her father standing with the president of the United States, read that it was about time for her to make the phone call. The picture had been taken at a fundraiser she and her family attended during the president's campaign. Olivia's father retired from the US Army as a colonel working for the comptroller's office at the Pentagon. He then became an influential investment banker and foreign affairs consultant working on behalf of the International Monetary Fund. Johnson's father reached out beyond just the voters in Washington, DC, and solicited support for the president that guaranteed his victory in the South. The payback to the Johnson family was significant but a sacrifice. Henry Compton Johnson had been nominated as chief of the Army for the Joint Chiefs of Staff, and Olivia had been fast-tracked to be nominated as director of the CIA. While her dad held the post for just over a year (he was considered a caretaker until some general without skeletons in his closet could be found for the post), Olivia had stayed to keep the CIA ship floating in the right direction. As the country changed so rapidly after the 9/11 attacks, Olivia Johnson cemented her reputation as a smart, responsible leader who oversaw the piles of new government layers to face the terrorist threat and worked herself to the bone to make sure the United States stayed safe. She had surrounded herself with knowledgeable, honest people who considered all angles and did not shrink from telling the truth. Congress and the White House continued to weigh options against the political fallout, but Johnson's analysts, case officers, and senior leaders made it clear that the threat to the United States was real and expanding.

Johnson sometimes thought that she was playing "Chicken Little" with all the threat information they were disseminating, but that thought disappeared one dreary afternoon when a senior member of the House Permanent Select Committee on Intelligence stopped in unannounced. The congresswoman, a stern but stalwart supporter of the CIA, had gotten a visitor's badge at the front gate and taken a standard elevator to the seventh floor. She walked in with all the grace and confidence of a powerful woman and placed a small paperweight on Johnson's desk. The item was a birdcage made of cheap pot metal; it was rustic and dark, with no shine or bright colors. Inside the cage was a single yellow ceramic bird, whose somber appearance and bright color stood out from its enclosure.

"Olivia, you are the canary in the coal mine. Keep up the good work" was all she said before she turned and walked out. No pleasant conversation, no hint of regret or disdain: one committed public servant to another. On that day, Olivia Johnson knew she was doing right.

As she contemplated what she had done—and not done—as CIA director, she picked up the phone and dialed a cell-phone number with a Maryland area code.

"General," said Olivia in a calm, steeled voice, "it's about an hour before their meeting. Would you join me?"

"Olivia, I'm at the back gate to the CIA right now, and I'm trying to explain to your officer that I've been invited. Would you talk to him?"

Johnson was both pleased and perplexed at this sentence. But as she heard the cell phone being handed to someone else, she began to figure it out.

"This is Sergeant Melnick, Security Protective Service; with whom am I speaking?"

"Sergeant Melnick, this is Olivia Johnson; do you recognize my voice?" The director had to tread carefully here, as she had not submitted a visitor request form for the general, and the CIA's police force, the SPS, was very proud of their requirement that any and all requests be submitted at least twenty-four hours in advance of every visitor's arrival. Johnson had not submitted the request because she was unsure who was monitoring her emails, even on the campus at the CIA. The general's visit needed to be kept close hold.

"Yes, ma'am" was the only answer. Melnick was a stickler; that's how he had been promoted so quickly within the SPS. The fact that he simply acknowledged her name and didn't flinch, didn't jump, said nothing after that—it proved that he wasn't putting up with any "executive entitlement" at his post.

And she was fine with that. She kept her tone level and professional. No barking or mewing.

"The man in front of you is an important visitor that I asked to meet with me today, and he is restricted from showing you his intelligence community badge. I neglected to notify the SPS of his visit, as I was uncertain he could even make time to see me today, and when I called him just now, he surprised me with his presence here."

"Okay, so I guess you need us to escort him to the VIP garage? Lights and sirens?" asked Melnick in a tired voice that bordered on sarcastic.

"Oh no. I ask that you provide him with a red visitor's badge and let him pull just beyond your gate and park where you can observe him. I will send my protective staff officer to collect him and bring him to me. I can't thank you enough, Sergeant, and I promise you this will never happen again."

"Yes, ma'am" was all Melnick said into the air as he handed the phone back to the three-star general.

Johnson then clicked off and changed phones to her secure phone. She dialed the number for the chief of her protective staff, and when he picked up, Johnson said, "Bob, I need you to take a car and go to the back gate and retrieve a visitor I just got inside the fence."

"Will do, ma'am," said Bob Raffleson as he stood. He was used to the director needing things right away. "Will I recognize the VIP?"

"He's a senior military officer with a badge that he can't show you. His clearance is higher than anyone you've met before. He's a great guy, but Melnick is out of joint because I didn't submit a visitor request."

"Melnick's an asshole, ma'am. I'm on my way."

CHAPTER FIFTEEN, MAY 6, 2003

The only true wisdom is in knowing you know nothing.

—Socrates

While DPS Senior Special Agent Bob Raffleson was speeding out of the VIP garage to pick up the visitor and chide Melnick for making any demonstration that he was "out of joint" with the best director they'd had in years, a pair of dress-shoe heels were clicking out of the elevator and heading toward the Office of General Counsel at CIA HQ.

The heels stopped at the outer door, and the doorbell ring resulted in the door being buzzed open. Into the OGC office stepped Michael Benson, the deputy director of the Counterespionage Section of the CIA. Known unofficially as "spy-busters," the CIA/CES had a very serious and autonomous mission to ferret out leakers, spies, and outright traitors who threatened the security of the finest intelligence agency in the world. They were normally very dismissive or reluctant to look into most tips they received, but when something as explosive as this case was involved and the request had come directly from the White House, they plunged into the investigation with both feet. They had done quite a bit of research into the people involved, and it was clear that a very serious security violation had occurred at the most senior level. This revelation, once admitted and quietly forwarded to the White House, would satisfy the requirement laid out a month ago: find some reason to fire Olivia Johnson.

Benson had arranged for the chief of the OGC, a career lawyer with CIA named Alicia Sebring, to accompany him on this surprise visit. Once they gathered their materials, Michael asked, "So, Alicia, are you ready to do this?"

"Oh, I am so ready for this," said the smiling chief of the OGC. This was going to be fun.

Benson and Sebring walked side by side down the hall of executive offices on the top floor of CIA headquarters, then into the office of the director. The anteroom outside the director's office was empty except for the executive assistant at her desk. This was fortuitous, as normally there would be people sitting around in the anteroom waiting to see the director, or there would be those stumblebums in her DPS security office lounging around. Benson and Sebring strode defiantly through the anteroom and right on by the executive assistant, fully expecting her to stand and express objections to someone barging into the director's office. As this matter had most everything to do with the executive assistant's actions, they had decided that they would say nothing to her until it was time for her arrest.

"Go right in; she's expecting you" was the sole comment from Marjorie Jenson. She never looked up from her computer screen as the two senior officials passed her by to enter the DCIA's office.

This was a bit unnerving to Benson, as this was supposed to be a surprise visit. They continued into the office and stood beside the dark-red-leather wingback chairs that were normally for those who visited with the director. These chairs were slightly less comfortable than the tufted two-person couch along the far wall of the office, but that was the way Johnson wanted it.

Olivia Johnson was sitting at her desk, leaning back in her chair when they entered. "Good afternoon, Mr. Benson, Alicia. It's good to see you both."

"Director Johnson, we have come because we believe that serious security violations have occurred at the CIA, and those violations have come from within this office." Michael Benson was all business and immune to idle chatter and polite greetings. Next to him, the powerful reinforcement of the most senior lawyer at the CIA proved that this was no routine or random accusation. It was time for heads to fly, and Alicia Sebring's slight smirk showed that she was happy to be there when it happened.

Johnson leaned forward in her chair slowly and folded her hands in front of her on the desk. "Oh? And who in this office has committed these violations?" Johnson had rehearsed this line a dozen times this morning, and it still seemed to be droll when she delivered it.

"A woman who has been very close to you and your family for several years. We have surmised that your executive assistant, Marjorie Jenson, would not have leaked critical CIA information pertaining to sensitive operations and those involved without your knowledge and consent. This looks very bad for your leadership of this organization and the team that supports you." said Benson. His somber and even tone resembled the opening brief of a criminal trial.

Johnson listened to the broad statement, considered the range of issues that had been raised, and looked down at her phone. She picked up the receiver and dialed a number.

"Yes, you can bring her in now. We will debrief Ms. Jenson in here, in private, and have the requisite notations drawn up by Ms. Sebring's office so that formal charges can be brought." This was the hurried and almost excited statement made by Benson. Sebring actually smiled at this point and looked over at him. She was so excited by this she could hardly keep from laughing out loud. This self-important woman who prided herself on all the great things she had supposedly done for the Agency was going down, and Sebring would happily recount every detail over drinks at the Truluck's bar on K Street tonight.

"Okay, Bob, send him in" was all Johnson said, and then she replaced the receiver.

Benson was a bit thrown off by this response. He kept his cool, and Sebring kept smiling at him. And then the side door to the director's office opened. This door led from the executive staff section, and someone coming in from the anteroom wouldn't have seen anyone standing in this area. In stepped a man who terrified Michael Benson. The man wore the uniform of the US Army and displayed a dizzying set of medals and braids on the tunic that bore three stars on each collar. The senior military officer carried a briefcase and sat in one of the red leather chairs. He opened the briefcase on his lap and brought out several sheets of paper and a couple of pictures.

As Olivia Johnson opened a manila file that had been lying on her desk, she quietly said, "May I introduce you to Lieutenant General Thomas O'Herlihy. Michael, you may know General O'Herlihy from all the time you two spent in congressional briefings, as well as from the counterespionage center."

Alicia Sebring adopted a quizzical look; who was this guy, and why was Benson looking like he was going to fall down? Johnson allowed just a moment to pass while Tom O'Herlihy put his papers in the proper order, and then she looked to Alicia to explain. "Tom is a three-star general who worked at the rank of colonel here for a few years—working in CES, actually—before heading to Fort Meade as chief of their security office. Once he got his first star, he had to go into senior management, and since most of his experience was in counterintelligence and security operations, and the management at NSA refused to lose him, they nominated him to run the Investigations Division at NSA. He worked there until the previous president's administration made him work as the inspector general for the White House. Didn't you love that job, Tom?"

"With all my heart," said O'Herlihy. He was enjoying the career brief by DCIA.

"So when the most recent administration switched out senior leadership, they wanted their own person to look after the White House and nominated him for something else. The president pushed his nomination through Congress. Tom became the inspector general for the NSA a couple of years ago, and I have benefited from his oversight and counsel several times. As has the president and intelligence committees in Congress."

"Look, guys," said O'Herlihy as though he were in a hurry, "please tell me about what your office has come up with. If I can help at all, I will."

As Alicia Sebring began to mouth an objection, Michael Benson spoke up like a whipped schoolboy. He knew when he had been outclassed, as O'Herlihy was not just a senior military intelligence officer; he was a counterespionage expert who answered to nobody in the US government. O'Herlihy's access was absolute, and his experience with counterespionage cases all over the intelligence community facilitated the term "need to know."

"Director Johnson's executive assistant was recorded meeting with a non-CIA person in a semi private setting and discussing sensitive information about CIA personnel and operations" was the best he could muster.

"Was it this person she was meeting?" said O'Herlihy as he held up the file photo of Senior Special Agent Alexandra Stallings.

"Yeah, and Jenson was giving her information about one of our officers!" blurted Alicia. She couldn't help it; she had to make this matter a clear security violation.

"Was it concerning Randall Betts?" asked Johnson.

"Yes! It was about that rude-assed Marine who thought his shit didn't stink because he saved some Jordanian prince from an assassin! I had to take him down a notch then, and now he's tied up in some surveillance operation, and Jenson's telling your girl all about it." Sebring had raised her voice just a bit as she made this announcement, just enough to make the temperature of the room rise. Michael politely reached over and touched her on her arm to make her be quiet.

O'Herlihy turned to Olivia Johnson and feigned surprise. "He saved a prince? Olivia, you've been holding out on me!"

Then he turned to face Benson. "Sit down, Mike. Young woman, you can take the love seat." O'Herlihy politely motioned Sebring to sit on the tufted two-person couch across the room.

"This woman works for me. She is a trusted and responsible security agent who has worked some of the more gnarly cases at NSA," began O'Herlihy. "We are currently working on a very serious and sensitive case in which we believe that a surveillance operation inside the US has been undertaken illegally against Betts's family, as well as Betts himself. When my agent found out about the surveillance of Betts, she was unsure whether or not this constituted a crime and worked to keep the whole thing below the table. The Investigations Division stumbled onto this surveillance op because NSA employees were being paid, but not on any known payroll. Stallings looked into the matter and discovered our people were surveilling Randall Betts. She then edged a few corners from our admin staff to find out that Betts worked for the CIA, so she used a secure phone to contact her old school roommate and carefully seek out some info, while at the same time quietly alerting the CIA to the surveillance op against him."

With this revelation, Michael Benson looked at Director Johnson. She then picked up the paper that had been in the manila file and handed it to Benson.

"This is a dated, notarized security incident report provided to the Office of Security from Marjorie Jenson in which she described in detail that she had met this NSA special agent in downtown DC, and they shared information about Betts and the surveillance op against him. She came in and filed the report the afternoon of their meeting."

Michael Benson read the official document, started to get the various points about this meeting straight, and then looked up at the director to try and save some face: "And why is the counterespionage section just now finding out about this?"

"I ran the agent's name and background through CIA security. When everything rang true, it became apparent that no crime had occurred. Marjorie had an informal briefing from an NSA officer, but no sources or methods were disclosed. As the Office of Security documented the case of their meeting and put a letter in Marge's file about the incident, warning her about the wisdom of discussing matters specific to CIA outside compartmented facilities, nothing else needed to be done. I am forever grateful for the information provided by this NSA agent about the surveillance against Betts, and I have undertaken some steps to ensure his safety. By the way, Michael, how did CES become involved in this investigation in the first place?"

"You don't have to answer that, Michael" came the quick response out of Alicia. Her voice from the far side of the office had to be a bit elevated. It came out somewhat shrill.

Benson moved a bit in his seat. "We, uh, had an officer in the bar who observed Jenson come in and meet some stranger. She holds an important position here, so he took the initiative to—"

"Why?" pushed Johnson. "Why was your man there? Old Ebbit's Grill in DC? Why was he there? And how does he know Marge? She never leaves this office other than to go home and look after her family, and she is not a published member of the leadership team. Why was she targeted?"

Benson took some offense at this. "Director Johnson, our office has the responsibility to investigate any improper activity when it comes to this Agency, and hiding behind the Office of Security—"

That was it. Johnson suddenly stood up from her chair with such speed that it made Benson stop talking and Alicia jump from the love seat. She leaned forward with her arms straight as she put her weight on her fists, peering at Benson with a look that could easily be described as impatiently evil. Evidently, the director was going to pounce on Michael. For his part, Tom O'Herlihy started putting his papers back in his briefcase. This was going to be the opposite of pretty.

Despite her overbearing stance and stern look, Johnson kept her voice both level and malevolent. "Your office's independent status mandates that you coordinate any and all concerns about the security of this Agency with me, the FBI, and the Office of Security. As you have chosen to ignore those mandates and attempt this surprise meeting merely to smear a senior member of this leadership team, and include the Office of General Counsel, it is indicative of an effort outside of the protection of this organization to force a conclusion. Marge Jenson has been a close friend to my family for over twenty years. My father put her in for a promotion at the Pentagon, but she turned it down to come work for me." Olivia Johnson allowed the room to be quiet for one more moment before she sat in her chair and spoke again.

"Your so-called independent status has officially come into question, Mr. Benson. Let me ask you: Did you think that your communications with a senior adviser at the White House would not make its way to me?"

Tom O'Herlihy stood at that moment and graciously made his way out of the office. He went through the side door that he entered and found the chief of the director's protective detail standing nearby.

"Is she unleashing it?" said Bob Raffleson. He had seen this woman throw a fit, and she could do it so well.

O'Herlihy just put his finger to his closed lips and whispered, "I think she's gonna be in the mood to drive herself home tonight."

Raffleson smiled and guided O'Herlihy through a set of doors out of the executive wing and toward an elevator to the garage level where the general's car was parked. As chief of her protective operations staff, Raffleson had come to give up on certain evenings when the CIA director was so fed up with work in Washington that she got into the driver's seat of the Suburban follow car and insisted that she take out her frustration with I-495 Beltway traffic. He had argued with Director Johnson that she was not allowed to drive the armored beast and pointed out that the chief of security would fire the entire team if anybody witnessed them speeding on the Beltway in the armored limousine following the Suburban.

Back in the office, Benson collected himself and stood slowly. He drew a heavy breath and said, "Well, Director, I will be forced to report this to the chief of CES."

"A job you will never hold. Now get out, both of you," said Johnson coldly.

As the two made their way out of the room, Johnson waited until Alicia Sebring was in the open doorway to speak. "Ms. Sebring, your presence in this affair reflects poorly on your objectivity with the OGC as well as your dedication to the CIA. Along with your unsolicited and unprofessional opinions about a decorated CIA officer in front of an NSA official, I have lost faith in your ability to lead in your current position. You will have your letter of resignation on my desk in the morning, or I shall undertake to relocate you into an office of my choosing."

Michael Benson paused ever so briefly to hear what Sebring had been told, and then the two of them walked to the door leading to the hallway. As they left, they looked over in the waiting area and were stunned at who had been kept waiting.

"Thank you for coming in; have a nice day. Sir, the director is happy to see you now," said Marjorie Jenson from her desk.

* * *

As DCIA Olivia Johnson was welcoming her next guest, FBI Director Raymond Columbus, Earl and Randall Betts were looking up at the twelve-story Atlanta Veterans Affairs hospital in Druid Hills, Georgia.

Their three-and-a-half-hour drive here had been quiet, but the traffic had been chaotic. Betts had been checking behind them on the interstate, looking for any evidence of someone following their travel. He didn't relax until they were crossing the parking lot and entering the VA hospital. Once they were in the main lobby, Randall let his dad do the talking. "I'm looking for a patient here, James Obenshain Willis."

The woman working the information desk informed the two visitors that Willis was in the ward next to the ICU, and visiting hours wouldn't start for another hour.

"Ma'am, my dad and I traveled a ways to get here, and he's very anxious to talk with his old war buddy." Randall tried to make this as pleasant and positive as he could.

"War buddy or not, the visitation for this ward isn't for another hour!" The woman's response was the jagged edge of polite and parochial.

As Randall began to lean in to address this woman's unfriendly attitude, his father put his hand on Randall's chest and said, "It's okay, son. We can wait in the snack shop."

As Betts and his father sat in the small gift-and-coffee snack shop, the sudden stop to the day's schedule was infuriating. Betts was sitting still and quiet, but inside he was livid that this receptionist had held them up. His inner anger was only stopped when his cell phone rang. It was Alexandra Stallings calling to update Betts on the progress of her effort to find out who was trying to kill him and his father—and why.

"I've got all these leads and occurrences, but they're going nowhere," reported Stallings.

"Two dead guys isn't enough to prove it?" answered Betts.

"Every trace of what I've found—the vehicles used to follow you, the pictures of the people involved, even the ownership of the silencers— nothing ends up with a record. Somebody is pulling some really serious strings to keep this thing hidden." Stallings was both embarrassed and enraged about this. She knew where the money came from, but the "executive deniability" of the funding for cars, guns, and killers was so dark that proving it even existed was difficult.

"There has to be someone who can explain all this," said Betts as he watched his father rub his chin and look at his watch.

"There is, and I'm gonna get to him somehow. But it's going to take some serious collaboration to do it. What are you doing today? Are you being safe?" Stallings tried to change the subject.

"My dad and I are visiting an old pilot buddy of his from Vietnam days," answered Betts.

"Wow, more jungle magic," joked Stallings. "Get him to tell you who the traitor was. Maybe he knows something."

"Will do. Stay safe, Alexandra" was the last thing Betts said before he closed the call. The receptionist was waving them over to her desk.

Once they received their visitors' badges, they rode the elevator and came out onto what seemed to be another world. All the noise and bustle of the lobby was gone, and the movement of the doctors and nurses seemed to be in slow motion. As they walked to the room number for Willis, Randall saw that these rooms were all occupied with men and women in the last stages of life. This was apparently the hospice ward, and that would explain why it was so close to the ICU.

When they came into the right room, Earl moved his son aside and called out, "Hey, Creeper!"

No response from the shadow of a man under the covers. He was razor-thin, with a slight tuft of white hair. Both of his arms were outside the covers to expose the tubes in each arm, and the hum of the machines drowned out his father's hearty greeting. His eyes were closed, and his mouth was open. Randall thought for a minute that they were too late.

Earl then moved solemnly to the far side of the bed and drew a chair close. "Creep? Jimmy? It's me, Earl. I finally made it to see you!"

With this voice, Willis opened his eyes and looked anxiously over at Betts. As Earl took his hand and they exchanged warm greetings, Randall could sense years of pain and degradation lift from the man's visage. He was truly happy and relieved to see Earl.

"Early-Bird, did you get my notes? Get my stuff? Did you put that bastard in front of a firing squad?" Willis asked in a strained but firm tone.

"I'm working on it, Jimmy. We both are. Meet my boy, Randall, Jimmy. He's back from Iraq and helping me get everything squared away," said Earl in a hurried voice.

The wily, brave, industrious pilot turned to Randall with a look that was gracious but serious.

"I'm honored to meet you, sir," Randall said as he shook his feeble hand. Randall was ready to add some fluff about his dad's stories, but Willis grasped Randall's hand hard as he looked into the young Marine's eyes.

"You have to get this stuff out. Your dad has to expose that rat for all he did against us, against everybody!" Willis had raised his head and neck off the pillow to say these words.

"I'll do everything I can, sir, but please tell me what this is all about!" said Randall.

Willis lowered his head back to the pillow in an exasperated motion. He licked his lips and started speaking in a clear, strong voice that gave Randall goose bumps and gave his father memories.

"We were working in some of the most ungodly places along the border. Regular troops and Green Beret guys, they couldn't get in there. But we could. We gathered up all the mean-assed special ops guys, linked them up with South Vietnamese troops, Cambodian soldiers, even Hmong tribesmen, armed 'em with the meanest guns available, called them a 're-con team,' and shoved them out into Charlie's yard. No fancy uniforms or shiny boots; these were guys playing dirty in the jungle. The CIA was paying the bills, providing the overhead imagery and buying the right stuff, and they were making Charlie sorry he'd ever heard of the Ho Chi Minh Trail. I was there with my gunship, and your dad was there to keep them in touch. These recon teams got into such dense bush so far away from the border that their calls for help wouldn't be answered by big green. But your daddy was hearing them, and he was using everybody he could scrape up to get these boys out safely." Willis jerked his head over to shoot an admiring glance at Earl, who by now had tears in his eyes.

Willis's eyes narrowed as he continued, "The recon teams were well-trained and had infil and exfil plans, but Charlie was getting wise to them and trying to burn them every time they went out. The casualty rate for those teams was over 100 percent! Your daddy intercepted message traffic that big bounties were being offered for anyone who could give advance warning about a recon team's travel, and they started getting shot up pretty good. When it turned up that the gooks were getting too much good info, your dad and I worked out a system. I'd take off, and your old man would get on the radio and scold me for going in the wrong direction. When I acted like I was disagreeing, I'd say the unofficial nickname of a senior recon team leader in Vietnamese to make my case. You know, like I was arguing with him!"

Willis was getting more animated now, and Earl was grinning from ear to ear. "So your dad would check the NVA radio net, and sure enough, Charlie started moving in the direction that I was heading. They could monitor some of our traffic, but they'd have to send it back to Hanoi for translation. When I said the team leader's unofficial nickname in their native language, they jumped on it. This helped some of the teams by distracting Charlie about their true location, but it also proved that they knew our call signs and operations! This had to come from an American!"

Randall asked, "Did you report all this?"

Willis waved his bony arm so hard it seemed he'd throw out an IV line. "Oh, hell. Command just blamed it all on the South Vietnamese troops. It was true that the North Vietnamese had a lot of ARVN guys on their payroll, but short of isolating some of those guys, nothing ever came of it! They did all kinds of slack-job investigations of the ARVN and then challenged us to show more proof than that."

"And the proof is those boxes? How do they prove anything?" asked Randall.

"I stuck around after Nixon closed out the American fighting. Your dad left early, I guess to go home and have you!" said Willis as he pointed a thin finger at Randall. "I kept on flying for the South Vietnamese. Had some good fun with it too. Thanks to my experience with the border, I was using up a lot of left-behind ammo on the NVA. But they used so many Chinese troops and tanks, they finally took over Saigon. So I got into my Creeper, and I left for Thailand."

"Okay, the boxes?" said Randall.

Willis snapped his fingers and looked right at Earl. "Oh yeah. Well, working with the South Vietnamese Air Force, I saw a lot of cargo go in and out. This one shipment caught my eye 'cause it was English language covered in Chinese letters. This stuff was going to China. The manifest just read 'cultural exchange,' but I knew that was hooey. I got into one of the crates one night and found the proof. Every box in the shipment was high-end radio equipment. Stuff your daddy hadn't even seen yet. All this stuff was friggin' gold to the Chinese, so I wrapped it all up, used a pallet jack, and put it on my plane. I flew it out to Thailand with me, and held it in the hangar until I could sneak it all back to your old man. He'd know what to do with it!"

"I didn't get it until a couple of years ago," said Earl sadly. "It's been in that hangar all these years?"

"Couldn't move it until I got my dual citizenship!" said Willis. "I sent you as many notes on the QT as I could. I couldn't trust the mail, the phones; with you outside the military, I couldn't trust regular channels."

"Why not?" asked Randall.

"I was still in the system, Jimmy. I didn't leave the service just because I went home. I stayed on with the NSA for another twenty years," said Earl flatly.

"You did?" asked Willis in amazement. "I didn't know. Doesn't matter. I couldn't trust any regular way to contact you if the NSA was listening to every damned thing coming from overseas. Goddamned perverts, monitoring everything people say, and it's just gotten worse after 9/11."

As Willis sank deeper into his bed with these words, Earl tried to cheer him up a bit.

"Yeah, I stayed on and watched all the other guys we worked with get promoted. I even saw ole Polyander get his colonel's rank before I left."

With the drop of this name, Willis's head jerked toward his old communications specialist. "Polyander? That's the traitor!"

"What?" said Earl. Suddenly straight and focused, he clearly understood the ramifications of what Willis was saying more than Randall.

"Don't you remember? Didn't you read my notes? His ops name is on there! Didn't you read the labels? Haven't you gotten him arrested by now?" These questions flew out of Willis, and the beeps on the machines got closer together.

"Slow down, pilot," said Randall in an effort to calm him.

"Look it up, Earl! There was a CIA intercept of Chinese military officials talking about a shipment from their favorite source! The name the Chinese used was 'Mouse'; it came out in '73. Didn't you see it? You were still at the NSA!" Willis calmed a bit but remained emphatic.

Just then a nurse came in and insisted that the two visitors leave. They were getting erratic readings on the metabolism machines in this room, and they were evidently getting Willis too excited.

"Mouse, find the name. Mouse..." said Willis as he slumped back into his pillow.

"Copy all, Creep, RTB. Winds are light out of the south, and visibility is good," said Earl as he wiped the tears from his face and touched Willis's arm.

"God, it's good to hear your traffic again." Willis sighed. He was staring at the ceiling, worn out from the exertion.

They walked somberly out of the room without a sound, just the noise of the monitors.

Earl and Randall stood outside Willis's room for a few minutes, considering what he had said.

"Who is Polyander?" said Randall. The whole story was thick with questions.

"NSA logs guy in Da Nang," answered Earl. "He was running a little empire there, wouldn't let anybody check out any equipment that wasn't on the assignment list. He was a speed bump, son. I'd be begging for replacements for my equipment, and Polyander said I'd have to get it cleared with HQ first. It seemed to me that he was hoarding the gear, just holding on it for some other reason. He was a true asshole, but the brass loved him because he had them convinced that he ran a tight ship."

"What happened to him?" Randall was starting to understand the first part of this story.

"Oh, he got promoted. He made colonel before anybody else in his class. He was still running the intercept shop when I retired in '89," replied Earl.

"Do you think he's the same guy as this 'Mouse'?" asked Randall.

"I don't know. This intercept that Creep is talking about; I've never heard about it. We need to get that NSA agent working for us, see if she can do something more than sneak around and shoot people," Earl said with a *grumpf*.

"You oughta be glad she can sneak around and shoot people," said Randall as the two men turned to walk toward the nurses' station. Staying longer would not be productive, as it would just rile Willis up more.

When they got to the nurse's station, Earl asked, "Ma'am, is there any family or emergency contacts for James Willis?"

The nurse didn't even check her screen; she knew all there was to know about Willis. "He checked himself in here three weeks ago. He has no family, no wife, no kids, nobody. All he brought us was his discharge papers and military ID. We only know of one phone call he's made since he's been here."

"That would be to me," said Earl. "What is his prognosis? Can we check him out and take him with us?"

"He has stage-four pancreatic cancer, along with lung blockages and recurring renal failure. He won't be here to take home in a week," replied the nurse. She felt bad for the grumpy old guy with fantastic stories and carefree attitude. He was stubborn but not hostile, and he was pragmatic about his condition; whatever God wanted for James O. Willis, he felt that he was ready.

These words stung Earl. Now all he wanted to do was rush back into Willis's room and tell him all the things he had wanted to say when they worked together: how much he appreciated the dedication and courage to fly straight into antiaircraft fire and neutralize the threats against the recon teams. How the senior team leaders should applaud Willis's bravery. How the morale of the teams remained high because they knew somebody like Willis would come help them out a jam. All these things needed to be said.

But none of that mattered now, Earl came to understand. Willis wasn't interested in reliving his perils and problems in Vietnam. What was important now was getting the rat who provided all that information to the NVA. Earl finally understood that the accounting of the boxes wasn't relevant; it was getting to the bottom of the identity of the rat. As he stared blankly at the nurse, Randall's cell phone chimed, and he turned to answer the call.

"Randall, it's me, Marilyn. We need to talk as soon as possible. Are you with your dad?"

"Yes, Marilyn. We're together in Atlanta, seeing an old buddy of Dad's" was the cheerful reply from Randall. It was good to hear her voice.

"Okay, I got the tests back today from your dad's MRI. It's not good. When can I meet with you two?"

"What's not good? Tell me now," insisted Randall. He looked up to see his father walking in his direction.

"Not on the phone. I'll be at your dad's house when you return; we will talk about it then." That was all Marilyn said as she hung up.

CHAPTER SIXTEEN: MAY 7, 2003

Attack him where he is unprepared,

appear where you are not expected.

—Sun Tzu

The mountain air was clear and almost warm this morning. The travel from Nashville to Pikeville took about two hours, and the men inside these thick, heavy vehicles had the front windows slightly open to allow for a good airflow throughout the cab. The front windows were open, as lowering the rear windows created too much wind noise. The drivers didn't mind the road noise from the open windows as long as it didn't interfere with the encrypted radio traffic.

This two-vehicle convoy was transporting six special agents from the Nashville Field Office of the FBI (FBINash) to Pikeville at the direct orders of the FBI director himself. These agents, volunteer members of the field office's SWAT team, were geared up in flight suits with body armor and full weapons packages. Each vehicle carried three agents each, and they were relaxed but ready for anything. The director's briefing had been a rare event; these agents were summoned into the office of the Special Agent in Charge (SAIC) of the Nashville Field Office, and a secure call was set up on a speakerphone so that the SAIC and the six agents could listen. The director made clear that information from a top intelligence community source had detected an illegal surveillance operation in the area for which Nashville FBI was responsible, and the operation was being undertaken in Pikeville. The orders from the director were to stop this operation through a vehicle interdiction and very quietly take these surveillants into custody for extradition to Washington, DC. The perpetrators of this operation were reportedly well equipped and had undertaken violent actions against their target, so no aspect of this felony arrest was to be taken lightly, and the profile of this action was to be very low-key.

The agents chosen for this arrest were seasoned people with felony-arrest experience. The usual inclusion of fugitive-arrest teams was negated, as the low-profile nature of this action demanded that the agents conduct themselves with speed, surprise, and stealth. There were five men and one woman, three with master's degrees, two with language proficiency other than English, and all with exceptional marksmanship skills. This team was heavily armed and ready for anything.

The vehicles chosen for this arrest were also low-key; the lead vehicle was a GMC Yukon SUV that had been taken out of service due to age and weight. The vehicle was in good mechanical condition, but it had been fitted with Level II armor that added six hundred pounds to the vehicle's weight, making it ideal for issuance of high-risk warrants ten years ago. As armored vehicles had been improved (with some coming from military stock), this vehicle had been sidelined until this arrest plan came up. This vehicle looked like any family vehicle, but it would protect against most pistol rounds.

Following close behind was the newest version of armored vehicles, and it drove like a dream. After 9/11, the FBI had contracted with a relatively new company simply called "The Armor Group" (TAG). The contract called for dozens of various truck platforms that could protect from rifle rounds and low-explosive attacks without looking like the hulking armored Humvees currently in Iraq and Afghanistan. The TAG model provided to the Nashville Field Office was a Ford F-350 with no outward indication of its girth and ballistic resistance. The vehicle looked like any four-wheeler chosen by the youngsters in this part of the country, but inside, it was a thick beast that could travel at highway speed, absorb rounds from a heavy machine-gun, and stop on a dime if needed.

The team leader reviewed the satellite imagery that pinpointed the location of the average-looking van that had been proven to be the source of the electronic surveillance, and he checked to make sure he had the phone number for the closest wrecker company. He wouldn't call for a wrecker until they had cleared all the personnel from the sight of the arrest.

"Green team," began the team leader on his radio net to the agents in the TAG truck, "we are going to turn right up ahead and go up some dirt roads to get to the top of the rise. When we come over the top, we will be above and behind the van. We will proceed up behind, and the dirt road we're on will turn to hard pavement. When that happens, I want you to pass us and go around to the front of the van and pin him in. We'll come up behind and block his rear doors. The only way out of the van will be the side doors, so deploy quickly on the passenger side and we will deploy to the driver's side. Copy that?"

Two clicks were all he received, and that was exactly what he wanted to hear. No noise, no extraneous talk, no joking around. They had reviewed this plan before leaving the field office, and had even practiced the maneuver on some unsuspecting office workers before leaving the city limits. These folks knew what to do.

And the arrest went off spectacularly well. The two vehicles rumbling through dirt roads between farmland created very little interest from the locals, just some disdain for kids off-roading in the area. The pinning of the vehicle was textbook, and the agents disembarked and were at the doors of the van before the two guys inside were even aware that they had been blocked in.

The two men inside the van produced verifiable ID cards from a local cable repair service and provided paperwork that explained why they had been dispatched to survey an "RIS" (Reduction in Service) issue in the area. All these documents were provided by discovery once the two men were arrested, handcuffed, and heaped into the back seats of the FBI vehicles separately. They would have plenty of time to explain themselves and their work during the trip to a small airstrip nearby, where an FBI L-100 aircraft was standing by, ready to transport them back to Washington, DC.

The surveillance operation against Earl Betts had ended in seven minutes. The van was locked up, and the team leader called for a rollback wrecker to transfer the van to an address in Nashville. Very quick, very quiet, and very efficient. The agents involved would never have this arrest on their official record, but they would be summoned to the SAIC's office later in the week to be presented with certificates of appreciation from the Central Intelligence Agency. The agents were then informed that, as these certificates were classified, they had to return them so that they could remain stored in the SAIC's safe.

CHAPTER SEVENTEEN: MAY 7, 2003

Evil enters like a needle and spreads like an oak tree.

—Ethiopian Proverb

As Earl and Randall returned to the hillside property in Pikeville, they eased up the driveway to see Marilyn's blue Ford Explorer in the driveway. As he climbed out of the driver's side of his rented Jeep, Randall looked beyond the house to see something unusual. Marilyn was standing just outside the detached garage, staring into the opened vehicle doors. The shelves of small boxes were getting some light of day, and Marilyn was just staring at them.

"What the hell is that nosy nurse doing now?" demanded Earl as he shuffled by Randall and headed toward the garage. This time, he didn't pause to look to his right at the weeping willow tree. He marched up to Marilyn and said, "These doors do not need to be opened! I don't want anyone seeing these boxes!"

Marilyn turned slightly to Earl and spoke in a somber, sorrowful voice. "I finally remembered what the smell was. When I first saw all this, I knew they were electrical parts from the days when my dad was a TV repairman. But the smell in the garage, the faint smell coming from them, it wasn't right. I looked into it with some of the other Vietnam vets in the hospital, and it became clear. These boxes have been sprayed with Agent Orange."

Marilyn let that statement soak into Earl for a moment as she turned to face him. She spoke again just as Randall came hobbling up. "Mr. Betts, you have an osteosarcoma, a cancerous growth, on both the radius and ulna of your right arm. The cancer cells have moved from the area of your elbow joint into your bloodstream, and they will settle into any soft-tissue home in your body they can find. Sarcomas like this are fairly rare, but the primary cause for men your age is exposure to Agent Orange."

"I wasn't in the areas where they were spraying. I stayed away from that crap when I was doing radio work!" replied Earl.

"But you've been around these boxes for the past two years," said Marilyn in an even, almost calm tone. "You've been in here for hours each day, according to Randall, just trying to get the inventory straight. You've been in constant exposure longer than just the soldiers in Vietnam. And for the smell to last this long, they must have been heavily doused with the stuff!"

"Where else has it spread?" asked Randall as he tried to catch his breath. It seemed that the ringing in his ears was coming back. He was almost as unsteady on his feet as his father, who was being told he had serious cancer.

"I've arranged for more tests of other parts of his body," answered Marilyn. "The places we'll check first are the lungs and the pancreas."

"You mean I'll end up like Jimmy?" was the strained question from Earl. He knew what old age was and how it looked when young men got older, but the sight of the emaciated, discolored man that was his friend Creeper in that hospital bed shocked him.

"We're going to get you some great care" was the soothing statement made by Marilyn as she guided Earl back to the house. Randall followed behind, trying to squeeze his eyes shut and cursing the dirty, crusty cast on his ankle.

As they walked back toward the house, Randall could barely hear his father loudly spouting more radio traffic from his days as a signals intercept officer in the jungles of Southeast Asia. The ringing was a bit subtler now, a bit sneakier, but it rose to interfere with both his hearing and his vision. He wanted to sit, but he needed to get into the house first. He needed to avoid these boxes in the garage.

* * *

At the same time that Earl Betts was learning more about his illness, the section chief was rushing into the director's office at NSA headquarters.

"What is it?" said Polyander as he glanced at the pages in the section chief's hand.

"Just got confirmation from the voice lab," came the panicked response from the section chief. "We ran a check on the voices of the two women who visited Earl Betts the night of the shooting. One of them belongs to a regional field-care nurse out of Baltimore. The other voice, the one that did the shooting, was a special agent out of our Investigations Division! That's why she was there and making those comments about Earl; she knows all about what we're doing!"

"What's the agent's name?" asked Polyander.

"Alexandra Stallings. She was first in her class of special-agent training at Glynco and has been working counterespionage for almost ten years!" responded the section chief. The reference to Glynco was related to the Federal Law Enforcement Training Center in southern Georgia. This facility, part of the former Glynco Naval Air Station, had a reputation for the finest training in the country, and many of the federal agencies sent their police officers and special agents there for weeks of professional training and conferences.

"She doesn't know squat," replied the director. "If they knew something, that self-righteous prick O'Herlihy would be in here before now. With all the other parts shut down, they have no case, and once you get that garage burned down with Earl Betts inside, they'll have even less!"

The section chief looked down at this. It was his turn to start making Director Polyander happy. "I have been in contact with the female contractor. She knows what is expected: kill Betts and burn down the garage. She is moving in cautiously, doesn't want to bring any undue attention to herself—"

The director cut him off. "I don't care about her being cautious! I want that job done! Tell your contractor that we want both Betts men dead, as well as that field-care nurse!"

This thing was expanding, becoming more dangerous, and getting more complex. The section chief started thinking about a lot of details, including how he could extricate himself from this job. He used curiosity as a means to make sense of this obsession.

"Boss, can I ask why the stuff in the garage has to go? Couldn't the radio gear in the garage be part of the story about why these people killed each other?" The section chief wanted to be clear to the female contract killer he had hired to kill the Betts men, but the detail of burning the garage was a nagging one.

"No!" insisted the director, giving him pause and making him speak in a strained whisper. "That radio gear not only implicated me, but the boxes were treated with a special defoliant before I tried to ship them out. The simpleton who interrupted the shipment kept me from poisoning those Chinese fuckers who were working with the NVA. Don't you see? If that information gets out, along with the connection to me, it'll start all kinds of shit. That garage has to burn, and it has to burn hot enough to ruin the radio parts and kill off the defoliant!"

The section chief just stared. The question from the director was the only thing that jolted him back from his disbelief.

"Why don't you have a field report from the LP team at the Betts house?" demanded Polyander.

"I haven't heard anything from them today. I called their cell phone but got no response" was the answer.

"Send somebody else out there; get a handle on that collection effort. If this nosy bitch Stallings has told them anything, we need to know about it now!" said the director.

The section chief walked out of his meeting with a true sense of dread. His boss was tied up in some real bad stuff. This wasn't just stopping some old guy who could ruin the director and the reputation of the NSA; this was covering up both treason and murder.

As he made his way back to the language lab several floors down from the director's office, the section chief made a discreet call from his cell phone.

And as the section chief was making his phone call, NSA Director Polyander was checking all the communication databases for the inspector general's office. He wanted to see what Stallings and that holier-than-thou IG chief O'Herlihy were sharing. He went deep into the informal messaging systems and found some correspondence related to the "Southwest Project," and perhaps that was pertaining to the surveillance op against Betts. In switching to this title as a means to search for notes between the two, Polyander saw that they were slowly building a sizable case for presentation. This was trouble, the director knew, but he had a potential solution.

Polyander checked the messages between Stallings and O'Herlihy for other recipients and found none. Evidently, they had been keeping this matter close hold. And that was a good thing, Polyander knew. All he had to do was remove the evidence Stallings had compiled or discredit the findings of their potential report. If those didn't work, Polyander had one last choice. He knew of a way to eliminate the source of the report, and possibly O'Herlihy too.

Getting into the database to delete the conversations was simple; Polyander could erase whatever he wanted within the walls of the NSA. But the erasure would be tracked back to him, so that avenue was out. Discrediting the report was a bigger enterprise that would take time and resources to compile; making a case against Tom O'Herlihy, who had an ironclad relationship with the president and the intelligence community, would be a complex effort that might still backfire on Polyander. No, the sole choice for stopping this investigation would be eliminating the person who conducted it.

Alexandra Stallings must die, and it must look like an accident or some kind of criminal act. The director did not pick up the phone to get the section chief to handle this; it had to be done delicately. As Polyander recounted the steps it would take to make this "accident" happen, he discovered that his means of eliminating the special agent could work to eliminate O'Herlihy too. That would seal the case shut: if both of them died tragically, it would end any interest in Polyander's spying on Earl Betts and his family. Their deaths would be terrible, and possibly stain the image of the NSA a bit, but it would be worth it to get them out of the way. With them gone and Earl Betts dead due to murder/suicide, nobody would ever know about Polyander's collusion with the North Vietnamese government and their Chinese overseers during the Vietnam War. He had made some good money off this collaboration back then, but as the war was coming to an end and Polyander had to cease all contacts with the Chinese Communist Party (CCP), he had needed an exit strategy. What better way than to take their money for a promised shipment of high-end radio gear and then ship them spare parts poisoned with chemical defoliant being used in the jungles of Cambodia and Laos?

Polyander was proud of himself for coming up with his plan to get out of Vietnam and dispose of his Chinese handler to discourage any interest in keeping contact with the enemy; no way the Chinese would ever discover that their field personnel had been poisoned by the radio gear he provided, and if they did, so what? They couldn't get to him, and any diplomatic whining they would do after they helped the NVA take Saigon would be ignored by the State Department. Polyander was certain that the sole thread connecting him to his "cooperation" with the enemy was the shipment that had been forwarded to Betts. Polyander didn't know who had interfered with the shipment out of Da Nang to Beijing, but whoever it was would certainly die of cancer by being around those infected boxes. Earl Betts would die, too, but not soon enough. That blithering old bastard had to die quickly and without having the chance to disclose what he knew about Polyander. And killing his boy and that field nurse was all but assured as well. Now all the NSA director had to do was eliminate the resulting investigation. He arranged the details of his plan and accessed the informal messaging system within the NSA. With the right kind of message to the right person, he could use Jennings to set up the investigators for killing and nobody would be the wiser. This was going to be fun, setting this up.

CHAPTER EIGHTEEN: MAY 8, 2003

We are never deceived. We deceive ourselves.

—Johann Wolfgang von Goethe

Jamin Gemetar walked away from his uncle's house in Dundalk, Maryland, in a much better mood. He had paced in front of the house for almost an hour, working up the courage to knock on his door and ask for this favor. The uncle had been wary of loaning Jamin his pistol, but Jamin had convinced him that he and a good friend were going to a local shooting range and the ammunition had already been purchased. The uncle relented and handed over the pistol, but with only four rounds in the five-round cylinder. He hoped that Jamin was getting his act together, finally getting a better grip on his life.

Jamin drove from his uncle's house just outside downtown Baltimore to the large overflow parking lot for the Live! casino. Very few cars were here, but nobody paid any mind to a vehicle parked on the second floor of the parking garage. Now Jamin could sit and ponder his next move. He could concentrate on what he would do next rather than focus on the past. His memories of what had gone wrong with the relationship between him and Alexandra Stallings were a mixed blur of anxiety and overdoing his affection for her.

Alexandra and Jamin had met at an NSA offsite conference in 2000, and they enjoyed each other's company for the weeklong event. While they were affectionate with each other, Jamin had failed to move the relationship to intimacy, and that stung him frequently. The truth was that Stallings was a beautiful, confident, powerful woman who knew her mind and was dedicated to her work. Jamin was a data-management specialist who oversaw several of the information-storage sites maintained by the NSA throughout the United States. His work entailed some travel to these remote sites, but mostly his time was spent in the storage lab, where Jamin would ensure the security of the historical information stored in huge, climate-controlled buildings that could be called up when needed for research and verification. His work was routine, boring. Stallings's work with the Investigations Division was challenging and exciting. That was probably why she broke off their relationship: Jamin was just too boring for her. As he thought further about this, his anger and frustration welled up again inside him.

But now he had to focus on the present. Jamin reached into his shirt pocket and pulled out the copy of the message he had received in his work email and read it again. The message had been sent anonymously, with no name or office attached to it. He read the message over and over again on his computer before printing it out and cutting off the margins of the page. Jamin was uncertain about the validity of this note, but he knew from his days as a programmer that messages could be sent on the NSA informal messaging application that could be wiped clean of any sourcing. The note was very clear and addressed specifically to Jamin:

"You have been wronged by an indifferent and uncaring person. Alexandra Stallings rejected your sincere affection and is now secretly dating a very powerful man who manages her workload. This is illegal and immoral. Alexandra's lack of concern for security regulations, as well as your feelings, is an embarrassment to more than just this Agency and should not go unpunished.

"As proof of her careless view of what is right, she and her lover will be living the high life at the Live! Casino outside Baltimore while the rest of us work to preserve the security of this country. They will be staying in the penthouse suite, sleeping together like lazy pigs in a trough, feeding off each other and collecting senior pay while you toil in the lab as a responsible employee of this great organization. When they are tired of rifling through each other's embrace, they will go downstairs, probably about 3:00 p.m. today. Then they will gamble in the casino for the rest of the afternoon, using taxpayer dollars to frivolously cast off their devotion to anything responsible. Somebody needs to stop this. You know Stallings and what she is capable of. You need to stop them. Nobody else has the power and foresight that you do."

The note was signed "A Junior Employee." Jamin could not figure out who this person might be, but they had access to the NSA messaging system, and everything they said was right. Stallings had no business fraternizing with a senior executive, and certainly not engaging in intimate relations during work hours at some resort. It was criminal and unjust. And besides, Stallings had her chance to be close to Jamin, and she chose someone more important, more powerful. Jamin was going to stop this.

* * *

As Jamin Gemetar was walking from his parked car to explore the Live! Casino lobby area, DCIA Olivia Johnson was picking up the receiver of the secure phone on her desk. She dialed a familiar number.

"Bob, I need you in here" was all she said.

Bob Raffleson stood up from his computer and walked toward the

DCIA's office. Raffleson was finishing the approvals for the work assignments for eighty special agents over the next two weeks, ensuring that advance teams, midnight shifts, and relief personnel for the three VIPs and their families under his care were covered. But this would wait. The director's protective staff (DPS) at the CIA was Raffleson's office, and anytime DCIA Johnson called him directly, it had to be important.

Raffleson walked into the side door of the DCIA's office and observed a man he'd never met sitting in a chair across from his director. The man was somewhat nervous and avoided eye contact, but he had a green visitor's badge, and that meant that he had been screened for any criminal or operational activity and no problems had been noted.

"Bob Raffleson, I want you to meet Mr. Jennings. Mr. Jennings has a management position at the NSA. He leads a section that reports primarily to the director of the NSA, and he has shared some very disturbing news with me. Mr. Jennings, Special Agent Raffleson runs all the security operations for my office."

Raffleson shook the man's hand and sat in the red-leather chair next to him. This was not a routine visit, and evidently there were a good number of issues that Raffleson would have to address. He wanted to be in close proximity to this person.

"I came here because I have very few places to go, but something needs to be done right away because I fear for several important people," began the NSA section chief. He knew that blowing the whistle at NSA would not accomplish anything; his director would cover it all up. And running to the FBI or Justice Department would expose too many crimes that would take too long to unravel. Publicity is not what would stop this man; it had to be done quietly and directly.

The NSA section chief, known to the CIA as Mr. Jennings, laid out the entire affair: How Polyander had sold out to the Chinese Ministry of

State Security and the North Vietnamese, and that Polyander succeeded in getting his Chinese handler killed by the South Vietnamese. Polyander told Jennings that he had sold information and radio equipment to the North Vietnamese Army and the Chinese during the Vietnam War, how the last shipment that was saturated in the cancer-causing defoliant known as Agent Orange was planned but somehow foiled, how Polyander discovered that the shipment had been sent to Betts two years ago, and about the surveillance op mounted against the elder Betts and his family to discover where the radio shipment was being kept. This shipment, according to Polyander, linked him to the Chinese asset code-named "Mouse," and that meant that Betts had to die and the shipment be destroyed.

"Mouse?" said DCIA Johnson. This shipment links Polyander to a Chinese asset named Mouse?"

"Apparently so," said the section chief, "and Polyander has been going crazy trying to find it ever since. He has had me hire professional killers to take out Betts and burn the garage where the boxes are located."

Johnson and Raffleson looked at each other. This was getting messier by the minute.

"That's not all," said the section chief. This made the only two people in the world outside of NSA senior leadership that knew about this treachery lean-in.

"Polyander has another leg of this thing percolating. He had me write a note on the whistleblower network at NSA informing the inspector general that there would be a meeting between the NSA director and Chinese intelligence officers at the Live! Casino near Baltimore. Our director is certain that the inspector general himself will want to be there so he can catch the traitor red-handed. But I know it's a trap!"

"When is this alleged meeting?" Johnson was rising slowly from her chair.

"Today at three o'clock. That's two hours from now," answered the man facing serious federal charges.

DCIA Johnson never took her eyes off Jennings. She pointed to the door and said, "Bob, go get Mark Trout out of the command post at my house and get him on Interstate 95! Tell him to get to that casino and alert the security people there that a serious threat is underway against a cabinet-level officer! Text-message him a photo of Tom O'Herlihy while he's on his way!"

Raffleson was almost through the door in the time it took to give these orders. Trout was a dependable, fearless agent who just happened to be in the director's residence in suburban Maryland. He could make it to the casino faster than anyone.

"Mr. Jennings, I'm going to call in a stenographer from the duty office of our security department. You're going to replay this entire monologue for the stenographer while I make some very discreet calls," said DCIA Johnson. Jennings just slumped in his chair. He knew what was coming for him, but he was relieved that he could get this off him. The pressure had been building to an abnormal level, and just explaining all this, even to someone who would put him in prison for the rest of his life, was somewhat of a relief.

DCIA Johnson called the chief of the security duty office and instructed them to send a stenographer to her office; then she placed a secure-line call to the office of the director of the FBI to give him some baseline information along with a promise to tell him more. With that harried conversation complete, Johnson switched to her "black-line phone." This would reach out on an unprotected open line, just like a regular phone. She called a number she knew well. And when Marilyn Emerson answered, Johnson instructed her to get to Randall Betts as fast as she could.

As she was finishing her phone call to the only person she trusted who was located as close to Randall Betts as possible, the DCIA's executive assistant stuck her head in the door and said, "Madam Director, you have an unscheduled visitor from the White House."

DCIA Johnson hustled Jennings out the side door in the direction of Bob Raffleson. Once Jennings was safely locked into the secure conference room, she returned to her office and told Marge Jenson to let whoever this was into her office.

Into her office walked one of the most powerful people in Washington, DC. He warmly shook her hand and sat down without invitation. "Madam Director, thank you for seeing me without an appointment." This was the president's chief of staff. An extremely busy and politically connected man who concerned himself with the image and interactions of the most powerful man in the free world. Very few people knew him, but he had both the ear and the voice of POTUS.

"Good to see you. How can I be of help?" was the gracious and sincere-sounding response from DCIA Johnson.

"The president has instructed me to advise you that by the end of this week, your services to this Agency will no longer be required. You will submit a letter of resignation, explaining that you need to attend to family matters and expressing your sincere appreciation for the president's support over the last five years." This was his answer.

While not a surprise, the lack of warmth in this message was a hard pill to swallow. This man was a pit viper, and his reputation as a shrewd politician meant that his friends were more powerful than hers. But the lack of neither manners nor graciousness would move Johnson to show emotion. She was too good to let them see her flinch.

"Very well. Kindly inform the president that I shall deliver my resignation on Thursday morning."

"I know this sounds harsh," said the chief of staff in a faked show of condolences. "It is certain that the president will make the announcement with all the candor and appreciation for your efforts over the past five years. If it is too difficult or distressing for you, I can deliver the letter to the president if you wish. Or have one of your briefing staff deliver it to me when they come to the White House first thing in the morning!"

"Oh no, I'm certain you will be busy, and my briefing staff have plenty of things to consider when they brief the president. I'll deliver the letter myself," said Johnson, with the same confidence and fake sincerity. No way this asshole was going to speak for her.

The meeting ended with the same curtness in which it had started. DCIA Johnson had to think fast. She had some tough choices to make, and she had very little time to protect herself and her people. She called Marge Jenson in and started giving her instructions.

* * *

The Live! Casino and Hotel was a resort-sized facility in Anne Arundel County, Maryland, just twelve miles south of Baltimore. The full-service hotel was adjacent to the twenty-four-hour casino, and the proximity to such attractions as Baltimore's inner harbor and the Anne Arundel Mall made the property a popular destination for both gamblers and families. It was also a favorite meeting site for senior officers in the NSA, due to the short drive north from Fort Meade to a mecca of gambling and recreation.

Mark Trout rolled up in a dark-blue Chevy Tahoe with no external markings to show that it belonged to the federal government. Five minutes before arriving at the Live! Hotel and Casino, Trout had been moving in excess of eighty-five miles per hour with all the red and blue hide-a-lights activated. He used the Baltimore/Washington Parkway to get to the casino, as Interstate 95 was more open but much farther away. Once Trout turned the emergency lights off upon entering the casino's parking lot, it looked like any other large SUV. The sole giveaway was the solid black steel wheels and twenty-two-inch run-flat tires.

Trout checked his watch; it was 2:30 p.m. He still had time. Trout had called from his vehicle as he sped north on the parkway and had passed along all the threat information and the file picture of Lieutenant General Tom O'Herlihy. He parked at the north entrance, at the far end of the Anne Arundel Mall, and left the vehicle sitting there. When he walked into the casino lobby, he was met by a senior security official for the resort, wearing a subtle red suit and Jerry Garcia tie. "Nice touch," said Trout to himself.

Trout introduced himself and showed his badge that would allow him to carry a firearm anywhere within the boundaries of the United States. He dropped the name of the woman who had called them from CIA headquarters and showed the picture of Tom O'Herlihy on his phone to the security chief and the dozen security officers who were waiting with him. As they walked into the casino area, the security officers, some in red suits and some wearing a more discernible uniform with a pistol at their side, fanned out in a broad line, moving parallel at about ten feet apart. Trout and the chief started a slow, methodical walk down the center of the large room crowded with gambling machines and varying shades of lighting. The overwhelming sounds of music, loud conversations, and gambling-machine alerts made for lots of distractions, but Trout was focused on what he could find rather than what he could hear. Along the walls to their left and right, the uniformed security officers moved parallel to their security chief. They were looking for anyone suspicious and staying in radio contact with the security center, where facial-recognition software cameras and dense-metal detectors searched for known threats and weapons. The casino had quietly installed metal detectors in the entrance doorways years ago, but these were not the typical detectors used in airports and courthouses. These detectors worked in a "passive" capacity, utilizing the earth's magnetic field to detect dense-metal items such as knives and guns. Metal items of lesser density, such as belt buckles and watches, did not register as highly as concealed weapons, so customers could flow through the casino space without drawing any undue attention. These detectors were wired into the casino's security room so that the presence of any weapon would be noted without causing any alarm.

"If your guy is in here, we'll find him," said the security chief.

Trout tried the personal cell-phone number for O'Herlihy again. It was off, apparently, because every call went straight to his voicemail. It was doubtful that someone as powerful and in touch as Tom O'Herlihy would leave his phone at work, leaving Trout to think that he had turned it off intentionally. The best chance to find him now would be to spot him somewhere on the property, and Trout was running out of floor space to check.

* * *

Jamin found the soft red carpet and varied lighting in the casino to be relaxing. Even with the obscene, loud music and sustained noise of machines being played, Jamin was comfortable and focused as he roamed the casino floor. He wandered around the gambling room and various restaurants for a time, then walked back to the hotel entrance to scour the area once more for his target. Once he exited the casino area, the floor was hard and polished, but it was a bit quieter, so Jamin could concentrate better. The women in here were various ages and sizes, but Jamin knew he would remember exactly what Stallings looked like. She couldn't hide from him forever. Thinking about this, Jamin wandered over to a ladies' restroom in the casino entrance area. Maybe she'd walk out, thinking she was on top of the world, and Jamin would be there.

* * *

The security chief's radio crackled. The guys in the security center had gotten a "ping" from the metal detector at the hotel entrance to the casino well after Trout came in, and they tracked it to a guy who was just wandering around the casino without using any of the machines. Now they saw someone who matched the description of the guy lingering around the ladies' room on the west wall of the entrance leading from the hotel entrance to the casino. The security chief was dismissing this, thinking that the guy was just a crank, but the fact that the detector picked up a possible weapon made him a bit more worried. The time was now 2:45 p.m. Mark Trout was anxious for anyone acting suspicious, and he asked how he could find this bathroom. With the security chief pointing out the general direction, Trout moved that way while a uniformed officer was instructed to meet him.

* * *

Alexandra Stallings and Tom O'Herlihy were staked out in the back corner of Luckie's Café, between the casino entrance and the lobby of the hotel. When the whistleblower's note said that Polyander would be meeting with a Chinese intelligence officer at the Live! casino,, they surmised that the meeting would be in the café that was quieter and away from all the open gambling. When it got to be close to 3:00 p.m. and nobody was coming into the café, they started to get a bit antsy. "Maybe we are too exposed here," said Stallings. "I'll take a quick walk to the front entrance and see if Polyander is here. He knows you, but he may not recognize me, so you stay put."

"No, I'll take the far wall from you. We'll get more of a look if we split up," replied O'Herlihy as he stood up and drew out his cell phone. "I'll call the office and see if Polyander has returned to campus."

* * *

Mark Trout met up with the uniformed casino security officer just as he arrived at the spot where the stranger was standing, next to the ladies' room. The man was in his mid thirties, with dark hair neatly combed. He was wearing an untucked plaid shirt over blue slacks. Nothing about him said anything unusual, except that his eyes were looking everywhere except at Trout. "Good afternoon, sir," began Trout as he tried to look and sound as if he worked for the casino. "Is everything going well for you today? May I get you a drink? How about a free-play card from the casino?"

"I'm fine," replied the stranger with a nervous smile. He took a moment to glance at Trout, and looked away quickly. "I'm not used to gambling; I just came along with my girlfriend. She does all the machines. I'm waiting for her to come out," he answered, pointing into the restroom.

The response made some amount of sense to Trout; maybe the security office had clued in to the wrong guy. It was very easily understood that standing at the ladies' room entrance would appear curious, and the guy was just embarrassed. Just as Trout was ready to excuse himself, the uniformed officer asked, "Sir, did you get a free membership card when you checked in?"

As Trout looked away from the gaze of this troublesome interaction, he spied Tom O'Herlihy walking out of the café adjacent to the casino entrance. He was twenty-five feet away, saying something to a woman, and he had his phone to his ear.

"Hey, *gun!*" was the scream from the security officer as Trout became instantly aware in his peripheral vision of a hand holding a small blue-metal revolver pointed in O'Herlihy's direction.

* * *

As he was waiting at the restroom door for Stallings to walk out, Jamin was approached by two men from different directions. This was unnerving, but as long as he played it cool, there was nothing these parasites could do. Jamin was convinced that casinos were just a tax upon the stupid. As long as people thought they could become rich by taking chances with gambling, these vampires would do everything they could to steal their money. It sickened Jamin.

And then one of the men spoke to him in a sincere, friendly tone and offered him a drink. Jamin was startled at this, as these people were known to be selfish and indifferent. For a moment, he was close to taking the young man's offer, but then he remembered that they were paranoid remoras and wanted to see if he was some pervert hanging around the ladies' room.

Jamin just looked at this athletic stranger with a big grin and unfamiliar clothing. Normally, the casino employees wore red suits or uniforms, and this guy was wearing cargo pants and a faded blue sport coat. And his waistline had a slight bulge; this guy was armed. He had to get rid of him quickly. He provided a simple, rational, calm explanation, but the rent-a-cop in the red uniform wanted to know if he had something called a "membership card."

"I just told you I don't gamble!" said Jamin with exasperation. Didn't these bloodsuckers who made their living drawing money from poor people pay attention?

When Jamin turned away from this fake cop in his ten-dollar uniform, he saw his objective come around the corner. Alexandra Stallings walked out of the nearby café area, followed by a man in a military uniform on a cell phone. Jamin recognized the man immediately as one of the big shots at NSA. So this was the lover Stallings had left him for. This was the man she was hiding out with, suborning her work while shacked up with this overpaid bureaucrat. Well, their screwing the people and each other was over. Jamin drew his pistol and aimed carefully.

* * *

Trout didn't have time to draw his gun from its Kydex holster on his hip. The stranger already had his gun out and was squeezing the trigger as the casino security officer was screaming and trying to get his own pistol out of his retention holster. The first shot rang out as Trout flew into the man, and they both fell onto the bathroom floor. As they fell, a second shot was fired. Then a third and fourth. These last two shots slammed into the wall of the bathroom, as they had fallen out of sight line with O'Herlihy. The guy was just squeezing the trigger over and over, even as the last shot had been fired. Trout held him down and pinned his arms to the floor as the guy screamed something he didn't understand and kept pulling the trigger.

Finally, a second set of hands grabbed the gun out of the stranger's hands and helped Trout get him to his feet. An Anne Arundel County policeman stuck the blue-steel revolver into the small of his back and ratcheted Jamin's arms behind him. A set of handcuffs was quickly and roughly applied to the man's wrists, and he was trying to twist around from the wall he'd been put against. He wanted to see what he had done. He was still screaming something. He was trying to shout something at the people he had just shot. Mark Trout was forcing himself to react in a loud, bloody scene that had been a busy but quiet place for gambling.

"What's he saying?" Trout asked one of the security guys over the screams of the others in the casino.

"He keeps screaming something like 'Stallings'!" was the answer.

* * *

Stallings was just leaving the café, heading toward the casino entrance with her boss behind her. O'Herlihy had checked with Director Polyander's office before they left Fort Meade to investigate this whistleblower tip. Finding that he had left for the day and had not requested that his security team accompany him, O'Herlihy felt that it lent credence to the tip about Polyander meeting some Chinese spook at the casino.

Now they were going to spread out and see if Polyander was indeed here. As she turned away from O'Herlihy, checking on the director one more time, Stallings saw someone she hadn't seen in three years. She knew Jamin Gemetar from a government security conference in 2000, and they went on a few dates after that. Nothing ever came of their association, as Stallings was always busy with something, and Jamin never seemed to want to do anything but sit and talk. Stallings enjoyed talking with Jamin, as he was smart and dedicated to his continuity-of-operations work at the NSA. But eschewing movies, bowling, pinball, everything except to sit and talk, was tiring. Eventually they lost contact with each other. Until now. Jamin was here, and the look on his face was unsettling. And then Stallings saw Jamin draw a pistol from under his shirt and point it in her direction. She began to draw her own pistol when she saw that his sights had changed from her to O'Herlihy. Stallings stopped drawing her gun and turned to push her boss out of harm's way.

The first shot fired went to Stallings's right; the bullet entered just under her right armpit as she was turning toward O'Herlihy, and it traveled in a straight line across the top of her right lung before exiting at her rib cage and striking O'Herlihy in the lower center of his chest. The .38 caliber flat-nosed wadcutter bullet stopped just below the man's xiphoid process, cutting his left lung just below the heart.

The second shot sent a bullet to Stallings's left. The bullet was higher and skimmed along the left side of her head but grazed off her skull. Having torn open the side of her scalp above the temple, the bullet passed easily into the right eye of Tom O'Herlihy, just to the left of the cell phone he was holding to his ear.

Neither of them heard Jamin screaming Stallings's name. Tom O'Herlihy died on the spot, and Alexandra was unconscious from the shock to her system and the rapid blood loss from the gushing wounds.

CHAPTER NINETEEN: MAY 10, 2003

Truth is more valuable if it takes you a few years to find it.

—French proverb

With his dad in the hospital, Randall had gone around the house and tried to tidy it up for when Earl would get back home. As he worked to make some room in his father's bedroom closet, Randall saw a large cardboard box, just larger than a regular shoebox, on the top shelf. Taking it down and looking inside, Randall found himself sifting through a puzzle of items that was both curious and jarring.

The top of the box was a frame that fit the exact size of the box. It was a presentation frame that held numerous pins, service medals, and ribbons that indicated that Earl Betts had achieved the rank of lieutenant colonel when he retired. Inside the box was a jumble of military patches, cigarette lighters, deformed bullets, and lots of notepaper. Randall took the time to examine one of the patches. It bore the typical American eagle watching over the globe, but this eagle held yards of paper strip in its mouth and was buffeted with lightning bolts. Typical communications humor, thought Randall. Another patch held the crest of a lion, with the words "Vigilis Salutis" ("Forever Vigilant") on the bottom. The biggest patch showed a hand clutching lightning bolts over a green background with wording above and below. The upper portion of the patch read "In God

We Trust," and the bottom portion read "All Others We Monitor." These were fascinating symbols of the craft and credits belonging to those who operated listening posts in support of military operations all over the world. Randall was in awe of his father's affiliation. Formerly the Army Security Agency, it had been transformed during the Cold War into the National Security Agency. This organization had dedicated itself to collecting a huge number of overseas phone calls, civilian cables, and telegrams to report on any enemy activity against the United States. With the emergence of cell phones, text messages, and the almighty electronic mail, NSA had expanded to a powerhouse of vacuuming information and assessing it for possible leads and threats of America's enemies. In addition, NSA had been deemed to be "Cyber Command" for the military, utilizing a broad array of electronic sensors and tapping mechanisms in an attempt to stay ahead of the threats.

The notes and pages in the box were a blur of handwritten notes and simple one-sentence pages. Three of them simply read "The Proof Is Coming! The Traitor Must Be Punished!" and one finished a blur of hastily written sentences with "Polyander Is Mouse!" in large black letters. These were evidently the notes sent by James "Creeper" Willis. But without the proof, where was this all coming from? How did Willis know this? These sheets seemed to prove Willis was obsessed with an idea, but it was just an idea.

At the bottom of the box was a slip of paper that was wedged under the cardboard flap. It was barely visible, and when Randall pulled it out, it tore due to being stuck to the glue adhering the flap to the bottom of the box. The slip of paper had one sentence on it, and Randall recognized the importance of the sentence immediately. The sentence read "Director" and then a five-digit number, and then the word "Canberra" and another five-digit number; the end of the sentence was "DTD 03Jun73." The font and use of capital letters was very familiar to Randall; it was the document number of a finished intelligence report out of CIA headquarters, which was disseminated from a cable originating from Australia in early June 1973. This would prove helpful in getting to the bottom of what Willis was suggesting. Randall dug into the flap to retrieve the other portion of the slip of paper more carefully, but he saw nothing else written. All it contained was the document number for an old intelligence report. Now he saw that he had to do something, but what could he do? He was locked into Pikeville to keep tabs on his dad, and being able to stay put at this stage was a better choice than driving back to Langley, Virginia, to discuss this with the CIA. Even if he could get away, who would believe him?

Two days later, at the request of DCIA Johnson, Marge Jenson called Randall Betts and got him caught up on what had been going on, and finished by informing him of the shooting at the casino. Marge filled Betts in about the surveillance op initiated against him and his family by Polyander and included the details about the importance of the boxes in the garage. He then went through the events that led up to the shooting, how some emotionally challenged tech guy had been fired up about something and took it out on Stallings, and how he had successfully undertaken getting a gun into the casino and emptying it at Stallings. Marge explained how Mark Trout and the casino security officer had frantically applied bandages to Stallings's head and chest, and the emergency-services team had stabilized her before a Maryland State Police helicopter transported her to Johns Hopkins Hospital. Randall Betts was stunned by all this information and begged for any update he could have. He didn't know the NSA inspector general that Marge was talking about, and the death of such a senior officer in the intelligence community was tough, but the person he cared about was the woman who had kept him alive and unharmed in a previous gunfight. All the criminal stuff conducted against Betts and his family paled in comparison to his concern for Stallings.

"She's having surgery tomorrow to get the lung reinflated, but her vital signs are good, and the infection is being handled," reported Marge. "A plastic surgeon has been called in for the damage to her scalp, and the most I'm getting from them is that the damage can be repaired."

"When can I see her?" asked Randall as he computed travel time and availability. He promised his dad that he would come see him every day, but these severe injuries to Stallings were demanding his attention.

"Randall, you won't get in there for several days. They've gone all *Star Trek* on preventing any infection, and nobody is getting in that room. Please let me keep you updated, and they'll get you in there the second she can have a visitor," said Marge. With the promise to stay in touch accomplished, Marge rang off.

This news put Randall into a state of immobility and emotional fog. With his father in the hospital facing an aggressive cancer and a woman he cared about fighting for her life from serious gunshot wounds, he couldn't get his priorities or plans straight. He had all this information from his dad to report, but he couldn't do it on an open phone line, and he doubted anyone had time to fuss with some old intelligence report. He found himself flooded with information and reactionary emotions. He was trained to respond to any affront, to come at his attacker quickly and effectively. But this situation was all garbled, all thrown out of kilter. Betts couldn't leave, couldn't communicate some sort of response to the attack, and didn't have the tools to create a fix. Randall Betts found himself plastered in place without any outlet or resolution.

Betts knew the easy route: withdraw. When the forces against you are more than you can bear, then withdraw and return to battle another day. In this case, withdrawal meant the couch, cable TV, and cocktails by the dozen. But this wasn't that time. Betts had obligations, responsibilities; his dad needed him, and Stallings needed him (didn't she?), and he had begun to build up the courage to ask Marilyn Emerson out to dinner. He had seen lots of Marines withdraw and use the stress as a trigger to swallow pills and booze and pot. Betts knew that this path was self-destruction, even though the dopamine was alluring. So he stood in the kitchen, looking at the landline phone on the hook, and tried to make sense of his immobility. When a course of action had come to him, he was unimpressed with his choice, but it was all he had left. All he could force himself to do was go into the backyard. When things always seemed too crazy to solve, Betts knew he had a valve. He stepped out the back door of the house and admired the various kinds of trees in the area. He thought back to his schooling and remembered some important facts.

The southern magnolia tree, *Magnolia grandiflora*, is an American tree native to the southeastern United States. It grows as a thick, conical-shaped tower of little more than fifty feet tall, with a straight trunk and heavy, broad green leaves, which unapologetically kill every blade of grass under it. The fragrant white blossoms are also thick, but they bloom and wither quickly. Their only job is to attract birds and insects that will spread the seeds. The root system is strong and shallow to keep the tree upright, running four times as far along the ground as the trunk is tall, and it absorbs every drop of water as quickly as it can to survive. They are best used as barriers or boundaries due to their bold, thick build.

The weeping willow tree, by contrast, *Salix babylonica*, is a species of deciduous willow native to dry areas of northern China. Its slender trunk creates waves of thin, flexible branches that extend to the ground and catch every breeze that comes their way. It is a hospitable, peaceful tree whose roots go wide and deep and allow the tree to bend in the heaviest weather and seek water much deeper in the ground than other plants can reach. It demands sunshine more than water, growing to a height of more than sixty feet, and the thin, narrow leaves don't make the messes that the larger oaks and sycamores do.

Betts knew these facts from both his college studies in earth science and the lectures provided by his dad. Every plant had a mission, according to Betts's father, and the mission had to match the environment that it was planted in. The backyard didn't need any additional barriers or boundaries; it needed a graceful, long-living tree that required sunshine and occasional water to thrive. Earl Betts had brought the stub of a tree and attendant root system back with him from Vietnam, and he planted it in the backyard before Randall was born. As the tree grew, Earl explained the tree's importance to both of his children and imbued them with a love and respect for all the different types of trees and their importance. The magnolia, as Earl explained to his kids, was a tree that exemplified power, courage, and confidence. The willow was a gift that reminded us that we all need a little grace and peace in our lives. That was why Earl chose this tree for the final resting place of the most gorgeous person he had ever met.

Now, as he stood at the fully grown weeping willow tree in his father's backyard, Randall Betts stared at the stone bearing his mom's name and length of life, along with the inscription his dad had paid extra to have on the marker. The sound of the mountain breeze moving through the leaves and branches of the enormous tree created a white noise that soothed Betts's soul and allowed him to talk without anyone else hearing what he said.

"Mom," began Betts with a quivering voice and uncertain mind, "you gotta get me straight here. Pop has all these secrets and all these...boxes, and he's getting sicker every day. I know now that Dad was involved in some heavy stuff in Vietnam, and his past is haunting him to no end. We checked him into the hospital two days ago, and he just seems to be going downhill really fast. I know we all get older, but the process seems to have sped up. It looks to me like this sickness was just waiting for me to get here so it could eat him up. And a woman who has saved our lives is now lying in a hospital, all shot up! Help me, Mom. Help me understand it all; I can't figure stuff out like you could. You never shirked from providing help and advice to us. You always had an answer, whether we listened to you or not; you could always find a way to make things better. To make things understood. I need your courage, your brains, your quiet determination to do what's right. I miss you so much, Mom. God, I miss you so much!" He had to stop here as his monologue brought him to tears and sobs. He bent at the waist, propped his hands on his knees, and let it all come out; he couldn't stop it. His grief and his longing for answers swept over him like the powerful gush of air from that rocket attack on the enemy position in the Iraqi desert.

He had not been there for his mom's passing, as he was overseas at the time. He was heavily invested in a covert-action plan to disrupt millions of dollars coming out of the Tri-Border Area of South America to fund Hezbollah in Lebanon, and his work with the local intel service and police was getting results. The US consular office had a very small staff, and they had a devil of a time getting him out of there. By the time he could get his airline tickets rearranged to get him home, all the funeral planning had been attended to and arranged by Earl. The plot was dug and prepared in the backyard, and a small group of neighbors had been gathered. Randall always felt like he had never really grieved for his mom. Now she was gone, and he needed her quiet wisdom and gentle guidance now more than ever.

"Good afternoon!" came a sweet, lilting voice behind Randall. He quickly wiped his eyes and his nose to turn and see a short, sturdy woman in her late forties wearing a light-colored raincoat standing near the back of the house, about twenty yards away.

"I'm sorry to bother you, but Marilyn sent me out here to check on you. I think. Are you Randall Betts?"

Betts didn't reply at once. He found himself staring at the valley and the sky again, just like that morning when he and his dad drove to the hardware store. The sudden rush of beauty and peace swept over him. This time, Betts thought, it was truly his mom touching his shoulder.

When he looked at the woman and replied that he was Randall Betts, she walked toward him with a big smile and kind voice. She kept her distance from the weeping willow tree in an effort to show deference for

Randall's grief. She introduced herself and explained why she was there as she stood between Randall and the open-doored garage. She had a very clinical air about her; clearly, she had to be a medical professional, as she kept both of her hands thrust straight into the pockets of her raincoat.

Randall then moved toward the garage to close the doors. Yellow tape and cones had been put up to prevent anyone else from getting into the garage, and the doors had been left open by Marilyn, but right now they would just be a distraction for this newcomer. As he apologized for moving past the woman, his pace became strained, and his head started to spin. The pain and ringing in his ears was back, but this time it was almost electronic. Before it had seemed to be an organic buzzing in his ears, like water in his eardrums. But this was much harsher, much louder, much more invasive. Randall took another step forward and started to feel like he was falling. His eyes were shut tight, and he instinctively put his hands to his ears to shut out the pain.

It was no use. The screaming sound was creating too much pain, and Randall almost sank to his knees. He took a few more steps, but they were labored under the intense pain in his ears. He could hear the woman, now standing behind him, saying something. Maybe she was asking if he was all right, because clearly, he wasn't. But he couldn't catch his breath enough to speak. Something was burning into his head, coming in through his ears and trying to get his head to explode. Randall now fell through the yellow tape onto the floor of the garage laying on his side, holding his ears, and looked behind him.

The strange woman was walking slowly toward him, and he could barely make out what she was saying to him in that soothing, sweet tone. But the image was all wrong; she was bending at the waist slightly, about eight feet away from him, with her hands still in her pockets. And she was looking at Randall with a serious expression that demonstrated nothing of comfort. The smile was gone; she was looking at Randall like he was a lab experiment, as though she was waiting for something to happen. She was doing something to have this effect on Randall. He didn't know what it was, maybe something in her pocket. Her eyes were locked onto him as she spoke, and they displayed none of the warmth that she had displayed when she introduced herself. She was pure evil and moving slowly toward him. He was powerless to move, and he could feel the pain increasing the closer she got to him.

And then she removed one hand from her right-hand pocket, and Randall saw that it was a foot-long dull-red rod, a little thicker than one inch. It looked like a stick of dynamite. But it couldn't be dynamite. The woman took her hand out of the other pocket, and he could see that she held something that looked like a large TV remote control. This answer to why she had her hands in her pockets was even more confusing. What was she going to do with these things?

Keeping the remote in her left hand, she pulled the end cap off the long, thin rod she held in her right. She then struck the tip of the rod against the end of the cap, and it created a bright, burning light. It was a highway flare! The type someone would place on the road at night to warn drivers to stay away from the scene of an accident or emergency equipment. What the hell was this for? She approached Randall carefully with the lit end pointed toward him as the burning bits of sulfur fell to the ground. She was getting close enough that even with the loud ringing in his ears, he could sense the intense heat of the flare.

About two feet away from Randall, the woman's head suddenly jerked to one side. She stood still for a moment, and then she seemed to stumble to her left, and she fell to the ground not far from Betts. He could barely see the woman as all the loud ringing in his ears forced his eyes shut, but then he opened them enough to look where the woman had been standing and saw a different figure approach him. This figure was taller than the strange woman now lying motionless in the dirt just outside the garage floor, with a lit highway flare burning just beyond her. The new figure approached Randall at a much more hurried pace and reached out to him. With one soft hand behind his neck and one hand grasping the front of his shirt, he was pulled several feet into the backyard, away from the garage.

Things seemed to happen too fast. Randall was just thinking back to the glorious wash of light and beauty and happiness over him as he turned from his crying at his mother's grave to this crazy woman with the soothing voice and the highway flare. Now he was being dragged across his backyard by someone he couldn't recognize because of the screaming in his head.

His eyesight returned just a bit as the ringing began to diminish. The quieter the sound in his ears became, the clearer his vision. The figure had left Randall's side and ran over to the woman lying on the ground. The highway flare had been picked up and stuck violently into the ground. The burning tip was extinguished, and the flare was thrown off to the side of the garage. Then the figure moved to the woman lying on the ground and fished through the pockets of both the raincoat and her pants. Upon retrieving several items from the woman's pockets and retrieving the remote-control-looking thing from the left hand, the figure stood and turned to walk back to Randall. Once the figure was just a few feet away, he saw that it was Marilyn. She stooped at his side and asked if he was okay. Randall replied that he was feeling better and began to ask a question.

Before the question could finish on his lips, Marilyn stood and quickly pulled her cell phone from her pocket. With all the manipulation skills of a surgeon, Marilyn held the remote control and a wallet in one hand while she typed in a number and held the phone to her ear.

"Marge, this is Marilyn Emerson. I need to talk to your boss right now. No, I mean now. An attempt has been made on Randall's life, and she needs to hear how sick and significant this is." A moment went by, and Marilyn repeated that this was an emergency and she didn't care what Director Johnson was doing.

When Johnson came on the line, the background noise indicated that the call had been routed to her while she was driving in her vehicle. "Hey, Marilyn, what's up?" was the quick statement from Johnson.

"Olivia, I'm here at the Betts house. Someone else has made a run at Randall. This time it was a woman! She came out here with a highway flare and a hypersonic sound device." Marilyn let that statement rest so that Johnson could ask her question, then replied, "It emits a very high-frequency tone that can be discernible to anyone with a recent head injury. This woman knew that Randall was having issues with his ears ringing and his dizziness, and the device can create enough whining distress that it can immobilize the victim and possibly cause a stroke or a broken eardrum. She was standing close to Randall and had him on the ground, and she was going to burn the garage down with him in it!"

"Why wasn't she affected?" was the sole interrogative from Johnson.

"She had noise-deadening ear plugs in. That's why she didn't hear me come up behind her with a shovel. I took that shovel and knocked her out, Olivia! I swung that thing like a baseball bat and caught her square on the side of her head! I may have killed her; I don't know!" said Marilyn in a gush of shock.

Johnson took a hurried, deep breath as she negotiated Beltway traffic. "Okay, look, Marilyn. I'm out of it now. They've let me go, so I'm transitioning to retirement. Marge is closing up all my files and arranging for the new director to come in. So I can't do anything right now, but I have reached out to some friends for help. They should have been there before now. I'm sorry you had to go through all that. Marilyn, I am eternally grateful for everything you've done. I wouldn't blame you if you wanted to walk away from all this crap and return to the Maryland panhandle. All I ask is that you work with the VA to help the Betts men and keep me informed." This was the longest statement ever made to Marilyn by Johnson.

"You couldn't get me away from this with a court order," replied Marilyn. "I'm going to see this through. These two are being targeted by some pretty dirty people, and they need all the medical help I can give. Don't you worry about a thing, Olivia."

Marilyn Emerson had counseled all kinds of vets in her work as a field specialist for the VA. She had met with a broad range of military personnel, from enraged youngsters who couldn't figure out why they had lost all their earnings to quiet, simmering Vietnam vets who knew the score and were experts at manipulation. They all needed help, and very few of them knew the path to recognizing wellness. Through the pills, the booze, the gambling, the medical pokes and prods, these people were broken. Marilyn knew how to help, but it took time and patience. Therapy sessions were organized as more of an interview than a conversation, and it required a deft balance of questions and rationalization to guide the unwell soul to a place of peace and personal discovery. The VA, however, prided itself on reporting to Congress about success, and lengthy interactions to guiding disillusioned patients did not count as successes. So Marilyn was regularly informed that her work was substandard or nonproductive. The accuracy of her performance evaluations did not match the gratitude of the vets that she helped, but that was part of the work.

Marilyn wasn't letting go of these two men. She had been drawn to Earl Betts from the moment she read the inscription on his wife's headstone. She had to admit that she was drawn to Randall because he was open and honest, and he needed some good guidance. And he was attractive. That was enough.

Marilyn put away her phone as she walked over to Randall and moved to get him to stand. He was somewhat conscious, but he couldn't get to his feet by himself. Marilyn hooked her arms under his left arm and coaxed him up. It was dead weight. He could prop himself up on his right elbow, and his sight was returning. But his head was a fog of pain and surrender.

He couldn't get up, and Marilyn couldn't get a good enough grip to get him up.

Just then Marilyn felt the presence of someone else. She had been so focused on Randall that she had not heard the arrival of another vehicle or the approach of someone coming up on her. A sudden shadow and whisking sound of clothing behind her caused her to cry out and turn to stand. Marilyn immediately tried to adopt a fighting stance, like she had been taught in her self-defense class. She took a half step back with her strong-side foot and turned at the waist while moving her hands up into a boxing posture to undertake both a defensive block and an offensive strike, but it was too late.

The figure that had come up behind her simply stepped around her and scooped Randall up to his feet. Marilyn was left standing in her fighting stance as a huge man, well over six feet and stocky, bent to put Betts into a fireman's carry. With Betts limp across his broad shoulders, he stood straight, turned to Marilyn and announced, "Hello, I'm FBI Special Agent Troy York with the Nashville Field Office. Do you want him inside?"

Marilyn saw the badge on his waist but couldn't see the bulge of a gun. Randall was lying limp across massive shoulders, and the agent's narrow waist meant that a hip holster was less likely to protrude. Somewhat in shock and definitely in awe of the agent's size and quiet voice, Marilyn quickly replied in the affirmative and guided them to the front door. She had a spare key made for her frequent trips to the house and instructed York to put Betts on the bed.

"I could have used you a few minutes ago," said Marilyn as she admired the height and girth of Agent York.

"I've been on assignment in the headquarters building, and the director asked that I come out here because of my language skills," said York.

"Language skills?" said Marilyn.

"Chinese, ma'am. I speak Mandarin better than Cantonese, but I'm pretty handy with both."

"And that's needed here?" asked Marilyn. She was uncertain about where this was going.

"The director instructed me to come out here and take a look at some boxes that were stored on the property."

They left Randall on the bed and walked back into the backyard. Marilyn guided the young agent out to the garage, where the woman in the raincoat was just coming around. She was almost standing up when a quick flourish by York jerked her to her feet, and handcuffs were efficiently fastened to her wrists. As she blurted questions and obscenities, York escorted her promptly to the back seat of his Buick sedan and slammed the door shut. Returning to the garage with all the pace and patience of a predator, Marilyn handed him a cloth mask and informed him of the physical threat posed by the poison that had been sprayed on the broad array of boxes on the garage's back wall.

"It should only take a minute," replied Agent York. He held the mask to his face with his left hand while he took several boxes from the shelves, looked over them, and placed them back on the shelf. He chose one box and carried it back out of the garage to Marilyn.

"Most of the boxes appear to have the same label on the back," said York as he put the mask into his pocket.

"But these are all different components, aren't they? My dad had a TV repair business and was a ham-radio freak, so I recognize what they are. I just thought they were separate parts," said Marilyn.

"Oh yes, ma'am. You have a good eye. But many of the boxes I looked at have a label taped to the back of the box. It must have been slapped onto them while they were new. These labels are pretty faded."

"What does the label say?" Marilyn didn't recognize the language.

"It's Chinese, Mandarin. It says 'From your favorite Mouse.'"

Returning to the house, Marilyn and Agent York found Betts sitting on the edge of his bed, trying to get his focus back.

"What happened to me?" was the first question out of Betts's mouth. He had plenty more, but right now he was safe and somewhat sound in his bedroom, so trying to figure out why he had been so snookered by a little woman was first in line.

"The woman came here to knock you out and evidently burn you up in the garage," Marilyn answered. "She was using a device that is used to test sound suppression in commercial buildings. It emits a very high-frequency sound that is adjustable and can be recorded on the other side of a reinforced wall. I've seen them used in hospitals to determine if MRIs and x-rays affect other rooms. As a measuring device, it's very handy. As a weapon used against somebody with the battle trauma you have, it can make your head pop like a balloon. She was going to immobilize you in the garage and set it on fire, and your burned body would show no signs of foul play."

As Marilyn explained this to Betts, York looked beyond the bedroom window and glared at the woman sitting in his back seat as she hollered at the closed window. York was going to find a way to slam a DOJ door on this bitch.

"So you came along and saved me..." said Betts to Agent York.

"Oh no," said Marilyn. "I was coming out for a regular checkup on you and saw what she was doing. I took that shovel your dad keeps at the back porch and clocked her a good one! I don't know how I found the strength, but I hit her so hard I thought I killed her!"

Betts and York both looked at Marilyn with grunting admiration.

Agent York didn't wait for the next question. He spoke up with a slow Southern drawl that hardly reverberated through the bedroom. His soft voice and easy tone clashed with his six-foot, five-inch, muscular frame. "I got here just after she did. When I saw you laid out and saw the shovel strike, I radioed for an ambulance. When I saw that this woman had taken care of business, I stepped in just for the wrap-up. Should I cancel the ambulance call?"

"Yeah, I'm okay," replied Randall. "I'm Randall Betts; I appreciate your help. Who are you, and how'd you get involved with this?"

"Special Agent Troy York. I'm currently with the Nashville Field Office. I was on temporary assignment to FBI HQ when the director sent me out here. Seems that your boss, Johnson, is very concerned about your welfare, and she couldn't gather any troops to get out here to help."

"She's been removed as DCIA," said Marilyn flatly.

"What? Why was she removed?" asked Randall.

"Politics. The administration wants someone more...amenable to their wishes" was all that Marilyn could say. Olivia Johnson had been candid with Marilyn about the pitfalls of serving at the pleasure of the president, and they knew this day would come.

"Did she ask for you specifically, Agent York?" Betts was trying to sidestep the idiocy of removing Johnson from her post, and getting a sense of this big guy would help.

"Nope. I was sent by the FBI director as a favor to DCIA Johnson. Once I read your file and was made aware of the threats against you, I got out here as fast as I could. You know, we have something in common," said York.

"What's that?" Betts fully expected to hear York recite his Marine Corps rank and unit affiliation.

"I worked the New York Field Office before Nashville. My boss was Darryl Beeker," said York.

Randall suddenly summoned his strength, pushed hard to his feet from the side of his bed, and quickly grasped York's hand. From his rapid response to the name uttered by York, it was clearly someone important to both men. Betts's former commanding officer in the USMC was a natural leader and valued mentor. Darryl Beeker had left the Corps and had taken a job with the FBI as a counterterrorism team chief with the New York Field Office. He had been the one who had used his considerable contacts to get Betts employed with the CIA, and had given him encouragement and guidance through his early career as a case officer. Beeker had become promoted to Special Agent in Charge of FBI/NYFO, and on September 11, 2001, he was looking through the mass of messages and cables about a terrorist plot inside the United States when the planes had flown into the World Trade Center, right next to the field office. Beeker had ensured all the available personnel in the field office were accounted for and got everyone safely evacuated from the building. He was talking with FBI HQ on speakerphone as he was shredding classified documents when the South Tower collapsed and killed him. He was a casualty of the global war on terrorism that reminded Betts every day that finer men than him had made the ultimate sacrifice, and it was his job to pay the bastards back every day of his life.

"Darryl Beeker was the best." This was all that Randall could manage.

"That he was. When I saw your military record, and when I read your fitness reports signed by Beeker, I knew I was helping the right guy." York demonstrated both respect and kinship in his voice.

"And, Marilyn, I owe you my life," said Betts as he turned to hug his rescuer.

"Well, I can't have you disappointing your father. I went to see him today, and he really wants to talk with you. Soon," Marilyn responded. She was happy for the hug, but her tone implied seriousness.

"I'll grab my jacket" was the quick reply from Betts.

Before Marilyn could mount an opposition to this idea, York stepped in to slow Randall from rushing out in his condition. Flying down the mountain and driving distractedly when he had just regained his composure from an attempt on his life was not advisable.

"Staff Sergeant Betts, it'd be better if you give me a chance to book that lady with the Bledsoe County Sheriff's Office," explained York, "They may have some questions for both you and the woman who saved you, so give me a while, okay?"

Randall sighed and agreed. They headed out to the kitchen to say goodbye to York. Marilyn began to make a pot of coffee, and then she noticed that her hands were shaking. Now she began to see what adrenaline and cortisol did to the body. When someone is rushed into danger and chooses to undertake sudden, violent action in defense of self and others, the effects can be severe. The resulting rush for committing to action was a combination of stress hormones and physical response that had to wane eventually, and when it did, the human body experienced fatigue from imbalanced sugar levels in the blood. She had to take a seat at the kitchen table and get Randall to finish making the coffee. She tried to control her breathing and her heartbeats, and she was embarrassed when she looked up to see the two men looking at her.

"Sorry" was all Marilyn could say.

"We've seen it," said York as he looked over at Randall. "Just breathe slowly and focus on one thing."

"And have dinner with me" was the comment from Randall. He finally found the courage and clarity of mind to ask.

Marilyn was quickly stricken by two things. One of those things was that Randall Betts had just asked her out to dinner. This was an incredible but somewhat predictable phase in Betts's therapy. Having feelings for the therapist was not at all unusual in field medicine cases, but the result had to be that Marilyn must refuse the request. She had to reshape Betts's attraction to her; as long as she worked for the VA, she couldn't cross the line and become emotionally attached to a patient. She used the second thing as a way to sidestep her response. As she sat in the kitchen chair, lower than the two men staring at her, she looked at the bottom of the wall cabinet across the room from the sink and noticed a very small black tube.

"Randall, what is that?" asked Marilyn with all the honesty and distraction she could muster.

Betts walked to where she was pointing and bent over, looking at the three-inch-long tube intently. When he "Humpf"ed to demonstrate dismay, York stepped over and took a look. He quickly recognized the object and stood straight as he asked Betts, "Staff Sergeant Betts, did your dad install a high-end surveillance system in this house?"

CHAPTER TWENTY: MAY 16, 2003

mors immatura.

—Latin for "a death before someone reaches the pinnacle of their life"

Army General Thomas O'Herlihy was entitled to a funeral service at Arlington National Cemetery with full honors, but the timeline for providing that high honor was so far off that his family decided to have him buried at the cemetery near his hometown. Fort McClellan Post Cemetery was located just over an hour from Birmingham, Alabama, and was much easier for his extended family to attend the service. As news spread from O'Herlihy's family to the various relatives and school friends that his funeral would entail full military honors, several plans and locations for wakes and life celebrations were quickly established. Suddenly, relatives who had not heard from one another for decades were arguing over who would have the better event to honor "Big Man Tom," as he was called during his high school years.

Ultimately, it was O'Herlihy's ninety-year-old mother who settled the relatives down and got them all to agree to a wake at her small house in Birmingham. The details were handed out like demands from the matriarch who raised seven children, and her judgment and instructions pertaining to timing, attendance, food, and libations were not to be questioned. Very quickly, old promises to help out the family from distant relatives and various business leaders were called in, and Mrs. O'Herlihy was granted all the respect and allegiance she deserved. By a few days before the funeral, arrangements and supplies for almost a hundred people were provided to the modest three-bedroom home in one of the oldest neighborhoods in Birmingham.

For the senior members of the intelligence community and politicians who oversaw the intelligence budget, attending O'Herlihy's funeral at Fort McClellan was simply a chore, having to abandon their cherished empires and travel to rural Alabama. The pomp and circumstance of a parade of Washington, DC, officials took a back seat to the honorific significance of a military funeral, and everyone had to stifle their egos and attempts to one-up each other in this small but critical national shrine.

So it was handed down to subordinates to attend the funeral. The president assigned the job of attending the funeral to an assistant deputy consul of the chief of staff's office. The chairman of the Senate Select Committee for Intelligence sent a page from his office. The House Select Committee sent a junior congressman who had little experience with the intelligence community but represented a portion of Louisiana next door. The Defense Intelligence Agency sent a colonel; the Central Intelligence Agency initially was going to send an assistant director for intelligence, but at the last minute, the chief of the counterespionage center where O'Herlihy had worked before insisted that he represent the CIA at the funeral. The FBI instructed the Birmingham field office staff from the Foreign Counterintelligence Squad to attend. The sole representative outside of NSA who truly knew O'Herlihy and his accomplishments was an unemployed civilian, Olivia Baines Johnson, former DCIA.

She flew into Birmingham on a Delta flight two days before the service and spent much of her time with O'Herlihy's mother. Johnson helped out with arranging folding tables, getting chairs out of the garage, and polishing serving ware that had not seen the light of day for twenty-five years. Not all her time was spent with the family. On the day before the funeral, Johnson met quickly and quietly, in the lobby of the Elyton Hotel near downtown Birmingham, with a CIA tech officer. She thanked the well-dressed young man profusely for his support and swore him to secrecy before he left to continue his family vacation in Destin, Florida. Johnson needed a favor from the technical operations center, and they were happy to oblige the former director. Johnson had a plan, and it was a bit risky, but it would help fill in the gaps in sealing the case against the director of the NSA. She knew that Polyander had to attend the funeral, and it was here that she could make her efforts to avenge the death of Tom O'Herlihy come to fruition.

The service for O'Herlihy was a massive event for the small national cemetery. The cemetery staff had done all they could to accommodate the visiting throngs of people, and the usual considerations for immediate family and senior military officials were promptly overrun with self-important demands and auxiliary arrangements for the Washington, DC, crowd who wanted only to be seen in front of the crowd at the service. The final schedule for the service was completed the morning of the funeral, and the right people were afforded the right placement at the site of commitment. The flag would be handled by an honor guard from the cemetery, and it would be presented to Mrs. O'Herlihy. The sole impediment to this plan was the insistence from the White House that the president's representative be the one who handed the flag to the grieving mother. It took a visit to the Oval Office by the Secretary of Defense to convince the commander in chief that the flag was not a trinket to be handed down to a civilian at a military funeral. Finally, the president relented and passed on the message that the chief of staff's assistant should stand down.

When the service had concluded, the various officials moved quickly and efficiently back to their waiting limousines or rented sedans for transport to the airport so they could return to Washington. As NSA Director Polyander eased himself into the passenger-side back seat of the Lincoln Town Car his service had arranged from the NSA fleet of cars, he was surprised to find Olivia Johnson sitting in the back seat on the driver's side. She was wearing a somber two-piece outfit of deep-maroon velvet with white buttons and a matching hat. Her shoes and stockings were thick and black. The sole bright spot on her outfit was a flag pin on her lapel. She was, as always, dressed very well and had a plain brown-leather purse on the seat beside her.

"Olivia!" said Polyander with genuine surprise. "Thank you for coming! Are you riding with me to the airport?"

"Director Polyander, I speak for myself and the CIA when I tell you how sorry I am for the loss of Tom. He was an incredible asset and source of collaboration for your institution, and I know he will be hard to replace." This was the first thing out of Johnson. She went on before Polyander could respond. "As you know, I have stepped away from the CIA, so as a civilian, I cannot take you up on your generous offer, but I wanted you to know that I will miss Tom and look forward to doing all I can to continue his work to protect this country, even outside of the federal government."

"I heard that POTUS kicked you to the curb. Very sorry to hear that. Dastardly way to treat someone like you." This was the careful response from Polyander. "If you need anything from me, do not hesitate to ask."

"Thank you, Director. Just seeing you here to honor Tom was all I needed," said Johnson as she grabbed her purse tightly and eased herself out of the back seat.

The squeeze of the brown-leather purse was just a bit exaggerated, as Johnson had been instructed by the CIA tech officer earlier. The purse (which did not match Johnson's outfit) was a standard ladies' handbag that had been modified by the technical operations staff to include a small transmitter built into a thick plastic bladder in a side pocket. When Johnson grasped the purse, the squeezing action would push the transmitter, tuned to send data to a CIA satellite, through the false bottom of the purse and embed it between the seat and the back cushion of the Town Car's rear seating.

As Johnson walked from the limousine, she spoke into a cell phone to alert the communications office to undertake collection of the data transmitted from the back seat. She knew the collection might be short-lived, but her presence and her comment about continuing O'Herlihy's work would rattle Polyander and hopefully cause him to make some calls that would incriminate him.

Olivia Johnson made one more stop after the funeral before returning to Washington: she went to Mrs. O'Herlihy's wake. She spoke with the siblings, aunts, uncles, and numerous relatives at the ornate party that had spilled from the house into the backyard, and she shared her (unclassi-fied) stories about Tom's service and incredible career in the intelligence business. None of Tom's relatives truly knew what he did for a living, and Johnson found herself debunking the various conspiracies about his work, more than providing the truth about a military leader who had earned the respect of everyone who served under him. Subject to social media drivel and pompous speculation, the people here were dumbstruck to hear this well-informed African American woman speak volumes about intelligence collection and the goals of the government to detect, deter, and deliver to justice the enemies of this country. Johnson was a lifelong resident of Washington, DC, and held no Southern accent, but her delivery of the truth about Tom O'Herlihy's service and career was well-received. Olivia paid earnest and tearful respects to O'Herlihy's mom and made a quiet exit for a cab to the airport. On the way, Olivia Johnson started making phone calls. The next phase of this operation required a lot of help, a lot of very senior help. And she would squeeze every bit of help from the upper echelon of the US government, just like she squeezed that purse to plant a bug in Polyander's back seat.

CHAPTER TWENTY-ONE: MAY 17, 2003

The truest wisdom is a resolute determination.

—Napoleon Bonaparte

Later the next day, Randall found the focus to call Olivia Johnson and report to her what had happened. She was still traveling from Alabama when she received his call and made quick notes as he spoke. Betts told her about the female assassin sent to kill him (which she already knew from Marilyn) and about FBI Agent York stepping in to help. He reported that York had found three different sensors in his dad's house that were wired to a broadcast antenna mounted behind a trunk in the attic. Johnson confirmed that they were most likely the microphones placed by the NSA surveillance team and assured him that the listening post for those sensors had been shut down. Betts then talked around the matter of the document information he had found in his dad's box, and Johnson expressed great appreciation for that. Now things could fall into place to implicate Polyander in treason and murder. Johnson reported to Randall that Stallings was recovering slowly, and her prognosis was good.

What Johnson could not bring herself to tell Betts was that the doctors at Johns Hopkins had met with senior officials at the NSA about the extent of Stallings' injuries and the long-term limitations caused by those injuries. Based on what the doctors said, NSA had determined that Stallings could no longer carry a gun for the government. The damage to her lung would take some time to truly heal, and it would impair her ability to requalify for armed service as a security agent at the NSA. The disfigurement to her scalp may never completely heal, and Stallings would have a permanent part in her hair above the temple on the left side of her face. The plastic surgeon brought in for repairing Stalling's scalp, a talented and experienced expert from the Mayo Clinic, requested that a dermatologist assist in the surgery to replace the damaged skin, and together they had employed stitching that was almost microscopic. The resulting patch was hardly noticeable, but the hairline would not grow back.

But she didn't have to tell Randall this; he already knew. He had seen firsthand the disfigurement from bullets and shell fragments and shards that cascaded into the bodies of men and women in combat. His brief time in the hospitals at Ramstein and at Walter Reed had convinced him that these people's lives were altered in a way that few people could ever understand. Simple tasks like putting on socks or buttoning shirts would now become chores that would prescribe how one's day would go, and personal affinities such as vanity or pride had to be discarded in favor of valuing one's courage rather than their appearance. And now Stallings was one of them, the victims of battle with an evil foe. Set apart by culture and society's desire for "perfect people," these warriors were now considered the detritus of horrible encounters that darkness couldn't hide and medals couldn't cover. Just the thought of Stallings lying in a hospital bed, barely alive and fighting for the chance to live a normal life, was an image that soured Betts's stomach. The anger welled up in him again, but he took a deep breath and thanked Johnson for the call.

"You called me, remember?" was the response from Johnson. "Whatever you need, Randall, I'll try to help."

"I won't need your help," said Randall to himself once the call was finished. "I'll need your forgiveness for what I'm about to undertake."

In the back of his head, Randall began to feel an acidic train of thought building. A snake of dark, thick revenge was starting to uncoil in his brain. He began to push the grieving and uncertainty aside to make room to concoct a plan. The Marine in him was preparing to unleash a tide of vengeance and justice against those who attacked him and his family, and the case officer in him was building a list of the things needed to prepare the plan. Randall Betts was considering violence, and the value of those thoughts was giving him some peace.

CHAPTER TWENTY-TWO: MAY 18, 2003

The best candle is understanding.

—Welsh proverb

Earl Allen Betts awakened with a start. He was lying in the same hospital bed, and he had the same leads and tubes hooked to him, and the background noise of the hospital had not changed. But something startled him awake, and he turned quickly to see his daughter standing beside his bed.

"Hey, Carol Baby!" His earliest nickname for her had stuck all these years.

"Hi, Dad. I came as soon as I could. You know, with the kids and the end of the school year, it's just been crazy, and everybody wanted to come, but I said no because I wanted you to be...ready to see everyone, and all that activity, and the kids say hi and they love you and I love you..." rambled Carol as she finally bent over the bed's rail and lay across her father and cried loudly. Carol thought she was prepared for this visit, but the image of how sickly her father looked made her very unsettled. Her sobs and tears were a release for both of them, as Earl had always missed his little girl. She had grown up full of life and opinions. Carol had spent the rebellious years of her youth seeking to learn from her parents instead of pushing the limits of their patience. This created a girl who wanted everything out of life, and staying at home wouldn't satisfy her. When she left to take a job in the admissions office at University of Richmond, the atmosphere was not a happy one; Carol was busting out on her own, and she was determined to make a life for herself. Her mother was worried that the cruel world wouldn't treat their baby girl well, and Earl tried his best to stop her. The years had softened that separation anxiety, and Earl was left with just the wish to see the second-favorite female in his life. The death of his wife was a terrible setback for Earl, and he searched for a solution to that loneliness and pain. He had undertaken plans to travel to Richmond to see Carol and her family once the count of the boxes was done. Now, as she sprawled across him as he lay dying in a hospital bed, he clutched her as best he could with all the lines going into him, and he patted her back and told her how good it was to see her.

When she stood again and wiped the tears from her face, Earl was right back to family business. "How're the kids? And Kevin? How's he doing? Did he get his teaching certificate worked out?" The ensuing conversation was good for both of them.

Finally, Carol sniffed and said, "Randy is coming here; he called me and said you wanted to see him. I guess I'll let you two guys talk." The hint of sarcasm hung heavy in the air. She didn't turn away dejected; she was willing to stand her ground and be a part of this conversation.

"I need to talk to Randy alone, honey, because he is going to solve a crime that was done to your dad before you were born. I need to see you because I have little else of value in this world but you," said Earl patiently. He was being truthful; all that was left for him were his adult children. Grandchildren were great, but they were no replacement for the legacy and learning that Earl and his wife had tried so hard to make right. The fact that his children were thriving was like a treasure at the end of a hard climb up a relentless and unpredictable mountain. So much of parenting was trying to set some pathways for the children to follow, and the paths that Carol and Randall had chosen made him proud. Even though he rarely saw his kids, Earl Betts had fulfilled his obligation to his parents and his country. For this, he was comfortable that anything else life threw at him was just noise.

And then a noise startled him. Randall Betts rushed into the room with a flourish and hugged his sister tightly. After a few questions and answers between them, Randall turned to his dad.

"Randy," said Earl in the best voice he could find. "It's good to see you!"

"Hey, Pop" was the smiling reply from Randall. He had returned to the hospital after getting a restless night of sleep after Marilyn and FBI Agent York left him. The phone call he made to Olivia Johnson had not eased his mind. The next morning, before Randall left to visit his dad, he received a call on the house phone that was more bad news, and Randall was starting to feel the back pressure in his brain: too much grief, too much suffering.

"What's new?" said Earl in a chipper voice. It didn't match the visage of Earl's emaciated body and whiskered face.

"Pop, I got a call this morning from the VA hospital in Atlanta. James Willis passed away last night."

Earl's facial expression changed from pleasant to grim. He squeezed his eyes shut, then opened them and quietly said, "You are clear for take-off, Creeper, clear skies and fair winds; you were the best." Carol didn't understand this statement, and she began to worry that her dad was going into some kind of spell.

"I had something else to tell you," said Randall, as his father didn't seem to notice. Earl was looking at a spot on the far wall while he was told about FBI Agent York deciphering the Chinese language on the box labels. Randall avoided mentioning the damage done to various patches of Sheetrock when York tore the listening devices out of the house. Randall also omitted the part about the strange woman who tried to kill him and burn down the garage. When Randall said the name, Mouse, that was listed on the labels, Earl seemed to perk up a bit.

"Mouse! That's the name of the traitor that Creeper was after! He had proof that it was Polyander! He told me about some intercept that proved Mouse was Polyander! Now he's dead, and we'll never get to the bottom of it. If I could just have finished the count of those damned boxes, I'd have solved this puzzle!" Earl was both excited and frustrated; his voice level was stronger but was still strained.

Earl and Carol bent close to calm their father down. "Pop, don't worry. We have the evidence" was the soothing statement from Randall.

"You do? You're going to fix that bastard? You're gonna make him pay for what he did to us in 'Nam?" asked Earl eagerly.

"Don't you worry, Dad; he's gonna pay for what he's done." This was the somber yet measured response as the planning for his next few steps began to take shape. The look of easing his father's anxiety would allow him to create a great deal of pain on Polyander's face.

Randall had been pushed enough: the attempt on their lives, the eavesdropping on his family, the shooting of Alexandra Stallings, the strange woman with the highway flare—these were all from the evil desire of Keith Polyander, and it was time for the Marine to counterattack. No more waiting for the cavalry, and no more being told to stand by so that somebody else could take care of it. Randall wasn't precisely sure of what he would do, or what he could do; he was just certain that he would do something to avenge the evil brought to his family, and that something would most certainly include violence.

Randall and Carol finished their visit with Earl and had lunch together at the hospital café, with Randall doing his best to calm Carol's concerns about their father. The thin, pale man that Carol had seen in the hospital bed was nowhere near the vibrant, upbeat role model that she had encouraged her children to contact on Skype. Randall couldn't deny this, but he promised Carol that their dad had all his faculties, and he was not on the verge of any breakdown or mental collapse. Carol did not seem convinced, but she was thankful that Randall had spent this much time with him and respected her big brother's opinion.

"I'm going to go home and demand that Kevin and the kids come back with me to see Dad," said Carol with determination.

"He'd like that, Carol. He's always bragging to me about you and the kids. I spent all that time overseas. I missed Mom's passing; I've been no help. You are the one who has succeeded, according to him. I think he's disappointed that I haven't settled down and had kids of my own," said Randall.

"He was never disappointed in you, Randy," said Carol, leaning forward to speak earnestly. "All he's ever known is family and work. He devoted so much to both that he had no time for office parties or midlife crises or fancy clothes. All he wanted was for us and Mom to be happy. He knew you were dedicated to your work, that you were gaining ground in a career that you enjoyed and he secretly coveted, and that sooner or later, the family would come. You have nothing to regret, Randy, not when it comes to his love."

Randall sat back as his sister told him these things. He felt the slight, cold throb in his ankle and listened for a moment to see if the ringing was there. And it wasn't. The passing of the information to his dad had eased the back pressure in his brain. He was starting to feel like himself again, like he had something to look forward to. That's when he felt that maybe he had turned a corner in his "treatment." For all the therapy sessions and serious discussions with Marilyn, for all the Tylenol PMs and all the late-night sips of good Kentucky bourbon, nothing had done the trick quite like getting some family time. The sheer joy of an honest conversation with his kid sister, and having his dad around for another day—that must have been the magic sauce that helped him focus.

Focus. That realization created another discovery; maybe it wasn't the family time. Maybe clearing the air with his sister and talking with his dad were the results of feeling better, but they weren't the *cause* for feeling better. Randall found himself focusing again on his plan, on the favors and revelations and tools necessary to carry out his new plan. As the idea was complicated and required some moving parts, Randall found himself lost in thought as his sister suddenly caught his eye.

"Randy, am I upsetting you with this?" said Carol with a serious note of concern. Her comments about how she felt about her dad's illness and the apprehension about her children seeing their grandfather in such an emaciated state—these were all lost on Randall as he lined up whom he would call next. Her question brought him back.

"Not at all, sis. I'm just as worried about him as you are, but he's getting the very best care that this regional hospital can provide, and the shaded portions of his lungs are being hit with radiation. It's a necessary part of reducing the cancer in his body. We just have to see how he handles it, and he's a tough old bird," said Randall with an air of confidence that did little to ease Carol's concerns. It might have been the curious conversation he had with Earl, something about FBI agents and "the Mouse." Her big brother was lost in thought about something, and she was unsure what it was.

CHAPTER TWENTY-THREE: MAY 20, 2003

Even though you know a thousand things,

ask the man who knows one.

—Turkish proverb

Benjamin Sutherlin was a USMC three-star general, and as deputy director at the NSA, a large part of his job was keeping Congress happy with his employer's efforts. Arranging the leads and revelations created by the humongous number of intercepts was both an organizational tool and an operational one. By listing these intercepts in a favored order, the Senate and the House Oversight Committees would know which intercept was most important but also create questions and "suggestions" from the Congress. In this way, the NSA could be better armed for the collection of intelligence that was important on Capitol Hill.

Sutherlin studied his sheets of notes but could not concentrate on the task of prioritizing them. He had just been visited by someone from the attorney general's office, and the brief meeting had been odious.

The first question posed to him was whether or not he had spoken with NSA Director Polyander in the past forty-eight hours. When he answered truthfully that he had not, the follow-on questions about "Operation Mountain" and an asset named "Mouse" were barely understood.

Once he answered that he knew nothing about these topics, the AG representative provided a business card and recommended that if he heard anything from Polyander he was to contact this number immediately. The AG rep further sought Sutherlin's assurance that the confidentiality of this meeting would be honored.

As he opened the door to wrap up the meeting, any further comments were vanquished by the AG's rep departing rapidly through the front office and toward the hallway with such stealth and efficiency of movement that Sutherlin was left standing in his doorway with the remnants of a smile leaving his face.

Sutherlin returned to his desk and turned over his notes to continue his assessment of the intercepted intelligence. He couldn't focus on which piece of information was more important than the others; he was suddenly fixated on the idea that he would soon be promoted to the director's position. Whatever Polyander was mixed up in, or whatever he had done, he was going to be out, and the NSA would be looking for a new director.

CHAPTER TWENTY-FOUR: MAY 22, 2003

The true path to heaven is through your parents.

—Japanese proverb

The mountain air was tainted this morning with the slight smell of burning wood. Probably a nearby farmer trying to clear some land before the farm bureau forbade outdoor fires later in the season. When the air and land got really dry and the wind still picked up, the threat of forest fires in the Sequatchie Valley of Tennessee was a real one.

Randall Betts had finished his first cup of coffee and checked his watch. The reservations desk at the car-rental agency where Betts had rented the Jeep was probably open by now, so he called and got the electronic tree for the rental agency. Once he was put on hold and reminded of all the great benefits of renting from this particular company, Betts put the phone on the counter and went to pour himself another cup.

He was heading back to the phone on the counter across the kitchen from the coffee maker when he noticed that the phone was buzzing. This was odd, he thought as he picked up the cell phone and looked at the screen. It read that another call was trying to connect. As Betts had already been on hold for a couple of minutes, he didn't want to lose his place in line.

And then he saw the number trying to dial in. It was a Tennessee area code and a prefix from a nearby town. Betts was dubious about answering, but then he thought it might be that muscle-bound FBI agent trying to reach him. So he pushed the button to disconnect from the rental car agency and connect to the new number.

"Hello, I'm calling for Randall Betts," said the unfamiliar woman's voice. When Betts confirmed that she had reached him, she rushed into her message: "Mr. Betts, this is Nurse Lloyd at the hospital. Your father has taken a very bad turn and needs to see you now!"

Betts was at his father's bed in just over thirty minutes. Betts came down the mountain in a hurry, reasoning that anyone following him today would have a hell of a time doing it. The traffic had been its usual terrible self, but the real delay was getting up to the hospital room where his father lay. Randall had pushed right by the information desk and the security officer, and he found himself in a shouting match to get to the elevator for the floor where his father lay dying. Only by being escorted by the security officer to Earl Betts's room did Randall win the fight.

"Pop, I'm here," said Randall as he pushed past the security officer and came alongside the bed. Earl opened his eyes and gently raised his left hand so his son could hold it.

"Good to see you, son. What's up?" was all his father said.

Confused, Betts looked around and noticed more machinery in the room. More invasive tubes were attached to his father, and a crash cart with AED paddles was in the far corner. All the chairs had been removed, and the bed pillow had been replaced with a folded blanket. Evidently, they had encountered some resuscitation efforts involving his father and were prepared for more.

"Pop, they told me you've had some trouble. How're you feeling now?" asked Betts.

His father swallowed hard and began a long sentence. "I want you to listen to me very carefully. I'm really tired, and I think that if I go to sleep,

I won't wake up. They've got all kinds of painkillers and heart stabilizers in me, but I feel that it's wasted."

As Randall began to protest and tell his father that it was going to be all right, Earl cut him off and continued, "You will tell your sister that it was too late when you got here, and then tell her that I've loved her with every fiber of my being all my life. You were a blessing to us, son, a strong, relentlessly energetic boy with more curiosity than fear. But a daughter, that's what makes a man's heart shine. We loved you and Carol equally, but you never had your father wrapped around your finger like Carol did."

Betts's eyes had begun to glisten, and his father saw it and reached over with his right hand so he could clasp both hands together on his son's arm. "You have become such an excellent person and dutiful son that I can never tell you how proud we are of you."

"I wasn't there for Mom, but I'm here for you," said Betts in his best effort to avoid crying.

"You were there for everybody, Randy. Your mom and I worried about you going overseas and dealing with all those people, but we never lost faith or pride in you. The day your mom passed, the last thing we talked about was wondering how you were and what adventures you were up to."

"I thought the last thing you guys talked about was the line you posted on her footstone," said Betts suddenly. He never knew where that beautiful line had come from. All he knew was that it wasn't Shakespeare.

"Hmmph," scoffed Earl softly. "That's a line from an old Bob Marley song."

"What?" asked Betts incredulously.

"Yeah." Earl chuckled. "Something your mom loved. I never understood it, but she got it. She insisted that her grave site include that saying, and I wasn't about to deny her anything. Anyway, when she passed away, the neighbors all came together for me, and that was all that I needed. If you'd have rushed back in time for her passing, you'd have felt like you were either overlooked or in the way. People around here loved your mom, and helping with the arrangements and the digging and the service and the wake, that was all a labor of love for them."

Now Earl leaned slightly toward his son. "So here's the plan: I have written a will that names you as the sole executor, leaves everything to you and Carol, and instructs you to cremate my body and put me next to her, understand?"

"Yes, sir," said Betts as the glistening in his eyes began to turn into tears.

The urging and earnestness demonstrated by Earl seemed to deenergize him. He sank back into the bed and took his hands off his son, and couldn't seem to find the next words.

"Pop? You okay? You want me to get the nurse?" said Betts as he wiped tears from his eyes.

His father looked at him with an eager look and nodded slightly. Betts hurried out of the room and eventually found a nurse in an adjacent hallway. The nurses' station was empty, and the nurse that Betts found was pushing a rack of lunch meals down the hall. He was trying to get her to come to his father's room as she was explaining that she had meals to deliver. Suddenly, the conversation was overtaken by an alarm from the nurse's station. One of the monitors on this floor was going into arrest. Betts left the nurse standing there with her apologies and ran back to the room to find his father had sunk even farther into the covers of his bed. His eyes were barely closed, and his mouth hung open at an almost exaggerated angle. Another nurse came quickly into the room and rushed by Betts to check on Earl. She stood finally, and asked Betts to leave the room.

Betts's protests were not loud or belligerent; he just wanted to stay with his father. Then he felt a hand on his elbow and looked to see the same security officer who had escorted him to the room. When Betts snatched his elbow away from this attempt at comforting him, the nurse stepped up quickly and spoke in a soft, clear tone: "Mr. Betts, please understand that we have things we have to do for your father. His last instructions to us were 'DNR,' and that means that we have to work to prepare him for transfer. We have to prepare paperwork for the coroner's office. We're truly sorry, but you have to let us do our job here."

Betts looked at her and replied, "I need to say goodbye to my father."

"Of course. I'll be just outside," said the nurse as she and the security officer left the room.

Betts walked to the bedside and took his father's cold, limp hand. He stood there and told him how much his love and guidance had meant to him all his life. He thanked his father for teaching him how to tie a necktie, and he thanked his father for teaching him to keep his hands off his face when in public. He assured his father that he would tell his sister all the things that he wanted to tell her, and he added that he secretly knew that Carol was his favorite as they grew up. Betts then surmised that maybe that was the reason he had always pushed to be somebody that his parents admired. Next, he told his father how proud he was of his service and his work ethic and his lessons to Betts about putting family before mission but honor above all. Betts continued by updating his father about his current employment status and used that to assure him that he would continue to take care of the house and the weeping willow tree and the grave sites for him and his wife of almost forty years. This led to a weather report about the mountain air and new growth in the flower beds, along with a forecast for the upcoming week. These were standard updates that Earl had come to rely upon to know what was going on. Betts then made a promise to his dad that he was going to settle down and marry and have all the grandchildren he could stand, and added that he had found the right girl. He then added that she didn't know it yet, but she would as soon as he could get her out to dinner. Betts was running out of things to say, but he finished by repeating the things he had said at first, and added that the evil motherfucker than poisoned him would face Betts's wrath.

Betts then walked out to the hallway and asked the nurse, "All right, what do we do next?"

CHAPTER TWENTY-FIVE: MAY 22, 2003

If you lose it all, find yourself first.

—**Bhuwan Thapaliya, Nepal**

The truck sent by the mortuary service was modest in that it would only carry one body, and the crew that came with it was two people with less-than-athletic abilities. As the hospital would not allow the gurney to exit through the emergency-room entrance, Betts found himself helping the mortuary crew move his father's body up a small set of stairs to reach the hired ambulance through a side exit.

Betts followed the truck to the mortuary facility near Pikeville, where the offloading and transfer into the facility was much easier. The gurney slid easily from the back, and the facility had a carpeted ramp into the rear of the building.

The mortuary director and his aide introduced themselves to Betts, but their greetings and names and quick expressions of condolences were never heard: Betts was thinking, and he was concentrating, and he was pushing past his grief to get to the bottom of how his father had died and who was responsible.

In the processing room, where normally bodies would be examined before being forwarded to the funeral home for burial, the mortuary director and his aide had been informed by the hospital that Earl's wishes were for cremation. They informed Betts that this could be done at this facility and offered to show Betts the range of urns available to hold his father's ashes.

Betts answered by going into "orders mode." Betts began by instructing the two men to undertake a thorough examination of his father's body and seek any anomaly or injury, whether it contributed to the death or not. Betts continued by providing examples of places where unusual activity could be found, such as under the arms or between the toes, and he then gave strict instructions that tests of the blood and organs were to be conducted for chemical analysis, and those results had to be provided to him before they were shared with the local authorities. Betts had rehearsed this speech while he was driving behind the truck that bore his father's body here, and it was time that Betts started taking charge of discovering any foul play. He thought back to the woman who had tried to kill him by immobilizing his body with a sound device and then setting him on fire in the garage. If any other dubious or subtle injuries had been effected on his father, he wanted to know about it.

When Betts was nearly done giving orders to these two people, the younger of the two, a portly man in his early twenties whose wrinkled dress shirt did not completely cover the tattoo on his neck, looked down at Earl's body on the table and adjusted his eyeglasses. "Well, Detective Columbo. Don't you worry. We'll look into it."

That's when it happened. That was the point at which it all welled up inside him. Betts had been unknowingly making a list, building an internal headache about the lackadaisical attitude of those around him, and now he had a heartache that bulged from the death of his father to the refusal by Marilyn to accept his dinner invitation. The incidents of indifference, like that prick doctor at Ramstein, to the attitude of disrespect from the clerk at the hardware store—they all bubbled to the surface. This wasn't rage; this was pushing out his refusal to accept the garbage that was coming from everyday life, along with the disappointment and disillusionment with a culture that failed to recognize the sacrifice and service of people that gave up a lot to keep this country safe from its enemies, foreign and domestic.

Betts looked at the young man with a vigorous disdain and started a rant that built to a point where the walls were surely reverberating from the pain and anger being spilled:

"You listen to me, you blowtarded piece of shit. You only wish you could ever be someone as good as my father. He raised a family with love and patience that slack-jawed assholes like you can't begin to achieve! This is a man who was poisoned by people he swore an oath to protect! He lived a life of service and duty that you couldn't possibly attain or understand. He was awarded more medals than someone like you could even lift, much less carry, and more than that, he was respected for his expertise, and people counted on him to stay alive. Can you say that, you candy-eating worm?"

Betts was 75 percent done with his purging of his anger when the mortuary director, the older man standing between Betts and the dumb-founded aide staring at this sudden explosion of vitriol, stepped closer and gently put his hand on Betts's wrist. His hand was warm, and his grip was very slight, but it worked to get Betts to look in the older man's direction and diminish the speed and edge of his speech.

"Young fella, we are completely sympathetic to your concerns about your father, and I can only promise you that we will conduct the very best examination and autopsy that we can. You can stand down on any suspicion that we will overlook anything when it comes to any harm that your father encountered. Now, may I ask about your father's service?" This was the calm, soothing voice of the older man. Betts was distracted by his uncertainty of the man's question.

"Service? You mean the burial at our yard?" said Betts, suddenly quieter and more cooperative.

"No, we'll get to that. I got the sense that your father served in the military."

"My dad worked SIGINT and ground support for MACV-SOG in 'Nam" was the quick and efficient answer from Betts.

"I was there from 1969 to 1971. The Battle of Khe Sanh almost ended us. Radio folks like your dad saved the day bringing in the air support we needed. How about you, soldier? Where'd you serve?" said the mortuary director.

Betts shook his head. "Not soldier, sir, Marine. Weapons support battalion second MEU. Took a hit in Iraq and they washed me out." The disdain for not being allowed back showed in his answer.

"That's where my other boy is!" said the older man suddenly. "Ricky here is learning the ropes of the business, but his brother is over there now, going into some little place called Fallujah."

At this point the younger man, Ricky, leaned forward and offered his best apology for appearing disrespectful to Betts. Betts was already in a state of extreme shame for his outburst. He took a deep, cleansing breath and waited for a minute to see if the ringing in his ears had returned, if the back pressure in his brain was still there. But he couldn't sense it, not right now.

"I'm hoping he has the same good troops around him that I did, and I wish for his safe return" was all that Betts could muster.

CHAPTER TWENTY-SIX: MAY 23, 2003

There is no shame in not knowing;

the shame lies in not finding out.

—Russian proverb

The Bethesda neighborhood consisted of fewer than fifty homes on generous lots just north of the Interstate 495 Beltway around Washington, DC. Built in the late 1950s off Wisconsin Avenue, they were seen as a true upgrade to the inner-city living in DC, allowing successful people to build in Prince George's or Montgomery County, just outside the District line but close to the action. Olivia Johnson's home was one of these homes. Nestled in Montgomery County with close to an acre of land and softly rolling landscapes, the house boasted convenience and concealment, thanks to the winding roads through the development and mature cedars. Olivia's father had bought the house upon landing his first consulting contract with the US government, and her parents gifted her the house she had been raised in when they needed much less space to enjoy senior living.

With a basement the same size as the living floor above it, the house contained almost four thousand square feet and a two-car garage attached at the eastern end. Much of the basement held the accumulated furnishings of the Johnson family, as well as a sturdy bar and card-table space for entertaining. The basement had one recent revision: the construction of two secure walls at an angle to the western end of the foundation. This allowed the CIA to build a fully functional and secure command post once Olivia had been confirmed as DCIA. After 9/11, the command post had undergone even more reinforcement measures, such as anti vibration flooring and soundproofing insulation, making the basement command post a contingency location for continuity of operations in case the WDC was attacked.

But today it was all being disassembled. Communication technicians and field engineers were removing hundreds of yards of wiring and large sheets of radio-frequency-blocking materials from the six hundred square feet of space, while computer experts from the CIA's Office of Security were clearing the machinery of any hint of classified information in preparation for being removed to a secure warehouse south of Alexandria. The walls that had been built to facilitate the command post were left in place, but the torn holes in the Sheetrock were not repaired.

Olivia Johnson cared little about any of this. Her only concern was that the removal crews did not damage the original walls or doorways as they stripped everything CIA out of her homelife. In some ways, she was happy to be rid of the command post. While she enjoyed the extra security of a staff of federal agents where she slept, and the ability to send and receive secure communications from her home, the fact was it was an anchor that took her away from her family and her personal space. This chapter of her life, watching over the intelligence-gathering and co-vert-action programs of the CIA, was a rewarding but gut-wrenching flow of success and tragedy that never seemed to end. The past few years were a blur of endless encounters and challenges and meetings that required both boldness and stealth. As these two qualities were mutually exclusive, Olivia Johnson had used every bit of guile, curiosity, and tenacity to keep the watchers watching, the fighters fighting, and the thinkers thinking.

This was the requirement for such an incredible but difficult post. She had learned as much as she had given, and the toll on her was indelible. She had sacrificed much for this job, and now she was being tossed aside for political expediency.

And so was Randall Betts. One of the last emails Johnson had received in her office was that the office of personnel was transitioning Betts from "military service leave" to "leave without pay" (LWOP). This would result in almost no salary going to Betts, and his security clearance was suspended until he was considered fit to return. Official personnel records indicated that Betts was suffering from extensive PTSD and had exhibited "aggressive" behavior during his hospital treatment in Germany. She knew this was all BS, that they were throwing Randy away like trash once DCIA Johnson was not there to defend him. It made her sad that the organization could be that cold, but after all, business was business.

Some of the greatest value she had earned from the job as DCIA was meeting some of the most incredible, dedicated people in the world, from junior officers to senior government officials. Olivia had learned to size people up quickly and determine their value to the job. This was essential, as those who saw the value of their positions as more important than their accomplishment could not be tolerated. Olivia had built tremendous relationships with friends and foes, as those relationships were critical to leveraging the policy needs of the United States.

Tonight, she was calling on those relationships. Once the CIA people were out of her house for the day, Olivia was bringing together a small but incredibly powerful group that she needed. She was certain that all the microphones and sensory detectors (another small sacrifice to her personal life) had been removed, and she could entertain people whom she had come to call true friends over her years of service.

The DPS had removed the standby limousine, a beefed-up Chrysler minivan, from the driveway to make room for the Cadillacs and town cars that would deliver her guests. Olivia had been working in the kitchen all afternoon to prepare cheese wedges, hummus dips, grilled flatbreads, finger sandwiches, and stuffed peppers for a spread that would convey warmth and welcome to those who accepted her invitation. All the food, wine, water, and place mats were arranged in time for the meeting to start. Johnson avoided putting out a porcelain vase given to her by the Greek PM with fresh flowers on the serving table, as someone would surely suspect a microphone was hidden inside.

Her guests were unaware of the hidden agenda of this meeting. Most of the guests had accepted the invitation out of the desire to wish Olivia well and commiserate about how badly she had been treated by the White House. While these sentiments would be expressed and appreciated greatly, Olivia had a slightly darker objective. She was going to trust these people with some of the most sensational and unconventional accusations of the past generation. Save for the terror attacks of 9/11, this could shake the USG to its very core.

First to arrive was Raymond Columbus, director of the FBI. He was always prompt and generous with his time. Olivia could never understand how a man who oversaw the largest federal crime-fighting Agency always seemed to have time to meet and talk. Next to arrive was Marge Jenson, her former executive assistant, who had served Olivia's family for so many years. She brought along a locked briefcase and set it aside until later in the evening.

Soon after Marge's arrival was the deputy director of the Department of Justice. Val Clemons was an earnest but serious former prosecutor who thrived as the deputy, as he was able to oversee the actual cases undertaken by the DOJ rather than answer every request to update Congress about the state of those cases. He had served in the Army as a Green Beret before interning in the Supreme Court under Thurgood Marshall, and his experience with both the opaque and shadowy workings of the USG made him a valuable ally to Olivia Johnson. Soon after Clemons arrived, the doorbell rang, and Elise Summers stepped in. Known to everyone on Capitol Hill as "Lisa," Summers was the United States Attorney for the District of Columbia. As the WDC's attorney, she oversaw the local cases prosecuted in the District as well as any federal case arising in her jurisdiction. For such a small office and staff, Summers wielded great power in Washington. And she was accorded that respect; everyone liked her, and Johnson found her to be honest and dedicated to the letter of the law.

The least senior of the group arrived shortly thereafter. CIA Special Agent Mark Trout arrived in a suitably tailored suit and informed the former DCIA that he had checked the immediate area and found no problems or outsiders. Olivia had invited Trout, as she needed a witness to this meeting who could be counted on to testify or lie, depending on how the evening went.

The group was just getting their first mouthfuls and glasses poured when the doorbell rang again. Olivia opened the front door, and in walked a military man who made everyone in the room straighten up. Admiral Nicholas Kopernick was a Navy pilot who had turned a law degree into a career of advancing Naval policies and procedures that landed him the rotational assignment of chairman of the Joint Chiefs of Staff two years ago. His association with Olivia had begun when a Norfolk-based sailor was accused of treason by consorting with a Russian girl working as a hotel housekeeper in Virginia Beach, and it was the CIA that revealed the true and benign nature of the relationship. The admiral glided into the room and warmly shook hands with everyone, and the meeting was off to a good start.

At precisely 8:00 p.m., Olivia called everyone to a seat so she could express her appreciation to everyone in attendance. She stood before the assembled group sitting around her dining room table as they enjoyed the snacks and conversation. Johnson played this part masterfully, being genuinely appreciative for everyone coming together. It was just as she was getting past her comments about the great work done by the CIA that the doorbell rang again. This time, Olivia stayed in place and asked Marge Jenson to answer the door.

Everyone at the table turned in curiosity and became immediately uncomfortable as a slim, well-dressed Chinese man quietly entered the dining room and bowed slightly. Most of the guests didn't recognize the man, but one did. Admiral Kopernick became rigid in his chair.

"Folks," began Johnson to the assembled group, "I'd like to introduce you to Vang Yong Lieu, currently assigned as a political affairs officer at the Chinese Embassy. Thank you for coming, Mr. Vang; did you find a parking spot okay?"

"The driveway was full. I parked way down the street and walked here," said Vang with a slight Chinese accent and clearly discernible frustration. This flustered Mark Trout, as he had prided himself on ensuring the area around the DCIA's house was clear. He never saw Vang in the area.

"What is this?" said Admiral Kopernick slowly. "He works for the PLAN!"

"The what?" asked FBI Director Columbus.

"The Chinese Navy! He worked intelligence programs in Gdańsk and Bergen!"

As the others turned to Olivia for explanation, Vang moved quietly to a chair at the table and started loading a small plate of snacks.

"His background is in the Chinese Navy, but his assignment here in Washington has focused primarily on policies and coordination for the PRC," said Johnson. Vang wasted no time consuming the Manchego cheese and flatbread.

"Olivia, I'm sorry. I have to leave," said the admiral. If the news of any gathering at which the chairman of the Joint Chiefs of Staff for the

US military and a known Chinese intelligence officer were present, the resulting blowback would be career-ending.

"Admiral Kopernick, Nick, please. Have a seat; I'm the one who invited you all together because I have a terrible story to tell."

Suddenly the atmosphere in the room had changed. Those who thought this to be a social event were now discovering that the former DCIA had a trick up her sleeve, and it wasn't starting out so well. The only person unaffected by this announcement was Vang, who had moved from the finger sandwiches to the stuffed peppers. He had filled a glass with a Chilean red blend and was hungrily working on as much of the finger food as he could.

Olivia Johnson retold the story as related to her by the NSA section chief Jennings. The story of an illegal surveillance operation being wrapped up in Tennessee granted a nod from Director Columbus. He had been aware that NSA had mounted an operation in the United States but was unsure about the story behind it. The story laid out by Johnson was deep and dark, and covered over three decades of betrayal and subversion by NSA Director Polyander. From Polyander's work in Da Nang to his rise in the ranks in the NSA, Johnson outlined his efforts to conceal his collaboration with the North Vietnamese and the money he took from the Chinese government.

Now Johnson took a personal tack. She started in on Polyander's record as the head of the NSA and Cyber Command. Without missing a beat, she reminded every senior official at her party of why they hated Keith Polyander.

"Director Columbus," began Johnson, "Polyander is responsible for changes in the NSA's security policies that resulted in the exclusion of your agents from high-level meetings. He has cut you off from learning about his overtures to corporate America for enhanced cyber cooperation.

"Deputy Director Clemons, several investigations undertaken by the Department of Justice against senior government officials suspected of trading updated signals collection information to the Russians…those investigations were halted by Polyander's influence in the White House.

"Lisa, your office in Washington, DC was instructed by Polyander's office to stand down on any active cases involving the Libyan and Pakistani Embassies. When your office sought clarification, it was revealed to you that they had their own investigations and did not want interference from the District's attorney general."

And then she turned to face Admiral Kopernick. "Nick, part of your investigation that thwarted the Chinese spy ring in Bergen was with secure communication channels available by a high-Earth-orbit satellite. It's okay; Vang knows all about that. What he also knows is that the Navy was later refused bandwidth communication access to that satellite because Polyander wanted to change that bird's orbit to start cataloging the Arctic Circle." This last statement left Kopernick with a red face that he slowly tried to turn away from the table.

Everyone was shocked that Johnson knew all this, but it was old news. With national security articles written by the *New York Times*, and signal intercepts by CIA, these were episodic examples that reminded everyone in the room why they hated Keith Polyander. Almost everyone.

It was when Johnson spoke about the final betrayal of Polyander, about the final shipment of radio components to China, that Vang stopped eating and looked down at the table. He had been mute the entire time, but his chomping and chewing had been hard to miss. Now he was silent, and the other guests were formulating their questions to Johnson about why she was bringing all this up.

"My late father worked intelligence cooperation with the North Vietnamese during the war with America," said Vang finally. This shut everyone up as they stared at the least-welcomed guest. "He was married to a Vietnamese woman, so his collection efforts and meetings with the NVA were more easily concealed," Vang explained. Then he continued with an almost boastful air, "My grandfather told me all about a great case my father had been working, some American spy who was giving up in-depth information about special-forces troops working in the jungles of Laos and Cambodia, outside Vietnam."

"You mean MACV-SOG?" asked Deputy Director Clemons. His time as a Green Beret included work with the small group of fighters in enemy territory. Anyone associated with these units had been sworn to a twenty-year promise to say nothing about their missions. Their existence had just recently been declassified, along with the presentation of a Presidential Unit Citation.

"My father was reporting on troop strength, ammunition supply lines, air support, even details from their personnel files, everything," said Vang. "And then one day the American didn't show up for a meeting. The North Vietnamese said my father waited in Kampot for over two hours, and the American did not show. My father presumed it was because the American had been caught or reassigned or killed. He caught a plane back to Hanoi, and that plane was shot down near the Laotian border. They never found my father's body. The security ministry blamed it on the North Vietnamese and closed the case. Later, the ministry reported that the American had been paid a great deal of money for some high-end radio gear, never delivered it, and then skipped out to the US."

At this point, Johnson pointed out Marge Jenson as she unlocked the classified briefcase. Marge carefully brought out several copies of the same document and handed them to everyone except Vang. He simply leaned over to look at Trout's copy, annoying Trout to no end.

Johnson said, "Marge is handing out a finished intel report from 1973 that documents a CIA intercept of a PLA exchange in which the Chinese government accuses the North Vietnamese of stealing their payment to the American spy. The amount of the missing payment is listed in yuan, but the value at that time would be in excess of eight hundred thousand

American. The intercept identifies the spy as a senior logistics officer in Da Nang and gives a brief account of the large amounts of cash already paid for his information about our MACV-SOG teams, as well as for the radio gear that was in use at the time. This report was disseminated to the intelligence community, but it never made it out because the man at the NSA in charge of disseminating intelligence reports at that time kept it out of official channels. That man was Keith Polyander. He had climbed the ladder at the NSA to be in charge of community dissemination, and he kept this intercept away from the intel community to hide his work with the NVA. When he went on to become director of the NSA, he worked to shut down the last link to him and the contact with Chinese intelligence."

FBI Director Columbus leaned onto the table to ask Vang, "What did you ever find out about the American spy?"

Vang sighed as he washed down a mouthful with a glass of spring water. "All my grandfather was told was that he was the logistics guy for technical operations at the Da Nang airfield, and he had access to all the personnel files. This guy came to the North Vietnamese Army through some open radio traffic and met the Vietnamese in the Cambodian town of Kampot. My grandfather told me his information was good, but he demanded too much money and was too difficult to work with, so my father was brought in to handle him and broker the exchange of money for the radio gear. My dad once said to my grandfather that the spy was just interested in the money and didn't care about anyone. My father said he had no honor. My grandfather never knew the spy's American name; all he knew was the name he gave himself—Mouse."

Johnson stood rigid for a moment and addressed him directly. "Mr. Vang, the last shipment of radio gear has been found. It was forwarded to the garage of a former NSA employee in Tennessee, and the boxes all have a label that reads, 'From your favorite Mouse.'"

She let the assembled group see the connection, and then she continued. "All those boxes were intentionally contaminated heavily with a chemical defoliant. It has been officially designated as a cancer-causing agent. Everyone exposed to those boxes has contracted deadly cancer. If it had made its way to your dad, he would have contracted it as well."

The look on Vang's face changed slightly. The nonchalance was gone. He looked at Johnson with an intention and determination that was easy to read.

And then Johnson dropped the biggest bomb she had, "Jennings's statement about conversations he had with the director include an admission by Polyander that he intentionally missed a meeting in Cambodia so he could watch his handling officer get on a plane, and then called the South Vietnamese Air Force and arranged to have it shot down over the DMZ. He bragged that it was his 'patriotic duty.'"

Everyone at the table was shaken by this. They didn't know Vang, and had little love for the Chinese Communist Party, but this was further proof that Polyander was an evil bastard.

"As easy as this is to connect, Olivia, it proves very little. Any time you're going to accuse someone as powerful as the chief of NSA of wrongdoing, you have to have an airtight case," said Clemons.

Now was the point of no return. Johnson took a breath and announced, "Val, Raymond, this is where I inform you that I placed a bug in Director Polyander's car. I secreted a radio transmitter into the back seat and collected information about three phone calls that he made from the limo."

The deputy director of the Department of Justice and the director of the FBI looked a bit surprised, but they were not shocked. The chairman of the Joint Chiefs was shocked, but Vang smiled for the first time that night.

"So?" was all Columbus said at first. He would not be shocked by Johnson's effort, but he was anxious to hear more before he undertook to ensure charges were brought against her. Johnson was admitting to clandestine surveillance of an American citizen on American soil without a warrant, and regardless of Polyander's guilt, she had possibly committed a felony. But he wanted to hear more. "What did you pick up?"

"Director Polyander made three calls from the limousine. Unfortunately, he only rode in the car for about forty-five minutes before dropping it off at the local airport so he could fly back to Maryland. The first call was to the cell phone of the NSA section chief, Jennings, the source of this information, which we are now handing over to the Justice Department. Jennings had a part in these plans, and he has submitted sworn testimony regarding the crimes committed in this country. As this man Jennings was being processed for several felony counts, Polyander had to leave a message. His message instructed the section chief to call him and advise the status of the 'woman we hired.' It is relevant to report that a female tried to kill my case officer, Randall Betts, and set the garage on fire that held the radio parts. Polyander ended the call by thanking him for setting up 'those two whistleblowers.' I'm certain you read the news that Tom O'Herlihy and an NSA security agent were shot by a disgruntled NSA employee last week.

"The second call he made was to someone named 'Luke.' Polyander instructed Luke to get to the bottom of a missing team of technicians working a listening post at what he called 'the mountains.' This may be the pair that your team arrested in Pikeville, Tennessee, Director Columbus."

Raymond Columbus spoke up. "They have been transferred to a federal holding facility on Maryland's Eastern Shore on charges of trespassing and interference with local utility services. They maintain that they are utility contractors, but the local power co-op and the telephone company have no record of any contract with them."

The group was now enthralled. All the small pieces and accusations were coming together, and their dislike for Polyander was growing. And Johnson had more to report.

"The third call Polyander made from his car was to an office line at NSA headquarters. He spoke to the chief of the Investigations Division. He asked about the condition of Special Agent Alexandra Stallings, who is currently fighting for her life at Johns Hopkins after being shot by a disgruntled NSA employee named Jamin Gemetar."

At this statement Marge Jenson stiffened and drew a long breath. She had visited Stallings several times in the hospital, even before she had gained consciousness.

"Director Polyander went on to say that it was shameful that Stallings and O'Herlihy were sleeping together at the casino resort during business hours." Johnson let that statement sit.

"Wait, how does he know that?" said DOJ Deputy Director Clemons. "The suspect, Gemetar, just made that statement to my investigators yesterday. He's been mute since we took him into custody."

"That's right," said FBI Director Columbus. "The motive has never been released, and the press release from NSA was that they were meeting at a local casino with intelligence officials at the time! Trash research at the casino by the Baltimore Field Office found a note addressed to Gemetar about Stallings and O'Herlihy being at the casino, but there's no source to the note. How could he know about that?"

"And Stallings was not sleeping with her boss. She and O'Herlihy were working the case against Polyander, but they weren't involved in anything nefarious," said Marge sternly. She had heard enough of this nonsense about her former roommate; she was not going to let some worm like Polyander smear Alex's good name, no matter how powerful he was.

"The NSA section chief has given sworn testimony that Polyander was setting them up at the casino," said Johnson.

"Okay, Olivia, this has gone far enough. You have proof that Polyander has been involved in some underhanded and criminal events, but it is mostly circumstantial, and your surveillance of Polyander was just as illegal as what he's done to the Betts!"

This came from Clemons, and Lisa Summers quickly agreed. "Livie, you've admitted to a crime, and any effort you put forward to indict Polyander will result in a mistrial and one of us having to arrest you!"

"Who says I want to indict him?" said Johnson slowly. She turned her attention to Vang.

"What?" said Vang with an honest air of innocence. Johnson had made her famous stuffed dates for this affair, and Vang had one just ready to go into his mouth. He was unsuspecting of any undue attention to himself this evening. He had been invited to this gathering as a farewell to Olivia Johnson, not to get accused of something going on over thirty years ago.

"Suppose we find a way to draw Polyander out into the open, into the public, and a very quiet but efficient team removes him to the country that's still waiting for those radio parts?" Johnson had not moved from her place, but the eyes of every person in the room switched to Vang.

"Do you know what you're proposing?" said Lisa Summers.

"Don't you see any other way to do this?" said Chairman Kopernick.

"Let the GRS do it, boss; we can slam this door shut and keep our mouths the same way," offered Mark Trout.

"Why would my government entertain such a move?" said Vang as he put down the stuffed date.

"Because when all this comes out, and it will, the old scars of Chinese involvement in Vietnam and stories of special operators being betrayed by a USG official will have horrible repercussions for both of us," said Johnson. She knew Vang was a senior intelligence officer for the Ministry of State Security at the Chinese Embassy, and her honest discussions with the Beijing government after 9/11 had resulted in Vang becoming a reliable contact. He toed the PRC line, but he was a realist, part of the post–Tiananmen Square generation, and his dedication to his country included being open to all points of view. Johnson respected him for that and hoped that he would be interested in avenging the double cross applied by Polyander, as well as arranging for Vang's father's death and the "fuck-you" message of poisoning the last shipment of radios. What she was seeking now was to leverage that respect in hopes of removing a corrupt official without any TV network fanfare or courtroom scandal. If this plot was ever uncovered, the media scrutiny would be extensive, and the resulting congressional meetings would rival what Senator Church had done to the intel community in 1974.

"Yeah, but you're talking about turning over the chief of US Cyber Command to the CCP!" said Admiral Kopernick.

"Somebody who violated his oath of office and participated in serious crimes in his home country. Anything he offers by way of updated intelligence should be regarded as questionable, and Mr. Vang would back me up on that assertion," said Johnson as she looked at Vang. His face was a mask of concentration and coordination. He was beginning to see that it could be done, as long as the Americans would allow it to happen.

"Can such a thing be done? In public, like grabbing somebody off the street and shoving them into a white van?" asked Lisa Summers. As a member of the bar in Washington and after moving to the DOJ as an assistant to the director, she had read many cases involving criminal activity. This was the first time she was seeing one being formulated.

"No," said Vang with a voice level and motivated. "You dope him up and hustle him out of a public bathroom with some homeless people, and nobody will take notice."

Johnson was the sole person smiling at this point. Vang was lost in organizing such a team in his head while the senior leadership of the United States justice system was staring at him. This was a major crime on US soil being contemplated, rather than just snatching somebody off a back street in Cairo, and the presence of these officials implicated them in the plot. Olivia Johnson was asking a lot, but if it worked, everybody would be a bit better off.

"It would sure as hell solve a lot of issues with very little daylight," mused Kopernick. He had begun to admire this plan and would be cautiously interested in how the PRC could pull it off.

"I've never heard of such a thing," said DOJ Deputy Director Clemons. "The idea that this could be done, in public, with all the cameras in many public places, it could be too easily observed!"

"You've never seen what they do in the District, Val," said US Attorney Summers. "The gangsters whisk people off sidewalks and out of stores, and the police never get a decent description. With the idea of being disguised as homeless people, nobody would look their way."

The conversations took on a mind of their own as Johnson's guests started to talk among themselves and get their heads around what she was proposing; rather than building a complex and confusing legal case that would cover decades of history and risk the exposure of huge amounts of classified information about sources and methods, it would work more simply to have a team of professionals with no ties to the US government simply disappear with the offender, and nobody would ever want to know why it happened.

"Mr. Vang," said FBI Director Columbus, "may I offer you a ride back to your car?"

In the midst of death, life persists. In the midst of untruth, truth

persists. In the midst of darkness, light persists.

—Mahatma Gandhi

Earl Betts's funeral was three days after his death. The coroner's office had printed a certificate saying that his death was from natural causes, and the probate office at the courthouse accepted his will as proof that Randall would execute his estate legally. To do it properly, the probate office provided extensive instructions and timeline expectations to ensure that Earl's heirs and the local government would be afforded anything to which they felt entitled.

As requested, Earl's body was cremated and placed in a sturdy but plain enclosure. Calling it a "jar" would make it sound like it stored fruits and vegetables, so the funeral service responsible for his commitment always called it an enclosure.

Randall took a call from the nearest VA hospital, where a clerk happily explained that "Section 501 of the Veterans Benefits Act of 2003 allowed states to receive a plot or interment allowance for the interment, in a state cemetery or portion thereof used solely for the burial of veterans, of any veteran eligible for burial in a national cemetery." This allowed for

Earl Betts to be interred at the national cemetery of the family's choice, at no cost. When Randall replied that his father's body would rest in the backyard of his own property, the clerk nervously responded, "Well, you have to make sure you're abiding by all the regulations and requirements of the county. We take care of all that for you, you know."

"Yes, ma'am, I will ensure that all the codes and requirements are met," replied Randall.

"Are you certain that you want to do that? Don't you want him to be laid to rest by the service he represented? And rest with those with whom he served?" was the response, somewhat half-hearted.

"Ma'am, he's being laid to rest by his family, who he served all his life. And he's resting next to his wife, whom he loved more than anybody in the military." This was Randall's slow and deliberate answer before he pushed the red button on his phone, ending the call.

The plans for Earl's service were set and established easily. Randall was somewhat surprised at how many neighbors appeared at his doorstep well before the service, offering tables, chairs, linens, food, even an amplifier for anyone who wanted to speak. All he needed to do was provide a time and date, and everything else just collapsed into place. For all the grief and sadness of an event such as this, the community seemed ready and anxious to get it done, and done properly.

The day of the actual service, cars lined the curved road leading to the Betts house. The neighbors and locals in attendance remarked that more people turned out for Earl's service than for Louise's. That surprised many, but not Randall. The US Army provided a two-person honor guard, two senior sergeants who jealously insisted on an agenda that included playing a taped recording of "Taps" and a formal flag-folding that would culminate by handing the flag off to Carol and her family. Word had spread beyond Pikeville about Earl's passing, and three shaggy men in their sixties arrived wearing M65 field jackets adorned with a variety of medals and patches.

They explained nothing about themselves and spoke only to Randall and Carol, stating that they had served with Earl and found him to be a solid, reliable man of honor and trust. Nobody from the CIA came, and Randall understood why. His only contacts with the Agency were busy going after the guy who had caused all this. Marilyn Emerson was there, and she hugged Randall tight as she expressed her condolences and tried to explain why she couldn't accept his dinner offer. FBI Agent York was there, bearing a handwritten note from the SAIC of the Nashville Field Office offering whatever help Randall might need. Randall knew the offer was hollow, but Troy York followed up by adding his sincere offer to ensure that the SAIC kept his word.

Randall was touched by all of this, and the service itself turned into an informal gathering that even drew in the three older vets. These stoic, somewhat withdrawn men became more interactive as the gathering continued into the afternoon. After everyone was seated and the flag properly handed off to Carol, the neighbors began to stand and tell the stories about Earl and Louise Betts. They shared stories about Earl's devotion to his family, and the "confidential" asides about Earl's reaction when Louise became pregnant with Randall two weeks after Earl returned from Vietnam—they were all glorious tributes to the man they knew.

The second-most profound thing that happened was when one of the three older vets, who had shunned contact with everybody else, finally stood up in front of the group and spoke into the microphone that had been hooked to an amplifier. His voice was steady and lean, and it dipped slightly when his presentation was ending.

"We were assigned to CCS during Thanksgiving of '68. My recon team was dispatched to find a bunch of gooks that the Army lost track of. They needed us to find these guys, so they dropped us into a rice paddy fifteen klicks from the highway on a cloudy night. Just me, one Yankee named John, four little people, and Earl Betts. His job was to keep HQ apprised of what we found and provide the coords so the Army could find 'em again. We quietly moved to a VC camp and couldn't find nobody to fight! Charlie had gone, so we took a rest in a dry spot. The next morning, over a thousand slopes came streaming into the camp we were sitting in. Couldn't see nothin' but black pajamas and straw hats. We were staying low, radioing all the info and trying to get air support, but we couldn't get nobody. Damned State Department said they didn't want a bunch of American helicopters flying into Cambodia, so we were on our own. Then one of the Cambos in our team started insulting the NVA soldiers standing guard. All those Cambodian guys wanted to do was fight. Well, the fuckin' firestorm kicked up, and we lost half our team in the first two minutes of the firefight. I got hit twice in the legs and was running uphill through elephant grass as fast as I could. My one-two was using what was left of his good arm to throw frag and Willie Pete as far as he could and Early-Bird was screaming about a prairie fire. We were flat-out going uphill and trading fire with every slope son of a bitch we saw. When we finally hit cover at the top of a hill, I could see that not all of Charlie was up and chasing us. We was calling the OV-10, and Earl Betts was whispering some of the craziest shit they'd ever heard in their life. Earl was amazed that big green wouldn't send in air support, but he was there, and he was broadcasting. He finally got a sympathetic shiny on the line, and they said they'd see what they could do. The gooks just couldn't believe that a small group of Yankees and ragtag irregulars could get so close to them. But they were mounting up. I looked down the hill and could see platoons of NVA regulars getting lined up to search for what was left of us. Once they started up the hill toward us, finding the bodies of all their buddies we had shot through and blown up, they found a pathway to us right quick. I thought we were done for, because the four of us were wore down, injured and bleeding out, and had no place to go. And then we heard that sound. That sweet sound that sent officers running and soldiers screaming and vehicles starting to turn away. A stinger came in at treetop, followed by a Kingbee helo. They weren't 'American' helicopters, so that was okay. That stinger cut and pitched and whirled and fired and just made the most godawful noise. All so we could escape. Earl told us to find a clearing and pop smoke, and fuckin' A, that's what we did. The Kingbee had a McGuire rig, and we grabbed onto those spikes and never looked back. Took almost an hour to get back to camp. Couple of us almost fell off the damned thing, but we made it back. We lived and Charlie died. Our kill ratio was over fifty-to-one, and the intel guy that sent us there got sent somewhere else. Not everybody came back from missions like that, but those of who did raised a glass every night to 'Early-Bird Betts, the guy who saved us from what we do.'"

Most of the people in the crowd were lost on this story, which came out in such riotous slang that even the terms that folks could understand were somehow missed. Carol's husband, Kevin, leaned over to Randall at one point in the story and asked if he knew anything that this crazy old guy was talking about. While these folks looked at each other quizzically and feigned offense at the salty language, the two sergeants in the honor guard stayed at attention with tears in their eyes. Randall had the same glisten in his eyes hearing the story, but he pushed it aside when he heard Marilyn Emerson say, "My God, what these men endured can never be forgotten."

The most profound part of the service came even before the crowd was seated. The local funeral service had sent a "crew" to prepare a site for committing Earl's enclosure to the earth. When two youngsters showed up one hour before the commitment driving a twenty-three-year-old pickup truck bearing a gas-powered auger, it was apparent that this would not be a good part of the day. The first thing the two youngsters proclaimed was that the root system beneath the willow tree was too thick, prompting them to offer to make a hole next to the garage. When this was soundly rejected, the two auger-drivers marked a place at the very top of Mrs. Betts's grave site. When the explanation was "Well, if the hole has to be here, then neither of them should object as long as they're together," Carol had to be restrained from slapping the face of the author of this incredibly offensive statement.

This resulted in the two young men, their truck, and their auger being sent away, and the men of Pikeville took off their coats. With sleeves rolled up and every pick, axe, and shovel retrieved from next door, the neighbors and vets carefully prepared a hole of suitable width, depth, and distance from his wife's casket to ensure that Earl's wish was fulfilled safely and properly. The tree's roots were respected as much as possible, and the commitment of the enclosure was a group effort that drew applause at the end.

With all the speeches done and the day's sunshine dimming to a golden hue, the funeral service for Earl Allen Betts was a testament to his hard work and loving nature. The comradery of those gathered and the revelry of consuming the locally prepared dishes brought to Earl's house was an emotional outpouring of love and support that Carol and Randall would treasure forever.

CHAPTER TWENTY-EIGHT: MAY 26, 2003

It's not enough to learn how to ride,

you must also learn how to fall.

—Mexican proverb

Washington, DC, in late spring is a truly gorgeous town. The grand architecture, complex street design and powerful government structures are mere distractions when compared to the beauty of nature that blossoms this time of year. After the middle of May, the tulips have finished their bloom and given way to the ground-cover flowers in adjacent beds. The stunning cherry trees around the Jefferson Monument have dimmed to a subtle pink. Once the dogwood blooms pop out along the reflecting pool, the serenity and beauty mask the politics and criminality of the city. The influx of new growth on the older trees that line the streets, the various shades of mature azalea bushes, and the new summer blossoms create a panorama of color and texture so intricate that artists struggle to catch it all on one canvas.

Randall Betts tried to appreciate the beauty of the landscape as he sat on a concrete bench next to the Jefferson Memorial. It was Memorial Day, and the city was crowded with tourists and speeches. This memorial stood in front of a small tidal basin where paddleboats could be rented. The area was called Hains Point, named for the Army engineer who laid the plans for this peaceful, engaging spot for the National Park Service. Everything around him contained color and architecture unlike any in the world, but all he could focus on was waiting for his friend to arrive. Betts had arrived two days before and stayed at his Falls Church apartment. It was a short but frustrating trip into Washington, followed by more anxiety finding an open parking space. Only then could he enjoy the wondrous walk to this meeting site. His call when he got into town had been a chaotic mix of greetings and catch-up with his trusted friend, which then led to explaining how his friend could help him kill Keith Polyander.

The sole firearm to which Betts currently had access was his father's hunting gun. It was a Model 336 lever-action rifle chambered in .30-30 caliber, manufactured in 1976 by the Marlin Firearms company of North Haven, Connecticut. The Kwik-Site rings had been accurately set on the rifle to hold a powerful nine-power scope and still allow the shooter to use the rifle's original iron sights as well as the image shown in the scope. Even with the old canvas two-point strap, it was a beautiful combination of power, accuracy, and graceful lines. It had brought down Betts's first deer, and his father had kept the rifle clean, oiled, and put away.

It was now covered in an old moving blanket in the back of Betts's rented Jeep. He knew that he could easily take down a target at three hundred to five hundred yards; all he needed was a spotter and support guy to get him into a position where Polyander would be in the open. The rifle would do the rest. He trusted this friend to allow him to complete this task of vengeance, and Randall was waiting for him at the appointed place.

Randall had abandoned any hope of continuing any kind of life after doing this. His offer to take Marilyn out to dinner had been refused. She explained that she had feelings for Randall, but her position as a veterans affairs' health provider forbade any personal contact with her clients. Upon driving into the Washington metropolitan area after his dad's funeral, Betts took the 495 Beltway north to get to Johns Hopkins

Hospital to see Alexandra Stallings. She was barely conscious, and the mask and heavy tent around her head prevented him from being able to see her very welll. Her voice was thin and strong at the same time, and all she wanted to know was about Randall's well-being and his father's. With the assurance that everybody was fine, Stallings just turned her head and fell back asleep. Randall walked out of the hospital with even more burn and determination in his heart.

The people he really cared about were either taken away from him or in a hospital fighting to live. And this wasn't a quirk of bad luck or fate; this was the result of one evil man and his criminal appetite to stay alive and rich. Keith Polyander was going to die, and die horribly. Betts had the training and the skill to pull this off, and he had something in his favor that his enemy did not: he had nothing to lose. Everything was going to be forfeit, and nobody could change his mind about it.

It was at the point that Betts had assessed his situation and said, "Fuck it" to himself for the third time that morning that his friend appeared. Out of the throng of tourists slowly making their way around the pond at the Jefferson Memorial, Jim Brewer raised his hands and made his way to Betts's bench. They hugged tightly and slapped each other roughly before sitting down to business.

Jim Brewer was a retired Virginia state trooper who had joined the CIA and had gone through operations training to be a case officer. He and Betts were "battle buddies" throughout the training, and they had kept a close and continuing dialogue as they wound their way through separate overseas posts. He was the closest thing Betts had to a brother, and he needed Brewer now to help him complete his mission.

Brewer looked around as Betts laid out the plan, and finally said in a low, flat tone, "Brother, are you fucking nuts? Do you know what they'll do to you? I couldn't hide you under a Klingon cloak of invisibility and get you out of something like this."

"I know that, and I'm not afraid of what they'll do. This guy has ruined my life, Jim. I'm no good to anyone anymore, and this piece of shit gets to count the money he made betraying his country while poisoning my father? Oh no, Jim, he's gotta go." This was all Betts said as he sat forward on the bench, flexed his arms, and squeezed his eyes shut.

"And what about the rest of your family, Randy? You're still mourning the loss of your dad; how about your sister in Richmond? Her kids, your nieces and nephews? What about them?" asked Brewer. He could sense the finality in Betts, that he was a man with no other objective than mission success.

"I can't do anything for them. I'm worthless to the CIA, to the Marine Corps; I couldn't help my dad do anything but pass away peacefully, and even then, all he wanted was to be buried next to Mom..." That's when Betts started to cry again. He couldn't help it; the image of his parents under the weeping willow tree in the backyard was too painful. Betts bent farther forward and held his face as he sobbed openly.

Jim Brewer had seen lots of men cry. He had seen drunks become tearful from remorse in the courtroom when they were sentenced to ten years for causing a fatal accident, as well as the cries of the family of those killed by drunk driving. He had seen other troopers cry at the funerals of comrades killed in the line of duty, and he had seen his father cry the night Brewer's mother went out for a pack of cigarettes and never returned. These were nothing compared to the raw emotion and sorrow and grief that his best friend was experiencing on this bench. Now he knew what he had to do. He was going to make Betts think that he was going to help him assassinate this prick, Polyander, and prevent him from following through somehow. He didn't know how yet, but he was determined to keep Randall Betts safe and out of prison. He reached over and patted Betts on the back.

"Okay, Randy, you call the ball. Tell me what you want me to do, and I'll do it," lied Brewer to the man with whom he had sworn a lifelong friendship. When they sat on the roof of the Hilton McLean Hotel in Tysons Corner in 1998 and watched the sun go down, Brewer and Betts had pledged to always be there for each other. They had gone through a hell of a time foiling a plot to blow up an American embassy in Addis Ababa, and their mettle and devotion to each other had been cemented.

And then Brewer had a thought. He recalled more about that time on the roof of the hotel and recalled the myriad details and people involved in that plot. He ran through a list of people and things they had encountered and survived, and then it came to him. He knew what he had to do. It would not be easy, and it might jeopardize his clearance with the CIA. But it would be worth it if it saved Randy Betts from going through with this shooting.

The two men stood after a while and walked together back toward Massachusetts Avenue, where Brewer had parked. Betts had cheered up a bit and was giving details and arrangements to Brewer that sounded more like battle plans than schedule arrangements. Betts was clearly back in the Marines, and he was prepared to kill. The presence of cold, vindictive plans to remove the head of the director of the NSA concerned Brewer a bit. His best friend had become different. The stress and the grief had changed Randall Betts, and this wasn't post-traumatic stress; this was something different. This was clearly criminal.

PART THREE

CHAPTER TWENTY-NINE: MAY 26, 2003

Turn your face toward the sun and the shadows fall behind you.

—Maori proverb

Randall Betts watched the traffic in the rearview mirror intently as he maneuvered through the cars, vans, and SUVs plying the Capital Beltway. No active or effective surveillance was detected. The drive from Hains Point back to Falls Church should have taken less than twenty minutes, but due to the various side routes and cover stops to detect surveillance, it was closer to ninety minutes. When Betts returned to his apartment, he turned his cell phone back on and saw that he had missed a call from Marilyn Emerson. Maybe she had thought better of her rejection of Randy's offer to have dinner; maybe she wanted to just check up on him since he was so bitterly disappointed by her refusal. Either way, he'd talk to her later, when he felt like it. The lighter ACE bandage on his ankle was the result of Emerson's recommendations to the VA doctor, and he was appreciative of the ability to wear a more normal shoe. He climbed out of his shoes and socks and lay on his bed. The raising of the ankle made him feel much better physically, but his mind was racing and full of plans. Now that Brewer was on board and coached on what was needed, Betts was more certain than ever that his plan would succeed. His next step was to make one more trip to see to his dad's estate, followed by a call to his sister, Carol, so he could update her and encourage her and her family to visit their father's grave site in the future. These were the steps needed to exclude him from the equation, to let everyone else get on with their life while Randy calmly and carefully ruined his.

When Jim Brewer returned to his office, he looked up a phone number to call. He looked on his computer for the office that provided language support to CIA officers going overseas. He looked down the list until he found the name of an interpreter whom he had worked with in Islamabad. Calling the number, Brewer quickly heard the greeting from Roger Hamadi. Brewer and Hamadi exchanged greetings (Brewer's Urdu was the worst, despite Hamadi's best efforts), and then Brewer told him what he wanted. A very simple task, and it took all of Brewer's coaxing and coddling to convince Hamadi that what he wanted was not illegal or a horrible prank being played on someone. He dared not explain why he needed this favor; all he could do was promise him that he would not get into trouble doing it. Brewer told Hamadi exactly what to do and explained that he needed it right away. Keeping Betts from ruining his life was a critical matter right now.

The next morning, Betts was up early, showered, and dressed. He rewrapped the ACE bandage on his ankle and headed out the door to travel back to Tennessee. He did not savor the idea of another ten-hour drive, but the plans were in place, and Polyander could live a couple more days. As Betts was climbing into his Jeep, his cell phone rang and displayed a number he did not recognize. The area code was local, and the prefix was a well-known number from CIA headquarters, but the last four digits were unknown. Betts mused that it must be those bureaucrats in the office of personnel, calling him to ensure that he had gotten their letter informing him that he was no longer welcome at CIA.

When he answered, his world began a spin that would leave him confused, unconnected, and completely discombobulated.

"Hey, is this Randy?" said the husky voice with some degree of confidentiality.

When Betts replied that it was, he heard, "Randy, I don't know if you remember me, but this is Mark Trout. We worked together in northern Somalia a few years ago, and I gotta talk to you. Some heavy shit is going down, and like it or not, you're part of it. At least, you're connected to it. Are you coming to town soon? I need to meet with you right away if that's possible."

"Mark! It's great to hear your voice! Of course I remember you! Hey, thanks for looking out for Alexandra Stallings. How are you? Look, I'm at my Falls Church apartment right now! Can we meet for lunch?" said Betts with complete honesty. Trout was a trusted executive protection agent, and his reputation for keeping people alive in treacherous environments and high-threat meetings had not been overlooked by Betts.

After a pause, Trout said in a low tone, "Teddy Roosevelt monument, forty minutes." And then he hung up.

Whatever this was, thought Betts, it was urgent and confidential.

CHAPTER THIRTY: MAY 27, 2003

Pretend inferiority and encourage his arrogance.

—**Sun Tzu**

At the same time that Betts was leaving the apartment for the twenty-minute drive to the Roosevelt monument, NSA Director Polyander was receiving a text message on his phone. The text simply read, "This is Jennings. The female we hired failed her mission, and now she blames me. I got death threats from her, so I have had to relocate to a place where she couldn't possibly find me. Randall Betts has been summoned to Washington for being AWOL, and he responded that he's coming in by train, arriving at Union Station tomorrow evening. Betts told his old boss at the CIA that he's going to bring proof about you with him, thereby getting his job back. I can't get to him, and all my contacts for sending someone have closed down. He doesn't know you, and this would be the best chance to catch him before he passes the proof to his boss."

Polyander stared at the message. He was sitting on the back deck of his vacation home on the Severn River near Hawkins Point, Maryland. The riverfront house was at the end of a crusher-run stone driveway that led from Route 173 and could not be seen from the road. Polyander chose to hide out here for a few days and let all the bad news percolate before returning and resuming his original task of overseeing the enormous intelligence-collection platforms at his disposal. There wasn't one piece of information broadcast, by electronic or spoken means, that he couldn't lay his hands on. The cyber threats against the United States had yielded great power to the National Security Agency, and unlike that stupid bitch Olivia Johnson, he wasn't about to disappoint the president or Congress with his leadership. The only impediment to his success right now was Randall Betts, and that stumbling jarhead was in his sights. With the old man gone and the garage burned down, there were only two people who could interfere with his success: Betts and that chickenshit section chief, Jennings. The latter impediment, Jennings, was easily sidelined because of his involvement with the surveillance ops against the Betts family and the attempted killings. His fingerprints were all over these criminal acts, and the funds necessary to support them had been drawn out of the director's discretionary fund without any electronic fingerprints from Polyander. Jennings would take the fall for all of this, and Polyander would express profound ignorance of the withdrawals from his discretionary fund and deep concern for Jennings's emotional state.

Now, as he considered the panic and distance demonstrated by Jennings, he found that the single most important impediment, Betts, had to be handled in such a way that it would appear Jennings had sent him to meet with Betts, and in an emotionally charged rage, Polyander had to kill Betts in self-defense. This might work, thought Polyander, but he'd have to get a few more pieces to fall into place. He was still in charge, and he would make this plan work, in spite of all the idiots in the government. Nobody would question his loyalty or his power once this matter was resolved; all he had to do was eliminate one crippled Marine maniac and pin the blame on the hapless coward Jennings.

* * *

In an office just south of CIA headquarters, seven people huddled around an enormous flat-screen monitor displaying the text message sent to Polyander. This building was a renovated central office complex for a large government contractor, and when they broke up their divisions to avoid SEC scrutiny over lack of competition, the huge complex had been left abandoned. After 9/11, the USG took over the building, getting it from a venture-capital firm for a very low price, and installed FBI and CIA personnel together to ensure better cohesion in the global war on terrorism. This was the National Counterterrorism Center, another layer of government designed to build power, not bridges.

The seven people crowded into the executive office space in this building and stared at the screen as it showed the message that had been sent from this room. A senior official had not been selected yet to occupy this space, so it was perfect for use as a one-time tech op that would show no trace of existence and leave no trace behind.

One of the seven people surveying the message and awaiting a response from Polyander was Olivia Johnson. Using the pretext that she wanted to say goodbye to the hardworking people that worked here, she was granted a one-day access to the facility. And one day was all she needed. She had assembled this group after the dinner party at her house and had received "tacit" approval for her plan to have Chinese intelligence agents capture Polyander and sneak him out of the United States to Beijing. This was an enormous risk for everyone involved, but they all agreed that the resulting scandal from openly indicting the director of NSA and laying out the case, even in a classified court setting, would be disastrous for the country and its government.

The sole person whom Johnson wished to be here was not; Mark Trout had declined to attend this portion of the op, explaining that he had little stomach for Polyander at all and expressing doubt that he would understand the technical jargon that would be required.

This was going to be a completely clandestine operation, totally away from any possible detection by the NSA, CIA, or FBI. The internet connection was through a dark-web address, and the author's identifiers were hidden in the broadcast. The ease with which these tech wizards had set up this message board to contact Polyander and still remain cloaked was frightening, and Olivia Johnson was glad that these guys were on the right side of the USG.

For a completely clandestine op, it sure had a lot of horsepower involved. Some of the people in the room were senior government officials who would have to lie under oath if they were ever to discuss the details of what was being done here. The most senior of these officials was the attorney general for Washington, DC, Elise Summers, who had agreed to be a part of this criminal act only if she could participate directly. While this sounded somewhat mischievous, Summers had explained that this experience would educate her better about the cyber threats the United States was facing every day.

The others in the room were in direct support of concocting the text message that would ensnare Polyander. The opening message had been formulated and approved by Jennings as he was being processed for confinement without bond in a federal prison facility in Maryland. Jennings had been helpful in pointing out how he would create the message's sentences and phraseology, and provided insights into Polyander's attitudes and opinions. These would be helpful in shaping the narrative so that Polyander would have little recourse than to come out into the open for capture.

Next in the room was CIA's top operational psychologist, Harry Stansfield. His work in assessing false and misleading statements had been a boon to the CIA's Office of Security for finding those who attempted to "cheat the box," or get past polygraph examinations. His job here today was to see if Polyander was buying the inducements being provided in these text messages. Stansfield was comfortable dealing with liars, cheaters, criminals, and traitors. He had been working for CIA security for over eighteen years and was highly sought-after for his expertise.

Standing beside him was an NSA administrative assistant who had been working with Alexandra Stallings from the beginning. He was well aware of the criminal actions undertaken in surveilling the Betts family, as well as the funding disbursed for vehicles and equipment that were used. He was recommended by Stallings once she had regained consciousness and was briefed on the plans to take Polyander down. Johnson had traveled to Johns Hopkins Hospital when Stallings was conscious. Johnson laid out what happened at the shooting, how Polyander had aimed Jamin like a weapon to do away with the people who were closest to catching him, and she assured Stallings that Tom O'Herlihy had been laid to rest with the honor he deserved. Stallings was relieved to hear all of this, but she did not get to her next question before Johnson quietly laid out the plot and the players being arranged to punish Polyander. Stallings had objections to the idea due to her firm belief that the Chinese MSS could not be trusted. Johnson answered that she had infused the Chinese team leader, Vang, with enough motivation to see the kidnapping through. This discussion proved to Olivia Johnson that Stallings was a tough nut and reliable resource. Stallings expressed confidence in this NSA admin officer's capabilities and his discretion, and that was good enough for Johnson. The admin officer's job today was to interpret any strange or NSA-specific code words Polyander might use if he distrusted the source of the note. He was most anxious to see what the disgraced NSA director might say in response.

Standing on one side of the NSA admin assistant was the senior technical operations officer from the CIA. He introduced himself only as "Ben," and he had much of the equipment set up before anyone arrived. Marge Jenson had arranged for his participation and assured him that no investigative smear would arise from this gathering. Ben didn't truly believe that was true, but he wanted a shot at doing this, and he had always liked Director Johnson. Now he stood at a small podium, which held a Dell laptop that would be processing the incoming messages and protecting the source of the outgoing ones. He stood ready, transfixed by what was about to happen.

On the other side of the NSA admin assistant was FBI Special Agent Troy York. He had been instructed by FBI Director Columbus to observe this tangled web of deceit and deception that was aimed at taking down a senior intelligence officer and whisking him away from media attention as well as the Justice Department.

Standing behind Olivia Johnson was Marjorie Jenson. Nobody in this room was trusted by Olivia Johnson more than this woman, and her ability to get things done at the CIA was legendary. Her goal in being in this room was to provide any historical background needed and ensure that nobody took an unnecessary interest in the activities of the assembled group. She stood firmly by the office door and checked to make sure that little attention was paid to this room. Beyond that, Jenson wanted to see the downfall of the criminal responsible for Stallings getting shot.

This assemblage was not unique: since the invention of an informal communication method called "electronic mail" in 1995, the counterterrorist center had been forming up small groups like this to assess and guide operational interest in strangers who were writing to the CIA over the internet. Once the Agency created a website with a "contact us" page, offers to work in the intelligence community and quietly provide information poured in. The Agency even got verbal offers from potential defectors, even though many of them were initially discounted as false-flag operations.

Soon after becoming DCI, Olivia Johnson was approached by a junior analyst proposing to create a small shop in CTC to engage with those who might be involved in terrorism but wanted a way out. Johnson was intrigued by this idea, and soon after the "Terrorist Defector Analysis" platform was established. Known informally as "The Today Show," it created a synergy in the cyber world that attracted some of the best minds to filter out the impostors and wannabes while making solid contacts with people caught up in the extremist trade looking for a way out. This effort had tremendous results, finding intelligence gold mines in people who had been marginalized by extremist leaders or pursued for sneaking funds out of terrorist organizations. The online conversations with folks that might have good information for the United States resulted in arranged meetings with case officers specially trained to deal with high-threat situations. Sometimes these meetings bore fruit, sometimes not.

"Here comes his answer," said Ben.

"Explain 'failed' to me. Wasn't the garage burned down? You mean Betts wasn't there? If she's upset, just don't pay her. She can't run to the police, and if she can't win against a crippled moron, how can she threaten you? It sounds to me like you're becoming soft on getting this done. Why must I get involved when you're the one who assured me that everything would be taken care of? Just catch up to Betts at the station and convince him of the way it has to be." This was the message from Polyander, displayed on the large screen for everyone to see.

Immediately, the interactions and opinions began to fly. Ben waited patiently as everyone argued over what Polyander meant to say, his frame of mind, and his gullibility. As a favor to the Betts family, SAIC Nashville contacted a news anchor with a local TV station and asked them to run a story about a garage burning to the ground in Pikeville. No mention was made of any injuries or fatalities. This story would be picked up by open-source research at NSA, and Polyander would know that part of the assassination plot had been fulfilled. Finally, when all the insights and suggestions were done, Johnson instructed Ben to respond with this message:

"The woman told me she killed Betts as you asked, and then set the garage on fire. When I saw on the news that the garage burned down but then intercepted the phone calls to Betts from the CIA, I knew she had lied, so I didn't pay her. Now she says she's coming after me. She doesn't know about you being in charge of this op. I'm afraid to show my face right now, and getting Betts at Union Station before he gets in a cab to his headquarters is the last chance we have."

Olivia chose this wording carefully to demonstrate that Jennings was too scared to complete the task, and bolster that fact that Betts had to be caught between the incoming train and the WDC cab stand outside Union Station.

The input from the group agreed with this move and provided guidance to Ben about putting in one or two typographical errors to show Jennings's anxiety. Once the group was in agreement about the content and intentions of the message, Johnson told Ben to send it.

Sooner than expected, Polyander's response was vulgar and vague: "Unsure what is meant by that. I only know that I have surrounded myself with spineless turds afraid of their own shadow. You have known from day one the importance of this project, and yet you have hired incompetent fools that have failed at every turn. Why must I be the one to settle this issue once and for all? You disgust me. Give me the fucking train number and go back to hiding out."

"Get him to admit that he'll be at the train station." recommended FBI Agent York.

"Yes, this isn't a real confession," added WDC/AG Summers.

"It's a good enough confession for me." replied Marge Jenson.

"Oh yeah, he's going to be at that train station." stated the psychologist, Stansfield.

"Thank him for personally taking the task of stopping Betts. Lack of a denial will be enough to convince me that he's going to be there." directed Olivia Johnson.

Ben typed up a one-sentence response and let it sit while everyone in the room agreed that it met the legal standard for setting Polyander up for being at Union Station. Ben then added the train route from Atlanta, the Amtrak Crescent train number, and time and track on which it would be arriving. Johnson gave Ben the word, and out it went. The shady part of this message was changing the arrival time for the train from Atlanta to 9:47 p.m. instead of 1:47 p.m. This could be explained as a simple mistake, but it was needed so that the kidnap team would do their job at night, when Union Station was less occupied. Very risky if he was to independently verify the arrival time for himself, but Stansfield opined that verifying the arrival times by looking them up would be considered admin work, and therefore beneath a narcissist like Polyander. The NSA administrative assistant agreed.

Now they knew exactly when and where Polyander would be on the following day. With no further message displayed on the board, Johnson walked out of the office and dialed a cell-phone number to advise senior Ministry of State Security officer Vang Yong Lieu that their op was a go.

While this gathering was breaking up at a government complex near Langley, Virginia, Mark Trout stood in front of Randall Betts at the Teddy Roosevelt monument on an island in the Potomac River and told him all about the plan to have the Chinese kidnap Polyander and take him to Beijing for debriefing and "trial." Betts was told about Johnson's plan to lure Polyander out with a farcical message that he had to go to meet Betts coming off a train. Trout explained that the Ministry of State Security would send a bunch of agents to Union Station in WDC and bundle him up as a homeless person, drug him, and whisk him to a waiting cargo plane at a hangar belonging to a CCP front company at Dulles Airport. The questions posed by Betts were all answered in full by Trout, and eventually Betts's plan to shoot Polyander seemed to become too difficult. The line of sight at Union Station would be too clogged with tourists and cops, and any idea of firing a rifle inside the terminal would be ludicrous.

The idea of having the Chinese punish Polyander cooked inside Betts for a minute. He could see the justice involved, and he certainly agreed that handling this matter outside of the US justice system wasn't a bad idea. But he began to see some collateral damage from the overall plan. Betts asked if there was a chance that any revelation of this kidnap scheme would later splash back onto Olivia Johnson.

"Randy, that chance is real. The US government can shut down the media if any wind of this surfaces, but there's too many people that will miss Polyander, and one thing the Chinese could do is gloat about having him in custody. If that happens, the spotlight eventually lands on Johnson, and she knows it," Trout replied.

"The idea is not a bad one, but I can't believe the DCIA would push it to the point where she could get in serious trouble over this. This isn't career-ending; this is life in prison," said Betts.

"She knows it. She confided to me that the list of characters who know about this plan, the Chinese and the Americans who are taking part in this plan, can't be trusted to keep their mouths shut or not point the finger at her the second a whiff of this comes out," said Trout flatly.

"What can we do? Can we do something to keep her safe?" Betts's mind was racing. He saw now that a great deal of effort and risk were being arranged to make Polyander suffer, and now it seemed that the simple idea of just shooting the guy at the entrance to Union Station was simple and effective but ultimately useless. Something had to be arranged so that this kidnap scheme was averted. Something had to be concocted so that Johnson and all these senior officials would be out of the loop, unconnected to the scheme. The Chinese had to be cheated out of their prize, and the National Security Agency had to be relieved of a scheming, disloyal, dangerous piece of shit that deserved to die.

Standing next to the granite statue that memorialized Theodore Roosevelt, Betts began to think about the breadth and width of the criminal actions undertaken by Polyander. He eventually broke it down to who was truly disserved by this man; who were the people most threatened by his treachery, his malice? He had arranged for the deaths of people Betts knew, but he betrayed a lot more people than that, and that betrayal was over thirty years ago. Then Betts thought about the promise he had made to his dad as he lay dying in a Tennessee hospital: the assurance that he would make Polyander pay for his betrayal of the MACV-SOG recon teams. As Betts formulated whether or not he should even stick his nose into this plan, he looked up and read a quote from Teddy Roosevelt inscribed at the statue's base: "Knowing what's right doesn't mean much unless you do what's right."

And that was all Betts needed for encouragement. He turned to Trout and surprised him with a sneering smile. "How about we cook up our own plan for this guy?"

Trout smiled back and asked Betts what he would need. They had to have something in place by 8:00 p.m. the next day, and it would be a covert mission within a covert mission. This sounded like a great idea.

CHAPTER THIRTY-ONE: MAY 27, 2003

Even from a foe, a man may learn wisdom.

—Greek proverb

The front yard and porch of Olivia Johnson's Bethesda home were all about color and texture. The various blooming flowers, along with the redbud trees and azalea bushes, all created a utopia of nature's hues, bidding welcome to anyone who visited. What real estate agents called "curb appeal" had simply been a labor of love for Johnson's mother. Now that the daughter owned the house, she tried her best to keep the colors and exuberant textures going.

The back porch of her house was all about business and efficiency. The sole color was the year-round green of the cedar trees and English boxwoods. The porch was all brick. The smooth squares of reddish-brown stones made up the floor, and the low walls were of curved bricks that spoke of a time when craftsmanship and brick mason talent were applauded. The steps leading down to a lush stretch of grass were also brick, and together the backyard architecture preferred serenity and safety over the colorful chaos of the front yard. It was here that Olivia Johnson enjoyed her solitude. The back porch had always signaled a slower pace of life, and she found that pleasure now that she was no longer DCIA. With all the technicians finished taking out the command post, with all the security techs certifying that the classified materials and commo equipment were accounted for, with all the nervous agents with guns moved to someone else's house, Olivia Johnson was finally alone. It was almost eight o'clock on a mid-May evening, and the sky was darkening naturally. The air held some humidity and the faint scent of a neighbor's fresh-cut grass, but the temperature was moderate, and the birds were less noisy. Now she could take out her secret pouch.

The day had gone pretty well. Her meeting to flush Polyander out into the public had worked, and Johnson had managed to get in one last visit to CIA HQ to say more goodbyes. Marge Jenson was staying on at the CIA, over the objections of Olivia's father. He wanted her back at the Pentagon, "where good people are appreciated," he said. Johnson said goodbye to those agents on duty and thanked them again for all their hard work and dedication. The DPS agents had come in two days before and all had their pictures taken with the DCIA. Last, Johnson stopped in at the office of the DDCIA. The deputy director, an Air Force one-star, always got along well with Johnson, even though he thought human intelligence gathering was a thing of the past. The future belonged to satellites, drones, and thermal sensors. Johnson disagreed with this, but it never interfered with her trust and sponsorship of the DDCIA's agenda.

And now she was home, and truly alone. With nobody worrying about her safety or her access, with no screaming calls from congressional oversight committees and no late-night reading of material destined for the president, Johnson could open her pouch without any prying eyes. Carefully and patiently, she drew out the silver butane lighter given to her by the Queen of Norway. Once she checked that the lighter still had the power to light anything in a windstorm, she reached into her secret pouch and drew out her favorite cigar. It was a very light smoke from the Dominican Republic, and Johnson found the honest aroma and satisfying burn of this brand to allow true relaxation. She didn't need brandy, although one snifter was indeed on hand this evening, and she didn't need mood music. She needed to sit back in her father's favorite Adirondack chair and enjoy a good cigar while listening to the quiet stillness of her backyard. Nobody to comment, nobody to judge her, nobody to suggest solutions. Just the peace of the backyard at dusk.

She quickly sat up in a start as she suddenly became aware of someone watching her. Somehow, someone had crept around the west side of the yard from the driveway and was standing twenty feet away, just over her right shoulder.

"Who is there?" demanded Johnson. She may not be a Washington power broker anymore, but she could hurt an intruder with a hot cigar or a swift elbow.

"Do you have another one of those?" asked MSS Agent Vang as he stepped up onto the porch, pointing at the cigar in her hand.

"Sorry, these are for enjoyment of solitude" was the answer from Johnson. She was still wary of Vang's intentions.

"Missus Director, please excuse the interruption," began Vang. "My men are briefed, ready, and prepared for the event tomorrow. I came by to tell you that, and to confess..."

Johnson continued staring at Vang, awaiting the rest. As she took a good draw on the cigar, he reached into his jacket pocket and brought out a small item in a cloth.

"I confided the plan you trusted us with to another," continued Vang. "My father would wish you to know how grateful he is for your consideration. You have settled a major impediment in his soul, and he can rest in peace knowing that the traitor who set him up will have justice."

Johnson took the small item from Vang and pulled away the cloth. Even in the diminishing light, she could see that it was a very small but ornate clear-crystal dragon. The head had a slight crimson tinge, but the body, wings, and tail were clear and very detailed.

"Vang, this is gorgeous. Thank you! I've never seen crystal this detailed before," said Johnson as she admired the Chinese symbol of good luck and cultural identity, so delicate and detailed.

"Oh, it's not crystal," said Vang appreciatively. "It is glass. It was hand-blown by my grandfather almost a hundred years ago. He presented it to my father when he married my mother, and it passed to me upon my father's death. My grandfather is gone now, but he always told me as a child that he holds no greater treasure in his heart than the one who values honor and prosperity over pride and power."

Johnson was almost overtaken with the sentiment. She could hardly handle this treasured piece of family history now that she saw the formidable patience and accomplishment of Vang's grandfather. She was honored and humbled by this simple gesture.

"You see," said Vang in an almost sheepish tone, "I am the product of a great family. My grandfather was an officer in the People's Liberation Army. He spent most of his career fighting the Red Guard in our country. My father did his job in the Ministry of State Security as best he could, and this asset Mouse was a burden to him. So I spoke to him spiritually about your plan, about your country discovering who this traitor is, and how your country will save face by slipping him off to us. I could sense that your plan would be joyous news for him."

"We are going to rectify this man's treachery, and you are going to help me avoid any scrutiny by *not* telling anyone else about this plan!" said Johnson quietly as she took another pull on her cigar, placed the small glass dragon on the side table, and dug in her secret pouch for another cigar.

* * *

"Hi, Randy, it's Marilyn. I hope I didn't disturb you or distract you while you're driving. I know you're heading back to Fairfax to clear up some things, and I'm not sure when you'll be back, but I need you to know something…Randall, my feelings for you are stronger than you know, and I have treasured every minute we've been together, but I had no choice but to say 'no' to meeting you for dinner. It has nothing to do with how I feel about you. It's just not in the rules for us who do the field-rep work. The VA is very strict about not getting involved with our patients, even when they're as kind, strong, and attractive as you are. Anyway, I wanted you to know that, and I hope you'll talk with me again soon. I miss you, Randy… and I'll just come out and say it: if you asked me to leave VA service so we could be together, I'd have to think long and hard about it. But it doesn't mean that I don't care about you. I mean that. Okay, so I'll hope to hear from you soon. Bye."

This was the message left on Randall's phone while he was meeting with Mark Trout. The message stung Betts, and he listened to it three more times before he sat in his apartment and drew up the list of things he would need to finish this thing. Betts was drawing up a final list of preparations to undertake violence and revenge against a man he had never met. But like any unseen enemy, Keith Polyander was going to suffer. The Chinese MSS couldn't stop him, Olivia Johnson couldn't stop him, and now, even Marilyn Emerson couldn't stop him.

CHAPTER THIRTY-TWO: MAY 28, 2003

The enemy of a good plan is the dream of a perfect plan.

—Carl von Clausewitz

Designed and built by 1907, Union Station in Washington, DC, is a monument to the city's achievements and failures. The destruction of entire neighborhoods and removal of busy street intersections to accommodate the tunnels and gates of the massive transportation hub was a demonstration of the sheer will of the government to consolidate the several bus and train stations in the city, and the recurring projects to renovate the structure had a cost that few people outside Washington would understand.

The most recent renovation of Union Station was a 1988 project undertaken not long after a renovation by the Reagan administration proved ineffective. This renovation, the most expensive undertaking in WDC's history, sought to incorporate Amtrak rails into the main station and to create a vibrant lower level with an indoor theater capable of making the station an attractive spot for visitors and rail/bus passengers.

The project had been completed, but the site attracted more than passengers. The open space and extended areas created a two-million-square-foot shelter under the station's dome that many homeless and indigent residents found necessary to attend. While many security plans, such as promised police patrols, numerous camera systems, and staged first responders, were somewhat effective, the true reason for the terminal was to allow bus, train, and cab traffic to flow with little interference. This was a constant challenge to the District of Columbia. As Amtrak Police, United States Park Police, and WDC Metropolitan Police patrolled the area, the spacious floors, open restrooms, and frequent corners made for all kinds of human mischief.

* * *

It was 8:00 p.m. at the East Hall of Union Station. FBI Special Agent Troy York sat at a small metal bistro table and held a commanding view of the interior space of the street level of this marvelous structure. This time of day held very few tourists, and the few passengers on the rail and bus lines attached to the station were dwindling. Families were still touring the facility, taking pictures of the grand hall and the statues of the Roman gods overseeing its safety. The crowd and resulting din of noise was fairly thin, but some activity was still ongoing. People were moving through the area, just not as many as the previous hour.

York was in contact with a two-man team in a nongovernment Toyota Camry near the roundabout in front of the station. The contact consisted of a small transmitter/receiver in York's ear; the guys in the Camry had handheld radios. Their job was to look for Polyander's approach to the station. York's job was to identify Polyander when he actually entered the station, and then leave. His sudden departure from the bistro table where he had been slowly enjoying a cup of coffee would alert the kidnap team stationed in the terminal. Once he moved from the bistro table, York's job was to leave the station, stand across the street from the Massachusetts Avenue exit, and ensure that three homeless men got into a waiting sedan nearby. Once the sedan pulled away, York would instruct the two-man FBI team to vacate the area. The lower a profile, the better; the kidnapping of a senior government official by a team of agents from the People's Republic of China under the nose of three separate police agencies was a daunting undertaking, and nobody wanted to attract anyone's attention.

The team included four well-trained MSS officers specifically brought in to assist Vang Lieu. Along with Vang himself and a driver, the six-man team did its best to spread out and prepare for the target to arrive. Vang had tried to bring in more agents, but Immigration and Customs Enforcement would only allow these four. They had been quietly vetted by the CIA, and the approvals for their "temporary visit" visas had been passed at the highest level. These men arrived on work visas for a cargo company operating out of a hangar at Dulles Airport, and their work on a critical conveyor belt assembly would take no more than three days. The cargo company vouched for the men and their transportation to and from the United States, certifying that the men would not leave the airport area during their work period.

Vang was stationed at the Massachusetts Avenue entrance. He could clearly see Agent York, but he could also see much of the grand hall himself. He wasn't going to trust the Americans completely in ID'ing their target. He wore his best suit, which was a light-beige polyester-and-wool blend that closely matched the color of the walls in the main hall. His white dress shirt and faint-yellow silk tie matched the suit but produced no brilliant hues. The sole color on him that stood out was the tourist map in his hands. His presence would go unnoticed, and his story for being there would correlate with his duties at the Chinese Embassy. Of the six men kidnapping Polyander tonight, he was the only one with a solid reason to be here.

The second agent of the kidnap team was stationed just inside the commercial portion of the station, overlooking the food-court area. Some concern arose that the target had arrived very early and camped out in the enormous lower-level facility, and this agent could spot him and assist in the capture. He had Vang in his line of sight, as no radios would be used for this op. He was the fringe agent, the oversight-and-assist function.

The third man was seated on the floor of the main hall, bundled in dark, dirty blankets, with an old baseball cap made dark with sweat and stains, watching with hidden focus all the foot traffic in the area. His apparent visage of a typical homeless person prevented anyone from taking notice of him. And as long as he bothered nobody and kept his mouth shut, the police wouldn't bother him. This was the contact man. He was the one who would take the target into the men's room for capture. The signal from York or from Vang would result in the man standing and approaching the target for money. Once contact was made, the target would be coerced to cooperate with this man's instructions to move to the men's room. This cooperation was guaranteed because this agent, named Lim, was the largest agent in MSS. At just over six feet, two inches tall, he was a former Olympic bodybuilder and wrestling instructor at the MSS academy in the Haidian District of Beijing. His slumped position sitting in a small corner of the main hall was hiding his size and strength, but it was incredibly painful.

The capture team was two MSS agents crouched on toilets in locked stalls in the men's room. The contact man would guide the target to the men's room, where these two agents would hear a one-word term from Lim that would hasten their move from the stalls into the open. The men would inject a serious tranquilizer into the target's arm, swathe him in old clothes, and hustle him out to where Vang was standing watch, and through the doors to Mass. Ave. and a waiting car, driven by the sixth agent.

The sixth agent was an actual employee of the cargo company at Dulles Airport. He held a valid Virginia driver's license and had been working at the cargo company for over a year. His ability to drive here, his knowledge of the area, and his ability to utilize the Dulles Toll Road were invaluable to the kidnap plan. The fact that he was an actual MSS agent working

250 | *Richard M. Timberlake*

under the cover of the cargo company didn't hurt. After this op, his cover
would be blown anyway, and he would return with the other members of
the kidnap team.

Vang would hold the door at the East Hall open for the three men,
and the two other remaining agents were to move together to the metro
train station on the lower level and ride to Alexandria for a cab ride to
Dulles Airport. There, they would assist getting the target loaded onto
the cargo plane, and all five members of the kidnap team would quietly
exit the United States with their captured prize.

The trap was set, and everyone was in place. They had been set up for
over an hour. Nothing.

Just as the door behind Vang was pulled open, York's radio crackled.
"I think your boy just got out of a cab and walked toward the building."
York looked over to Vang just in time to see a middle-aged man push
Vang out of the way and proceed toward the gate area of the terminal.
The movement and sudden appearance of the guest of honor surprised
York, and he struggled to slowly get up out of his chair to depart. He was
scared that the sudden lurch by York would trigger an anxious, suspicious
move by Vang. To York's relief, he glanced over to see Vang very casually
set himself back in place and fold up his map.

The folding of the map, the clear signal from Vang that the target had
entered, resulted in the big man, Lim, getting up from his spot to move to
the target. Just then, the effort to stand after being in a restrained sitting
position for over an hour took its toll on the muscular man. He stumbled
a bit, and had to work very hard to stand erect to start walking. He was
carrying his blanket over him; it would hide the target from the cameras.
As he was doing this, the target was walking faster than expected. He was
halfway across the main hall and heading for the gates where the passengers would be exiting the terminal. He was falling out of Lim's path, and
catching up to him would require some notable effort. Lim had started

from his sitting spot, but at the pace he was moving and the distance to the target, it wasn't going to work as well as planned.

As Polyander got to the halls transitioning from the main hall to the commercial area, the second agent turned from his position and moved straight across the floor to a young family taking a picture of their little girl in front of the statue of a Roman soldier. The MSS agent moved with purpose and agility, asking the parents of the little girl if they wanted someone to take a picture of everybody together. As he moved toward the family and volunteered to take the family photo, he clumsily ran into Polyander and stopped him in his tracks. Instead of apologizing to the middle-aged man that he had just run into, the second MSS agent continued to take the camera from the appreciative parents and changed his position so that the family was turned away from their original stance, and unable to see Lim catch up to Polyander.

Polyander's surprise at having this Chink idiot run into him and then just move off to talk to a bunch of strangers was replaced by terror as a massive grip from behind was placed on his left wrist and the arm attached to it was wrenched behind him in a fast, efficient move. Polyander tried to pivot on his left foot to gain enough strength to pull away, maybe even use his right hand to reach the revolver in his waistband, but he was quickly and quietly pulled off balance and herded away from his intended destination. The hand behind him, grasping his wrist, moved to grip the area between the thumb and index finger of his left hand and powerfully tucked his thumb downward, creating an immobilizing pain. As Polyander tried to cry out from the alarm and the pain, the person twisting his thumb and guiding him away from the train terminal entrance spoke in a quiet whisper from a mouth far above his ears. "Come with me and shut your mouth, or I'll break off your arm and shove it into your ass."

This contact, and the movement toward the men's room, was conducted just outside the main hall. This street-level area had so many turns and corners that almost nobody paid attention to the sight of a man being guided into a men's room. The second agent saw it after he took the picture of the smiling American family and handed the camera back to the parents.

Two other men took notice of it, and they split up when Lim started getting his target to the men's room. These two men were not part of the kidnap team; they were here to foil that plot.

As Vang watched, the large MSS Agent Lim caught up with the target and held his left arm in a restraining bracket that compelled him to do whatever Lim commanded. Lim and the target walked calmly toward the men's room and were out of sight as they turned the corner and the wall of the main hall obstructed his view. Vang relaxed and was back on his station, awaiting the group of three to come around the corner from the men's room so he could open the door for them and distract any interest or police scrutiny.

The second agent, having disengaged with the American family, was now heading slowly toward Vang's position. He would stay out of the way of the three-man group that would now be the kidnap team and the drugged target, going through the exit doorway, and then he and Lim would depart for the nearby metro station.

Lim continued to hold the target's left arm up and tight against his back, forcing the man to continue into the men's room area. This was an open bathroom, no door, just a path of tiles where the entrance quickly turned right into the tiled area of sinks and toilets. Lim got to the open entrance area and was ready to call out for the two kidnap-team members to come out from their stalls and take the target off his hands. Lim would plan to frisk the man for weapons and stand by, but he wouldn't be part of the team that took the target out of the men's room area.

Just then, an incredible force slammed Lim in his lower back, and his entire body reflexed in pain. A huge surge of power stiffened Lim into an erect posture that he was unable to control. His brain registered enormous pain, but he could not pull away from it; he could not react to it. All he could do was fall face-first onto the bathroom floor.

The loss of Lim's forceful grip on his arm made Polyander pull his left arm down and instinctively rub his left wrist as he turned to escape from this Neanderthal. Just as he tried to turn, an incredible wave of pain and reflexive shock went searing through Polyander's body, and he involuntarily stiffened and started to fall. He was eased to the ground, and his wrists were zip-tied behind his back, and a strap of duct tape was slapped across his mouth.

This treatment and chain of events was frightening. Polyander was filled with pain, revolt, and uncertainty as he could not figure out what was happening to him. Then he was pulled up and pushed back in the direction of the train gates. Polyander was really confused now; he was pulled away from looking over the train-gate area in anticipation of Betts's arrival, threatened with pain and violence, then taken to a bathroom, where his initial attacker was immobilized, and now he was being restrained and taken to the same gates that he was going to in the first place!

* * *

Randall Betts and Mark Trout stood watch over the scene at Union Station with some degree of admiration. For such a small team with almost no operational support, the guys lined up to kidnap Polyander were spaced properly and had most of the area covered. Trout pointed out Vang to Betts, and they presumed that the other Chinese fellows in the area were part of the team. They were nonchalant and very low-key. Betts was impressed with how well these guys blended into the environment. His plan to snatch Polyander out from these guys was going to require some quick movement and good timing.

These two well-trained CIA officers were almost invisible. Taking up a relaxed position looking at the train schedules, they went completely unnoticed by the locals and the agents getting ready to kidnap the man whom Betts was after. The Chinese would initiate their plan, but they weren't going to succeed, because Betts had two things in his favor: he had a complete backup plan to which he was entirely dedicated, and he had someone he trusted to help make that plan succeed. Just like an effective sniper/spotter team, these two men knew the stakes, knew the layout, and knew what they had to do to make their plan succeed. Mark Trout had come to the CIA from the Seventy-Fifth Ranger Battalion, and his experience with combat planning and execution was extensive. The Agency had taught him to hone those skills to a finer point, including some finer points about surveillance detection and countersurveillance operations. Tonight, he was armed with another skill the CIA had provided him: breaking and entering locked doors.

Betts's time in the Marine Corps had taught him to trust a good plan and have backup plans every time. His case-officer skills were about blending into an environment and attracting as little attention as possible. Betts was dressed in running shoes, blue jeans, and an Under Armour base-layer shirt covered with an oversize tan raincoat. Tonight, with all the planning and excitement, he was having some difficulty keeping those skills sharp. Trout had provided a file picture of Polyander, and now Betts was completely prepared for what he needed to do. He was ready to act, and seeing the others arrayed in the street-level terminal got him amped up for action. Betts was a combination of many things right now, all of them dangerous.

Betts pointed Troy York out to Trout and surmised that he was a one-man party inside with a SWAT team standing by outside if anything went to shit.

When Polyander strolled into the main hall, Betts took notice that the Chinese guy he pushed aside made a point to fold his map, and Trout observed York almost fall over his bistro table trying to naturally get up to walk outside. The scrape of York's metal chair on the marble floor was the loudest sound in the street-level terminal.

Betts moved his cross-shoulder bag to a position over his chest and got ready for anything. Inside his cross-shoulder bag were the items he would need to effect this plan. All the way to the end. Betts dedicated some time to being able to explain these items if he was arrested or detained for any reason, but after a while, he decided to forget the reasons. If he was asked why he was carrying these items, then by that time, the whole plan would have fallen apart, and it wouldn't matter. As long as none of the items in his bag were a firearm, he might be able to explain his way out of trouble. Betts's training as a case officer included learning to stay cool under pressure.

Betts adopted a stance of pretending to look at a printout of the Amtrak train schedule in his hands while he kept his eyes on Polyander's walk across the main hall. Trout had turned to look at the electronic board that read out the arrivals and departures, but he was focused on the reflection of Polyander walking their way.

Just as Polyander walked out of the main hall and into the commercial area, the two CIA officers watched an incredible ballet of movement and purpose. One agent stepped out and bumped into Polyander as he moved a family of onlookers away, while another person, the tallest homeless person they'd ever seen in their lives, grabbed Polyander and moved him toward the men's room. The choreography was smooth and barely noticeable. Betts was impressed but not deterred.

"Game on. See you at the door," whispered Betts as he moved toward the men's room and unzipped his bag. Trout said nothing; he turned and headed toward the train gates as he pulled a small pouch and a can of cooking-oil spray from his backpack.

Just as the tall homeless guy got Polyander to the entrance to the men's room, Betts knew they were out of camera view from the Amtrak police station monitoring activity in the train station. Betts came up quickly behind them as he drew his two-pole stun gun from his bag and slid it under the big man's shirt. He pushed it roughly into the skin at the base of the larger man's back. The shock to the big man's system took a moment longer than Betts anticipated, allowing Polyander to wrestle himself from the man's grip and attempt to turn away and escape. As the big man fell away and to the ground, Betts quickly turned the stun device on Polyander and thrust it into the center of the man's chest.

MSS Agent Lim had been a treasure to the ministry. His size and strength made him a dominating force, and once he could not compete for the Olympics, the MSS picked him up and made him an investigator with very little of the physical training required of other candidates. This meant that Lim had never encountered a Taser, had never experienced the body-disabling shock of an electric stunning device such as this one. The stun gun Betts had chosen for tonight was a strong one, a police model that advertised a delivery of over twenty million volts, and Betts knew he had to get the poles through the clothing and onto bare skin at the lower back region. With Lim's lack of understanding of what was being done to him, along with Betts's trained deployment of the handheld weapon, Lim was immobilized and left lying on the floor in a stupor.

Polyander also immediately stiffened and fell toward the floor. Betts eased him down so he could place him on his stomach and zip-tie his hands behind his back. Betts then returned the stun gun to his bag and fished out a short but wide roll of duct tape. He pulled off an eight-inch section and firmly placed it across Polyander's mouth. Betts then got up and pulled Polyander to his feet, put a fishing hat on his head, and hustled him back toward the train gates. The traitorous bastard wanted to see where the trains arrived, to see where he would ambush Betts and blame it on the PTS—well, this was his chance. The hat would help hide the tape across his mouth, but the stumbling gait and zip-tied hands were nothing he could hide. His only chance at this point was to move as quickly and efficiently as he could and hope that Trout had done his job.

As Betts guided Polyander north toward Gate A at the train terminal, he kept his posture as erect and normal as possible, avoiding any impression of rushing that would alert the security cameras. Out in the open train-gate area, very few people were sitting in the waiting area, and those who were there couldn't care less about two guys heading for a locked gate door.

But the gate door wasn't locked. Mark Trout had walked up calmly to the large glass doors at Gate A and picked the locks with tools from his pouch. Once the locks were disengaged, he stood the doors open and propped them in place before turning and strolling toward a line of small surveillance cameras overlooking the gate area. He quickly shot a fine mist of cooking oil at the cameras, blurring but not obscuring their view. This way, the Amtrak police monitors watching their screens wouldn't recognize the lack of clarity from the camera's lens until they really focused on them. Trout walked away, moving at a normal pace back toward the west exit onto Second Street.

Betts came into the area one minute later and pushed himself and Polyander through the open glass doors. Once they were past the doors, he turned and pushed his captive back into the gate area and moved smoothly to a staircase in the middle of the terminal. Betts bent Polyander forward into a duck walk as they hustled up the stairs onto the second level. Here, Betts pulled Polyander hard to his left and kept Polyander low as they walked along the second-floor railing and behind an ATM. This path, extensively researched and rehearsed earlier in the day, kept Betts and his captive out of the line of surveillance cameras overseeing the gate area. Once past the ATM, Betts headed straight for an alcove outside the gate area, where he sat Polyander next to a set of stairs. Next, he took off his shoulder bag and removed his jacket. Betts turned the jacket inside out, to display a dark-green, almost black color. Now he would not resemble the description someone would have seen on the cameras inside. Once he got Polyander back to his feet, it was a stroll down a short flight of stairs and into an open area that normally allowed cross-country buses to arrive and depart. Nobody was here this time of night, and the sounds of metro train arrivals and station announcements over the PA system seemed a bit louder in the cavernous bus terminal. Betts pulled and pushed Polyander along as he tried to scream through the duct tape and wrestle himself from his kidnapper's grasp. This was madness, and Polyander had no idea what was happening. He only knew that he was no longer in power, and the person controlling him was both careful in his planning and malevolent in his intent.

Back in the station, the two MSS agents stooping uncomfortably in their respective stalls were listening for the word from Lim. They had heard people come and go, and then they heard some commotion that sounded like someone quietly crackling a plastic bottle, and then some shuffling, but nothing from Lim. Suddenly, the sound of the shuffling became louder, and Lim shouted for them to come out. The kidnap team rushed from the stalls to find Lim sitting up but almost incoherent.

"They took him!" screamed Lim, and the two men rushed from the men's room in search of the target being taken out of the terminal. They were joined by the second agent, who was annoyed and perplexed that the kidnap team was running around the main hall without the target. This animated discussion, along with Lim staggering into view, was observed by Vang, who simply turned and walked out to the taxi stand. He would catch a cab back to the embassy, retrieve his personal vehicle, and drive home. For some reason, the kidnap plan had failed, and he was at a loss to explain it. But for right now, all he should do is extricate himself and remove any suspicion of his involvement with Union Station for the night. In the back of the cab, Vang pulled out his cell phone and made one call.

The Amtrak Police Headquarters security room held over a dozen monitors, which kept an eye on the station through several dozen cameras throughout the tenth-largest train station in the United States. The dispatcher froze the scan control on one particular camera and called one of the patrol officers who was at the eastern end of the food court. "Sector One, this is Control. I have two white males walking together out of the men's room by Gate A. One in a tan coat, one in a black coat, and the guy in the dark coat appears to have his hands tied behind his back." It would take the patrol officer almost five minutes to walk the distance from the east end of the station on the lower level to the gate area at street level.

"Two guys walking together out of the men's room, not unusual. But you say one of 'em has his hands tied?" was the response from the patrol officer's radio.

"Sector One, get over there now!" came the barking response. "Looks like they went through the gate doors! My cameras can't get any details of the floor area! Aren't you checking to make sure they're locked?"

The patrol officer hustled up to the gate area and found nothing unusual. Very few people were in the area, and none of them matched the description given over the radio. The gate doors were propped open, and at the urging of the dispatcher, he checked the area around the flight of stairs for any sign of people. He reported seeing nothing, and recommended that dispatch contact the WDC Metropolitan Police Department to have them check the track area outside of the station terminal. Amtrak police had jurisdiction over the track area, but the rest of the city was the responsibility of WMPD.

"If they've gotten down on the track area, there's no telling where they are! Get DC Metro and Park Police over here now," said the patrol officer. He wasn't looking forward to checking this huge track area alone.

FBI Agent York stood along Massachusetts Avenue, across from the cab stand outside the station, watching as the lights began to come on and darkness descended on Union Station. He could see the door that the team would come out of, and he could see the rented car awaiting their arrival. Then he noticed that the driver of the rented car was getting a call on his cell phone. He listened for a minute, put his phone down, started the car, and drove off. York was astounded. He thought that maybe the kidnap team had been wrapped up, but then he saw that no police response was going into the terminal. Everything was in place except for Polyander: What the hell happened?

After a minute, York saw two WDC metro police units pull up in front of the station and approach the other cops who were stationed at the first street entrance. Quick, hurried instructions were exchanged, followed by a hastened walk into the station terminal. This didn't seem like a big emergency, but then other cars started arriving, some of them with lights on, some more nonchalant. Strange, he thought. No sirens, no apparent emergency. It was when York saw a police van used to transport prisoners pull up in front of the station that he knew something had really happened. Out of the van came a half-dozen cops in utility uniforms carrying heavy-duty flashlights, and their procession into the terminal convinced York to walk over to where the other two agents in the Camry were sitting. He got into the back seat and recommended that they depart the area immediately.

* * *

After sitting in the bus terminal area for about five minutes, Betts stood Polyander up and pushed him toward the vehicle exit where buses would come from Second Street to this level. An SUV came up quickly from Second Street and came to a stop next to Polyander. Mark Trout unlocked the rear door, got out, and ran around to help Betts push him into the back-seat floorboard. Betts then climbed in and lay on top of him. When the tape was pulled off Polyander's mouth, the man tried to scream, but he was too exhausted from the forced march to the back seat of this SUV. Betts looked at him and checked that he wouldn't stroke out or have a heart attack in the back seat, and then he spoke. "Keith Polyander, you are a traitor to your country, and you're going to get a lot better deal than what the Chinese had planned for you."

Lim and the other MSS agents walked to the far end of the Union Station terminal once they could not locate their target and took the stairs down one level to the Capitol South Metro Station. Lim quickly stuffed the dirty blanket into a trash can and topped it off with the dirty red ball cap. They purchased their tickets and headed for the platform to await the shiny metro train to take them across the Potomac River. As they stood in the underground platform, they exchanged views about what had gone wrong and formulated ways to spend more time in the station looking for Polyander. In the minds of these highly trained agents, the second-guessing by their superiors would be blunted if they could explain that they had scoured the station more thoroughly. But when they noticed one Amtrak police officer running down the platform alongside a Washington, DC, police officer that was talking excitedly into a radio, they decided to keep their profile low and get on their train.

Polyander was trying to catch his breath from the exertion of all that walking. He was lying on the back-seat floorboard of somebody's SUV, still trying to figure out what this crazy man was saying. As he was telling Polyander to keep down and keep his mouth shut, the crazy man was pulling out Polyander's wallet, keys, anything that he had in his pockets. The man searched his waistband and found the .38 caliber revolver he planned to use tonight. Then he even took the belt that held his pants up! Everything was gone, and the man was pushing him down to the rear floorboard. The situation was dire for him, but it was clear that his only chance of escape was to scream and hope a policeman could hear him. They were moving now, and once they stopped at an intersection, he would call out for help.

Surely somebody would hear his cries for help and call the police. That's what responsible people did.

As Trout was pulling out into traffic, Betts looked up from covering his captive and saw over the back seat that police cars with their lights activated were moving toward Union Station. He turned to the front to check the route. "Aren't you getting me to Constitution Avenue?" asked Betts.

"I used Constitution to get us past the ellipse. Now I gotta drop you off on the south side of the street," replied Trout as he weaved and swerved through the throng of taxis and buses so prevalent at night in DC. "So I'm going up C Street and turning around just before the State Department."

"Okay, whatever. You let us out and keep going. I'll find my own way home," said Betts as he wiped his mouth and tried to calm his breathing.

"No way, mister. We agreed that I'd collect you near the Lincoln Memorial after this," answered Trout.

"Mark, the police are up and notified. They'll be looking for anyone or anything suspicious. I'm here to take my chances, but you're not. You can slip out of town on I-66 and be out of it. You've done everything you can, partner. Just make sure you throw this gun, wallet, and gear into the Potomac when you cross the bridge. Please let me finish this." Betts was getting his wind back, and he was pleading with Trout to prevent any further career damage tonight.

Trout was considering what Betts was saying as he eased to a stop at the red light on C Street next to Constitution Hall. Polyander took the chance to rise up in the back seat and holler as loud as he could. The sudden movement caught Betts off-guard. As he reached up to pull his captive back down, Trout turned suddenly with a vicious backhand strike that stunned Polyander into silence and impressed Betts immensely.

"Shut that running sore beneath your nose, fuck face!" said Trout as he pulled through the changed light and checked the intersection they were leaving. Nobody seemed to notice. The tourists were continuing on, and the buses were coming to a stop. No changes, thought Trout. Now, as he turned onto Constitution Avenue, Trout knew that the night was ending for him. All the fireworks were yet to go off, and Betts was going to do it himself, alone. Trout hated that idea, but it was the way Betts wanted it. Nobody had earned the right to do what he was preparing to do more than Randall Betts, and this Polyander asshole was completely unaware of just how much shit was going to be dumped on him.

CHAPTER THIRTY-THREE: MAY 28, 2003

If you want to go fast, go alone. If you want to go far, go together.

—African Proverb

Trout's SUV was right at the intersection of Twenty-First Street and Constitution, and he pulled to the right-hand side at a crosswalk. He offered to help, but Betts insisted that he stay behind the wheel as Betts climbed out of the back seat and jerked Polyander out with him. The last thing drawn out of the back seat was a filthy, smelly blanket they had taken from a ditch in Falls Church the night before. Betts slammed the door shut, and Trout headed off, seeking a right turn so he could leave the District on Interstate 66 East. Trout rolled down the windows as he drove away, hoping the night air would take some of the blanket's stench out of his SUV. This way, it would be easy to ditch Polyander's identity and firearm. Trout disassembled the small pistol as he drove, and threw the frame out one window and the cylinder out the other.

It was dark now, and the small throngs of tourists that frequented the area during the day were occupied elsewhere. Nobody paid attention to the two men shuffling along the washed-concrete pathway, dragging an ugly blanket as they got to the gray-stone squares that created the walkway to one of the most-visited memorials in Washington. Betts said nothing as they headed downhill to the apex of the Vietnam Veterans Memorial.

Designed by an American architecture student named Maya Lin and built in 1982, it was a controversial "gash in the earth" that eventually became a beloved symbol of the men and women who lost their lives in a war that began accumulating casualties in 1962. Betts stopped at the very center of the memorial, where the year "1975" was listed, and he looked briefly at the names inscribed on the walls.

"Here is where the men that you betrayed can't be listed, because they weren't all Americans, and they were sacrificing everything in an area outside Vietnam. They were fighting the fuckers that you were giving their information to, who were paying you quite well for your treason," said Betts as he stood Polyander to face the wall and drew out two forty-eight-inch zip ties. These were industrial quality and would not break or pop without a huge amount of power. Polyander didn't have that much power. As Polyander started babbling his denials to what he was being accused of, Betts dropped the blanket to the ground and slipped the two zip ties along the man's back, beneath his arms at the elbow joint, and closed their loop before he ratcheted the zip ties into a tighter circle. The resulting pressure of the zip ties at Polyander's elbows quickly drew his arms rearward until his elbows almost touched. The scream of pain from Polyander was muffled by Betts's gloved hand, but some of the sound reverberated off the wall that recorded the names of over fifty-eight thousand valiant Americans who died in Vietnam. It was as if the walls were just looking back at Polyander without pity. Betts hissed into the man's ear, "See? This was something they called the 'Vietnamese Rope Trick' at the Hanoi Hilton. POWs would be tied like this and suspended off the floor. It was terribly painful, but not as bad as this..."

Betts reapplied the stun gun to Polyander, this time into his back, and the man collapsed to the ground. Betts now drew two more zip ties; these were standard-quality eighteen-inch models. He tightened them around Polyander's ankles and turned Polyander onto his side. Now, with his hands tied together, his arms pinned back, and his feet together, the traitor could not move from this position. With his shock, his exhaustion, and his limbs immobilized, Polyander was unable to right himself or even roll onto his stomach. All he could do was scream and stare at Betts as he drew the last item from his bag. Betts glared into Polyander's eyes as he held up a translucent, tear-shaped bag made of thick plastic. It had a canteen top at the end, and the bag contained a thick orange liquid.

Betts could have smiled at this point; he had the man, had him pinned, and had him ready to face the final indignity. But Betts kept his glare as he explained, "See this? I used the bladder from an old friend's canteen and took it to Fort Detrick. Got a buddy out there who gave me a sample of one of the 'Rainbow Herbicides' used in Vietnam to clear jungle foliage. They would call it Agent Orange, but you already know what it is, don't you? You sprayed this shit all over the radio equipment you were selling to the Chinese, and it gave my dad cancer. You betrayed men in the field, and you killed people with this crap, so I'm giving some back to you." With this, Betts opened the canteen end and poured the two cups of liquid into Polyander's mouth. He gagged and coughed and tried to spit it out, to keep it out of his throat, but Betts was pouring it down into the back of his throat too hard. Polyander had no choice but to swallow. Once the bladder was emptied into Polyander, Betts retrieved one last strip of duct tape and sealed the man's lips.

Betts hadn't really had Agent Orange in the plastic bladder. He knew nobody at Fort Detrick, and he had not seen his VA rep begging for some of the toxic defoliant out of their lab. He had simply stopped at a car-parts store in Falls Church and purchased a gallon of antifreeze that was orange in color. This soupy liquid, along with a tablespoon of ammonia from under Betts's bathroom sink, looked and smelled like something odious, and Polyander had suffered as he swallowed it. That was enough.

Betts stood, placed the canteen back in his bag, and covered the whimpering man in the filthy blanket. He then walked away, heading east toward the Korean War Veterans Memorial, just before the Lincoln Memorial. From there, he would catch a cab home. He felt spent and worn as he walked away from the squirming, panicked man who now resembled just another homeless guy having a bad dream. But once he looked up at the wall and saw the light shining up on the three-man statue commemorating the soldiers who served in Vietnam, he straightened up and walked with respect for those honored at this site. He pulled off his gloves and threw them into the trash. Once he got to the Lincoln Memorial, he disposed of the plastic bladder with the remnants of the orange antifreeze. The stun gun would stay with him, for the time being. He didn't want to leave something like that in the District. With many of the contents of his cross-shoulder bag used or discarded, he raised his hand and flagged a cab.

When the cab dropped Betts off, it was at a shopping center along Route 7, a half mile from Idylwood Drive. He didn't want the cab company to have his exact address, and the walk along the noisy, busy street, even after 10:00 p.m., was a bit of relaxation and release for Betts. When he got up the hill off Route 7 and walked into the parking lot of the apartment complex, a light inside a sedan came on. Someone was climbing out of a car.

Betts didn't look up; he just kept walking for the door to his building. He knew this was it, and he had spent his time walking getting prepared for it. Someone would flash a badge and ask to speak with Betts, and the entire thing would come crashing down on him. Maybe a traffic camera caught him; maybe a tourist reported seeing him with a guy who was now lying in front of the memorial; maybe a real homeless guy complained about the screaming and gave the police Betts's description. However it happened, it happened, and Betts was okay with that.

"Randy! I've been waiting all night for you!" came the voice from yards away as Betts looked up and saw Jim Brewer walking toward him. Now Betts had gone from resigned to regretful: he had forgotten to tell Brewer anything about the change of plans. It seemed like a month since he'd convinced his best friend to help him assassinate Keith Polyander with a sniper shot.

"Jim! What are you doing here?" said Betts with all the enthusiasm he could muster. This wasn't going to be easy. He was going to have to spin Brewer off the course of helping him kill Polyander outright and still show that he was determined to punish the man later. Betts knew that this would be the theatrical performance of the year.

"Brother, I got a letter passed to me by a guy coming in from an overseas assignment. He brought it in the diplomatic pouch, and it's a letter addressed to you!" This was the earnest explanation provided as the two men walked into Betts's apartment. Betts was half listening as he hustled out of the double-sided overcoat and placed his shoulder bag behind the couch. He was not going to confess anything to Brewer, and hiding as much of the gear he used tonight as he could was key to that.

Brewer handed the folded and wrinkled paper to Betts, who unfolded it and read as best he could. It was late at night, and Betts was completely spent, and his ears were still calming down from all the traffic noise from walking home. But once he started, Betts was mesmerized. The note read:

Randall Betts, this is your old pal Munir Afridi. I'm writing to you from my hometown in the Frontier Province, but I have to travel to Peshawar to get it forwarded to you. I hope this letter gets to you, and I hope it finds you well.

I have lost my father. He was climbing the mountain behind our village to clear the snow from the roof, and he slipped and fell. I feel so lost without him. I wanted to write and tell you how much he meant to me.

My father taught me everything I needed to know about survival, even though my mother taught me how to live. He brought me so many good things in my life, and I thought I could never repay him for his teaching. But I was wrong. My brother Azzam has married, and they have a child that I adore. I will show him all the things about being truthful, being trusting, and being reliable to the family. Mostly, I will teach him how to be forgiving, how to turn away from evil and violence and find peace in this chaotic life.

I hope the same blessings come for you, Randall Betts. Our lives may change due to loss or sadness, but we must always look to the future with love in our hearts, and reject hate in our souls.

Your Friend Forever,

Munir

By the way, have you spoken with Krucic lately?

Randall looked down as he finished the letter, wiped his nose, and then he looked at Jim Brewer with tears in his eyes. Finally, he said, "Jim, you are a good man. My best friend."

"What do you think about that? Hearing from him after all this time?" said Brewer expectantly.

"This was a great idea," said Betts as he began to smile. "You outdid yourself with this one."

"What do you mean?" protested Brewer. "This is a letter from Munir!"

Several years earlier, Betts and Brewer had worked together to disrupt a terrorist bombing in East Africa, and Munir Afridi was the person who made it possible. Enlisted into the bombing plot by an extremist leader, Munir had shown bravery and tenacity in risking everything to stop the plot and do away with the leader. It was Betts and Brewer who pushed for Munir and his family to receive USD $5 million from the "Rewards for Justice" program. It was Betts who recruited Munir, and their work together saved lives.

"Munir didn't write this," replied Betts. "He was raised by his mother to be honest and useful. But his father taught him to be courageous and forthright. He would never reveal this much in a letter, especially to me. Sentiments like these are not the product of people that have relied on a hard life to sculpt their personalities. He's a great kid, and he deserved all the rewards we got for him, but those rewards would never soften him into gushing about love and forgiveness. But I tell you this: you are a true friend for coming up with something that would keep me from putting a bullet between Polyander's eyes."

"So you're still planning on killing him?" said Brewer sadly. He had put a lot of thought and effort into that letter, and he was pissed that it didn't work.

"Nope. Go home, Jim. Everything's fine. I'm not shooting anyone, for now," Betts said.

Brewer left the apartment, saddened that his fake letter didn't work. But more than that, he was puzzled by the attitude of his friend, who was ready to shoot this guy just yesterday. Now he seemed to be at peace about the whole thing. He couldn't figure that out.

CHAPTER THIRTY-FOUR: SIX WEEKS LATER

Memories are everyone's second chance at happiness.

—Britain's Queen Elizabeth, the Queen Mother

1. Change: July 12, 2003

As the master of ceremonies introduced her, along with a glowing overview of her career and service to the country, Olivia B. Johnson thought back to how she got here. She had left government service when the president found that he was no longer pleased with her service. She was contacted immediately by a DC law firm that had international clients and hired her as an "accounts consultant," making triple the money she had as DCIA. This led to invitations to speak at several conferences dealing with international issues, and Johnson found the need for an agent to coordinate a schedule and appropriate fees for the speeches. She kept her Bethesda home but lived mostly out of a leased row house on Sixth Street near Capitol Hill. She continued to be interested in improving the state of Washington, DC, regardless of how far her speaking engagements took her.

While her reputation as an outspoken arbiter of better negotiations with foreign nations grew, the political hacks on either side of the aisle were quick to condemn her as an agenda-driven opportunist trying to make the current administration look bad. But more and more people started listening to her common-sense approaches to monetary trends and political will. Through media scrutiny and a newfound internet presence, she became the go-to expert about international relations and fiscal responsibility. This reputation, along with a clear amount of influence from her father, made Olivia Johnson a household name for better politics and government accountability.

Now, as she began to stand when the introduction was complete, Johnson soaked in the applause and gave it a moment to convince those who were not applauding to join in with the crowd. When she started to speak, she found the room to be deathly quiet. People were listening to her, and she didn't have to command their attention or stoke their fears to get them to listen.

"Ladies and gentlemen, thank you for that warm welcome. I am here tonight to announce my candidacy for mayor of Washington, DC. I remember sitting on my grandfather's lap as a young girl, on the front porch of his house in Kingman Park, telling me the story of Swampoodle. This was an established but neglected neighborhood in DC, just beyond where the government printing office stands today, that was rife with poverty and crime. A thriving community of immigrants and working people who helped build the District of Columbia but were ignored by their government. With no sidewalks, sewers, or police patrols, it was a bruise on the reputation of this great city, and nobody in the DC government did anything to address the rampage of illness and injury being inflicted upon the poor. It took the building of a train terminal called Union Station to tear it down and displace over a hundred families. This was the result of government overreach and lack of concern for all the people in DC, and I am here to assure you that I want to work to avoid this kind of tragedy in this city. We are under the thumb of people in Congress who do not live here, and that needs to change!"

The applause was thunderous. Olivia Johnson was on her way to a new chapter of her life.

2. Challenge: July 14, 2003

Elaine Simons, senior sergeant at the First District Headquarters for the Metropolitan Police Department of Washington, DC, couldn't believe what she was hearing. The FBI fingerprint analyst on the other end of the phone was telling her that they did not have any records of the fingerprints sent weeks ago.

"Young man, we have kept this body at the morgue for way longer than any other, due to indications of foul play and lack of positive ID. None of the other databases, dental records, facial recognition—none of them have helped. So we turned to the FBI fingerprint records division in West Virginia for an answer. You have lost the first two submissions of fingerprints we sent, and now you're telling me that you don't have any records of this person?" fumed Simons. She had dealt with government ineptitude plenty of times, but this was the worst.

"I'm sorry, Sergeant. My records don't show anything related to the prints you submitted," replied the analyst.

Simons hung up in disgust. It wasn't fair that this much time and attention should be paid to a dead-end case, but foul play had been done to kill this homeless guy. He had been reported to US Park Police by a tourist who was appalled that a homeless person would sleep right at the apex of the Vietnam Veterans Memorial. Park Police discovered that the guy wasn't sleeping; he was dead. When they found the zip ties holding the guy's arms and legs, they called MPD to start a homicide investigation. An autopsy revealed poison in his stomach and throat, possibly antifreeze. So this guy was held down and made to drink toxic chemicals, very much an indicator of personal attack, not random street crime. The problem was, nobody knew where this guy came from. His face wasn't in any pictures at the local shelters, and he held no ID or property on his body. Nothing was ripped or torn to indicate robbery, and shakedowns of nearby homeless camping locations turned up no abandoned sleeping spot. No call-ins from missing persons of somebody matching his description. This guy just didn't exist until he died.

She had to finally report that this John Doe had been the victim of revenge, possibly something to do with Vietnam service. Maybe the Marine Corps, based on the discovery of a very small USMC medallion in the victim's shirt pocket. She had scanned reports dealing with Vietnam vets and attendant issues. Maybe a conference of veterans, maybe tied to the "Rolling Thunder" rally that just visited the city, maybe a crime of passion by a widowed soldier who wanted to send a message.

When a story had hit the paper about a missing director of the National Security Agency, she looked into connecting her John Doe to this missing director. Her inquiries were rebuffed by the NSA public affairs officer, as it had been determined that former Director Polyander had drowned at his Severn River home. The office of the new NSA director, USMC General Ben Sutherlin, faxed a copy of the incident report from the local county sheriff's office listing the former director's death as an accident, as a boat had been found unmoored from Polyander's boathouse. Efforts to drag the fast-running Severn River for the body turned up nothing, and eventually, the sheriff's department completed their investigation; Polyander was dead by drowning. Case closed.

Sergeant Simons's report would surmise the efforts conducted to establish an identity that could lead to a motive, and the negative results of those efforts would release the body for processing by the city mortuary.

It just struck Simons as strange. No records, no identity, no leads or interest from the dozens of agencies that document and list people all over the country. How was it that nobody knew who this guy was?

3. Church: July 18, 2003

The small crowd wasn't a problem at all. Randall Betts always thought his wedding would be a grand affair with a big church and huge crowd of friends, colleagues, and fellow Marines. After all, Betts remembered, the father of the bride would pay for it.

But his wedding ended up being a small, tidy affair at a Hilton Hotel conference room with a pastor, a best man, and a dozen coworkers, mainly from the bride's side. On the groom's side were Mark Trout, Troy York, and a tall black female that few people on the bride's side recognized. Betts's sister took the role of bridesmaid, and her youngest son served as ring bearer. In the hallway, just outside the conference room, Bob Raffleson quietly stood guard. He wasn't there to protect the wedding party; he was staying in the background as his new fiancée attended the ceremony.

The service would be followed by a stand-up gathering with finger sandwiches and a cash bar in the next side of the conference room.

"Aren't you going broke paying for all this?" quipped Jim Brewer.

"Hey, she had a hand in this too. It was a mutual choice," said Betts.

"Well, my friend, you are one lucky man," said Brewer as he grasped the shoulder of Betts's best jacket.

The two men stood together at the makeshift altar, next to a pastor who had done weddings at this hotel several times in the past. His experience with setting up a ceremony that was simple and effective was a great benefit to Betts and his bride, so that the rehearsal dinner was a much less stressful event. Now, as recorded organ music began to build in the conference room, the wedding could commence. The three men were staring at the conference room entrance from the hallway watching for the pastor to make the sign, and when the recorded music began to play the traditional march, he made a small wave, whereupon the bride and her father proceeded through two rows of sparsely occupied chairs to the altar. Everyone stood in reverence as the pair took their time approaching the altar. The bride was nervously looking down as her dour-faced father marched alongside her, the procession toward one man taking his daughter away, and the other man backing him up. The father's facial expression was fake. He was just past seventy and was overjoyed. He never thought this day would come when his career-oriented daughter would finally find someone with whom she could settle down. Now he and his wife would hopefully get the grandchildren they wanted so badly.

The bride's father had built his company from one D9 bulldozer to a regional powerhouse in the world of clearing and grading. His work with shopping centers, government buildings, and interstate highways left him comfortably wealthy, along with multiple accolades for work completed on time and within budget. His daughter's college debt was paid off, and his assistance with whatever house his baby girl wanted would be substantial.

The man his daughter was marrying seemed to be a decent enough guy; he just wasn't all that chatty about his background other than his time in the Marine Corps. He seemed to be happy about the marriage, and his daughter hadn't been this giddy since she got her reading tablet at the age of eight. At the rehearsal dinner the previous evening, the celebratory mood was interrupted by a solemn moment of remembrance called by the groom for all those who could not attend the wedding. Everything seemed to stop, and the room suddenly became deathly quiet. Toasts to people that the father had never heard of were long and a bit drawn out. The bride's father thought this was a bit much, but the bride and the groom were serious, and the few guests outside of his family stood and took an extra minute to raise their glasses and toast to those who were not attending this small but important event.

But now came the wedding, and all the rushing and gushing and blushing would be over with; his little girl would start a real life, not hurrying all over the place to solve other people's problems. His daughter was smart, maybe too smart, but she was getting married to a guy who loved her and didn't take drugs. And for the father of the bride, that was enough.

Finally, the father and bride arrived at the altar, and one man stepped behind the groom as the father took his daughter's hand and placed it into the hands of the groom. Now the pastor could start speaking. Now the bride looked up, and Randall Betts looked deeply into the bright-gray eyes of Alexandra Stallings.

EPILOGUE: APRIL 22, 2003

Examine what is said, not who speaks.

—Arab Proverb

Route 610, Garrisonville Road, in Stafford County, Virginia, is one of the rare places where a federally funded interstate highway intersects with a secondary road. Although the route number indicates that Garrisonville Road is a secondary route, the size of the roadway and amount of traffic has grown so much that it rivals any primary roadway in Northern Virginia.

Just over a mile along Route 610 from Interstate 95, a quickly built strip mall includes a restaurant that caters to the Marines who live in this area. About seven miles from Marine Corps Base Quantico, and with much less expensive real estate, the neighborhoods around this restaurant attracted many Marine Corps families and young officers.

At approximately 2:00 p.m. on a Thursday, a small but tightly gathered group of senior Marine officers walked into this restaurant to celebrate an awards ceremony they had just attended on base. They marched up the wide steps to the bar of the restaurant and proudly announced an order for a round of Four Branches bourbon for themselves.

The crowd today in the restaurant was light, just two couples at various tables and three young people standing at the far end of the bar, exactly opposite of where the group of officers was clustering. The three looked barely old enough to drink alcohol, and they were not noteworthy except for the fact that they displayed the cut and culture of Marines. One was thin and pale, one was a female with very close-cut brown hair, and one was a bit portly, missing the bottom portions of his legs, in a wheelchair. And they were all staring at the group that had just come in.

"I'd like to propose a toast to the major," announced one of the officer's group. "He was awarded his Silver Star for bravery in combat, and his achievement reflects well on us all!"

"It reflects all right, but the idea of it being an achievement is debatable," pronounced the female of the three standing at the far end of the bar. Her voice carried well, even over the clinking of the shot glasses.

This brought about the attention of the senior officers, all of whom turned to see what disrespectful maggot had dared to say anything in response to their celebration. The sole captain in the group turned his shoulders to face the youngsters at the far end of the bar and politely said, "Excuse me, who are you, and why are you inserting anything into this gathering of officers?"

"My name is Keane; my friends call me Izzy, and Colonel Brown calls me 'Sergeant.'"

The dropping of the name of the base commander at Quantico got the attention of the other officers. They now turned to see why this soon-to-be-demoted NCO was demanding attention.

"And how would you know Colonel Brown?" was the question posed by the lieutenant colonel in the group. As the most senior officer of the bunch, he would be the one to see to it that this lack of respect was punished.

"Motor-pool driver," said Izzy as she made a proper salute that nobody answered. "I take Colonel Brown everywhere. He insists that my duties revolve around his schedule. He put me in for every high-risk driving course he could find. He trusts my ability to get him in and out safely, and we talk quite a bit."

As the group turned around to return to their toasts, confident that this female pup would be driving wrenches in the small-engine repair shop by the end of the week, Izzy spoke again. "He told me all about your little ceremony; Colonel Brown knew y'all would be coming here for drinks. That's why he encouraged me and my buds to come set this straight."

The group of officers froze. They weren't going to turn and give this enlisted person the respect of their attention, but they were determined to hear what she was going to say.

"That major that you guys are celebrating with got a medal from MAR-FORCOM. Somebody knew somebody in the executive director's office and pushed the major's story through so he could get recognition for something that he observed, not something he did."

Izzy had them turning now. She continued while resting one hand on the man in the wheelchair and the other on the thin Marine staring at the group. "The ambush on Route One was a total shootout. They blew up our motorcade and had us dead to rights with an IED in the road, RPGs and two dozen Fedayeen assholes with AKs. They took out the turret gunners and were wearing us down to nubs with rifles and rockets. Me and Bucky here were in the rear vehicle, and we were shot up and screwed up trying to apply bandages. It was Staff Sergeant Betts that came and got us assembled and took it upon himself to draw fire at the end of the line of vehicles so that we could move to an evac point. All he had was a pistol, and he drew them away from us. Betts took a round in the ankle and got all chewed up from the attention he was getting, but he found the strength to climb on top of a burning Humvee and pull Sandy here out." She turned to the young man in the wheelchair so he could speak.

"I woke up with my legs on fire and a loaded Ma Deuce in my hands," said Lance Corporal Sanford Shoal with no emotion or guile. "The enemy was aimed at the far point of the motorcade from me, so I mowed them down like flowers on the freeway. The air support was inbound, but from two hundred feet up, they said they couldn't tell where anything was with all the smoke and sand and fire. But they reported later they saw the muzzle flash of my .50 cal and knew where the enemy was. They blew that place to shit just as Sergeant Betts reached into the turret and pulled my fat ass out. He carried me all the way to the evac site. I lost my legs to fire and shrapnel, but the staff sergeant saved me, not that major." Sandy pointed at the man who was looking away and sipping his drink.

"The major was the first one squatting in the shitter, and he didn't pull anybody in. He just sat in the helo and watched us get the fuck outta Dodge. That's the man you're celebrating today," said Izzy with a final wave of her hand.

One of the other majors in the group, in an attempt to draw a close to this embarrassing exchange of viewpoints, took a fresh shot of bourbon and carried it to a point in between the two groups. Standing halfway down the bar with his drink raised to the man in the wheelchair, he said, "You did good, Marine. Thank you for what you did that day."

"I kissed all my thank-yous goodbye, sir," said Sandy to the officer. "But if Staff Sergeant Betts told me tomorrow that he was going to hell, I'd grab a rifle and rip the legs off your mama's kitchen table so I could stick 'em on and follow him."

With nothing left to say, Izzy turned the wheelchair to leave, and she and Bucky eased their comrade down the steps to their van outside.

ABOUT THE AUTHOR

The author has an extensive career of over 35 years of service in the CIA. From personnel security to counterintelligence programs and clandestine operations, he has traveled across the country and around the world to collect the memories that have gone into this story. Since retiring, he has provided security training and consultations to various organizations and crafted several courses in personal safety and situational awareness. He is a Certified Protection Professional, and was listed in the 2023-2024 publications board of "Who's Who in America". He is married and lives quietly in the Tidewater region of Virginia.

Milton Keynes UK
Ingram Content Group UK Ltd.
UKHW032219231124
451423UK00014B/1376